THE TESTING OF ROSE ALLEYN

THE TESTING OF ROSE ALLEYN

Vivien Freeman

186 Publishing

Chapter One

Along with grey clouds and a consequent drop in temperature, there comes the return of what is never far away in these parts, a keen easterly breeze. Borne upon it, the plaintive sound of a concertina makes me think of the cold sea even further east. The tune reaches its conclusion as I draw level with the church and glimpse beyond it, in the school playground, a Maypole with its rainbow of ribbons. The end of each ribbon is held by a child who stands still in his or her starting place, returned from all the weaving intricacies of dance.

In the High Street, one of Gifford's windows is dominated by a large gilt-framed photograph portraying three young women wearing light-coloured dresses, intended, as our housemate Lettie has told us, to convey a sense of spring sunshine and youthfulness. They are seated as tradition dictates, with the queen at the centre, a crown of interwoven silk leaves and may-blossom perched on top of her hair, worn loose but drawn back to reveal her round, open face. A sash across her chest proclaims her: "Widdock May Queen 1900". Her attendants, flanking her, wear tiaras of a similar style and hair also down, but they are un-sashed, which absence allows my unimpeded scrutiny of Lettie's chest. I am enormously relieved and not a little satisfied, given the formidable challenge, to see that this presents a smooth aspect to the observer, the swell of her bust being hardly noticeable as her top-half descends and tapers towards her waist. Lettie and I are, as she was the first to acknowledge, chalk and cheese when it comes to shape. Where my bodice is a simple matter of slightly generous darts, Lettie's far ampler form required an altogether different construction. I came up with a kind of glove into which she scoops herself, this same being let into what goes on as the original bodice shape. Once she has her petticoat and dress on top of it there really is no reason, apart from the hint of a smile in what is otherwise a rather solemn tableau, to suppose that she is any differently clad underneath from the other two young women, no doubt encumbered by their corsets.

"This photograph doesn't do our Susan justice."

"Nor our Jill. Why, you'd never guess they're both strawberry blondes."

I have been joined by two matrons.

"It's clear he took a shine to this one."

"All that wild black hair, the witch."

I walk away.

"Good, I was hoping these would come through quickly," says Mr. Pritchard. "It's just what we need."

From its opening this January, the bookshop has benefitted from the fact that a course of weekly evening lectures commenced then and ran till Easter. I've been aware that, without the stimulus of the reading list for Mr. Philpott's Thinkers of Our Time, our sales have not been quite as buoyant over the last two weeks as previously.

"There!" My employer holds up one of the books, whose receipt he has just recorded, so that I can read the title on its maroon cover, Three Men on the Bummel by Jerome K. Jerome.

"Oh! He's the author of Three Men in a Boat, isn't he?" I say, "I rather enjoyed that."

"Precisely," says Mr. Pritchard. "The publishers have sent me a few copies of that too, just in case there's anyone who hasn't read it."

I'm looking again at the title. "Bummel, that sounds German."

"It is. The word means 'stroll'. This novel's about the three friends cycling around Germany, but I imagine the strolling idea is to make it seem casual – three chaps doing a spot of cycling." He says this in the light tone and accent which a gentleman of leisure might use, but goes on, "I'd be surprised if there weren't some unappealing caricatures of the German national character – unappealing to me, that is, as I don't find poking fun at foreigners amusing – but I don't suppose it will be truly insulting, and I expect the rest of it will be humorous."

"And a lot of people will enjoy it," I say.

"Quite right. So, let's get cracking and clear a space in the main window. We need to sell as many of these as soon as we can. It's just the kind of thing the station bookstall will cotton onto and they'll have no hesitation in knocking a penny off to undercut us."

We make a good display of the newly-published Three Men with the first volume just behind it, together with a copy of H.G. Wells's The Wheels of Chance which, although also some years old, is a humorous novel about cycling. Mr. Pritchard insists on redressing the balance, regarding humour, with a collection of German poetry in translation. "We must read some more Goethe."

He seems, today, almost hearty. I wonder if he, too, is trying to recover and step back from the heightened atmosphere of yesterday.

It is our custom on a Monday afternoon, when the shop is often empty of customers, to sit at the counter and read out loud a poem apiece which each of us has previously chosen, then to discuss it. We fell into this pattern early in the life of Pritchard's Bookshop and, although I still am nervous despite the encouragement of my employer, I thoroughly enjoy the opportunity to extend my education and to hear him read, for he has a lovely voice.

Yesterday afternoon, in that unseasonable heat, no one came to interrupt us, and Mr. Pritchard astonished me with a poem by the late Gerard Manley Hopkins called Spring, whose vibrant language thrilled me. How sad it is that we shall hear no more from that inspiring man. When my turn came, I felt compelled to read from Mother's anthology a poem called A Chanted Calendar. This records the arrival of spring flowers and has the lines, 'Then came the daisies, On the first of May,' which made it eminently timely. But something happened to me, perhaps engendered by the poem itself, or by our talking about it, Mr. Pritchard's deep blue eyes alight with passion for the subject of language; above all, though, by the childhood memory of dearest Mother reading the poem. Never far from the surface these last three months and more, grief threatened to overwhelm me. Seated next to me, Mr. Pritchard pressed his clean handkerchief into my hands. In his unusual inability to speak he seemed, for a moment, equally affected by emotion. The stimulus of discourse, the pain of grief, to which he is no stranger having lost both parents, the heat, it was all a little too much for us, perhaps, and yet a part of me feels strangely wistful for that evanescent mood.

As soon as I have closed the front door of Apple Tree House, the kitchen door flies open.

"Yes, it is," Winnie calls back into the room. "Come on, Rose, we've been waiting for you."

What she means, I discover after I've flung my hat and coat on the hallstand, is that although the four factory girls have eaten their first course and Lettie is just finishing hers, they are holding back from pudding because, as Meg tells me, we have a treat.

"So, your rhubarb tart lives to fight another day," says Priscilla, with a smirk in my direction. She starts clearing the dirty plates, as I sit down to eat my dinner.

On the day I arrived at this hostel, I learned from its landlady, Mrs. Fuller, that the cook had eloped with her truelove, each from old Widdock families who were sworn enemies like the Montagues and Capulets. Somehow, I took on the role of cook because I'd grown used to it during the times when Mother was poorly, or if everyone was home in our cottage at Markly. Now that my housemates in manufacturing are on their earlier summer hours and all five of my friends who live here get back ahead of me, tonight's dinner of bubble-and-squeak, although prepared by me, was cooked by them. I do my best to down the portion left for me in record time.

Jenny, who is Priscilla's office colleague at the toothbrush factory, comes in at the back door having fetched Mrs. Fuller from her studio in the garden. "What's all this about?" she asks. "I can't wait to be enlightened."

It turns out that Winnie and Meg have received an official commendation from their company, Hallambury's, which produces medicines and surgical equipment. They used to work in the packaging department but were promoted to the office, where they have been working for three months now. Not only are their posts confirmed but, because their

5

pharmaceutical knowledge is so good, since they are the daughters of a chemist, they have been told that they may draft proposed replies to enquiries and instructions to be enclosed with orders.

"Though our manager, Mr. Dixon, will have to approve and sign the letters, of course," says Meg.

"He put the idea forward to the Chairman, so he's just as pleased as us."

"I bet he is," says Priscilla, "if you care to think about it."

But the rest of us are congratulating the two sisters.

"We thought it was a rather special day," says Meg, "what with Lettie's lovely photograph as well."

"So, we rushed down during lunch break and begged Askey's to put these aside to pick up on the way home," says Winnie bearing in from the scullery, to our gasps of anticipated pleasure, a double-tiered cake-stand upon which are seven mouth-watering Swiss buns, arranged to point outwards as if offering their slim fingers for our delectation.

"We chose the ones with the most icing and asked the assistant to put them in two boxes," says Meg, "and we carried them really carefully."

"What a lovely idea!" says Lettie. We all murmur our agreement. "And you must let me pay –"

Winnie bats Lettie's offer away, together with her thanks and all of ours. "This is our treat."

Mrs. Fuller has fetched the finest tea plates from the dresser and, offered first pick, takes her bun and raises it by the underside aloft as if it were a wine glass. "A toast," we follow suit, "to the photographic muse," she nods to Lettie, then to Meg and Winnie, "and to your promotion. Well done!"

With buns raised, we echo her. There follows a period of relative silence, broken only by murmurs of appreciation. Askey's do make an exceptionally light Swiss bun, and they are generous with the icing.

"May we lick our fingers?" Jenny asks.

"Of course," says Mrs. Fuller. She is only halfway through her bun, having eaten it at a far more decorous rate than us. She raises the remaining half. "And here's a toast to all of you clever girls. Two scientists, two assistants in interesting shops and two office clerks. I call that impressive. To all six of you!"

After an hour's card-playing with all of us housemates, Lettie hardly can hardly wait till our bedroom door is shut for the night. "Did you see her face – " she breathes, "you know, when Mrs. Fuller - ?"

"I know." I say no more, uneasy as I always am, that we might be overheard by someone passing on her way to or from the bathroom.

"She looked as if she was sucking on a sour lemon. Trust her to be so jealous of Meg and Winnie's good fortune, she couldn't be pleased about Mrs. Fuller's toast to us all."

I simply nod and go to use the bathroom myself.

It is true that, in response to Mrs. Fuller's rousing affirmation of our achievements, Priscilla's first expression, swiftly blanked, did not echo the appreciation on everyone else's faces, but Lettie's deduction doesn't quite add up, and I don't want to dwell on any further interpretations. What remains uppermost in my mind's eye is how, when Mrs. Fuller included Priscilla and Jenny in the toast, Jenny's smile froze, as if in shock.

Mr. Pritchard's wish about sales of Three Men on the Bummel has been granted. We have had a busy week. The purchase of one book sometimes leads to that of another, just as the sight of customers contentedly browsing often attracts passers-by to step inside. There has rarely been a moment when the shop has not had someone in it. As a result, my employer has been in excellent humour even when his three sparring partners, Messrs. Nash, Davidson and Vance make their usual visit today, Saturday, and the latter upbraids him for "pandering to the public taste".

"It's not bad though, listen to this..." says Mr. Nash, quoting for the entertainment of all the bookshop.

"And please note my scholarly alternative in the other window," says Mr. Pritchard, "the essays of Montaigne – just up your street."

"I've read'em, of course," booms Mr. Davidson, "but it's a worthy gesture, educating the good folk of Widdock."

"Hear, hear," cries Mr. Nash, "God knows, we've been trying to do that all our adult lives!" He and Mr. Davidson are schoolteachers.

Mr. Pritchard laughs along with them. It's just the kind of mildly intellectual banter he enjoys with these three loyal customers.

As I walk home to Apple Tree House, I can only be pleased and relieved for both of us and the future of the bookshop.

I enter the kitchen, the aroma of fried fish-cakes making my stomach growl. I hadn't realised I was so hungry. I hurriedly wash my hands. There's no sign of Mrs. Fuller yet but the others have kept my dinner warm, so I join them at my set place. Lettie uncovers the plate in front of me, releasing even more appetising scents of spring onion. They are all in the process of passing round the custard for their slices of tart, rhubarb again this time of year. I went down and pulled it when I got home last evening. No one says a great deal while we all enjoy our food but when we have finished our respective courses, I ask about their day. Meg and Winnie spent their afternoon browsing the shops, Jenny reading in the park. Priscilla says, "Nothing interesting." Lettie has been unusually quiet. It comes to me that she looks just like the cat that had the cream.

"Your friend came into the shop, Priscilla."

There is something about her tone which makes me pause, my hand on the jug of custard.

"You know, the one at the back of the group, last Saturday. The one who didn't really want to be involved. We had a nice little chat."

Lettie had confided this humiliating incident to me, that evening, while we walked alone beside the river. She had been dressing Gifford's window, when she noticed Priscilla staring at the window in the next shop, pretending not to have heard her name being called by a group of young women, clearly fellow employees from the toothbrush factory. Priscilla had glanced up, catching sight of Lettie witnessing her discomfort. The fact that Lettie was standing in the window, where soon the photograph would be displayed, must have been a bitter reminder of our housemate's good looks, popularity and, as Priscilla would think of it, her complacent self-regard, something which would have to be taken down a peg or two. So, Priscilla greeted her co-workers, led them into Gifford's and encouraged them to ask Lettie to get out every frill and ruffle, knowing that she could not refuse a potential customer, and had to remain polite. Then, when the group went giggling out again, having bought nothing, Priscilla knew that Lettie would have to wind the trimmings patiently back onto their cards and store every item neatly in its place.

All this flashes through my mind as Priscilla is answering. "She's not a friend of mine. No one likes her much. That's why she was at the back of the group." Priscilla looks at Lettie eye to eye, as if willing her to falter.

I stare at my pudding. Suddenly, I am no longer hungry. I look up and see Jenny's ashen face. Meg and Winnie exchange an anxious glance.

Lettie savours her moment of suspense, then she says, "I learnt from your co-worker on the factory floor, Prissie, that you're not a clerk at all. You're a nit-picker! You pick creepy-crawlies out of the hog's hair for the toothbrushes!"

Jenny utters a little squeak. Meg and Winnie look embarrassed and worried, Lettie triumphant.

The words have hit home, but Priscilla keeps her tone expressionless. "She's a liar. She would make up something like that, she's jealous. Why don't you ask Jenny if I work with her in the office?"

Lettie turns to Jenny. Winnie and Meg are now looking down at the hands in their laps, a picture of discomfort.

I have had enough. "Why don't you — " I begin, addressing Priscilla, but Jenny gives a heaving gulp, dashing her hand up to her mouth from which issues a gush of clear liquid.

"Oh God!" says Lettie. She scrabbles for her handkerchief, which she thrusts in Jenny's direction.

I am already on my feet, as Jenny's body convulses again.

"Oh dear," she whispers, eyes closed. Behind me, as I run to the scullery, there is a general commotion of jumping up. When I return with the bucket, Winnie and Meg are taking Jenny's bodyweight as she slips into a faint. They ease her from chair to floor, Lettie assisting with her legs.

"On her side," says Winnie.

"Get that cushion, please," Meg tells Priscilla, who seems frozen to the spot.

She grabs a soft one from Mrs. Fuller's rocking-chair, and Meg places it gently under Jenny's head. She lifts Jenny's wrist and feels for her pulse, then starts undoing the buttons on her blouse.

"Can you loosen her stays, please, Rose? I'm going for the smelling salts," says Winnie.

I start to do so. The corset is not heavily laced, but any constriction on her vital organs must, clearly, be relieved.

"Jenny? Can you hear me? It's Meg. You're going to be perfectly all right. You just rest and, when you feel able, open your eyes. Someone else say something. Keep talking, quietly."

"I can do that," says Lettie. "It's me, Lettie. You look lovely, Jenny, just like a romantic heroine."

I fetch a glass of water. When I return, Winnie is back with the salts. She wafts the little glass bottle under Jenny's nose. Jenny opens her eyes and groans. "You stay there as long as you need and we'll be right here with you," says Winnie, but Jenny has seen the water and tries to sit up, reaching out her arm.

11

We cradle her between us. I hold the glass and Jenny sips. She smiles at me. "Thank you," she whispers.

"You're doing very well," says Meg.

After some time has passed, Jenny feels able to stand and we help her to the armchair opposite the rocker into which she sinks.

"Would you like a cup of tea?" I ask, poised with the kettle.

Jenny smiles again, the thread of her voice says, "Ooh, yes, please."

"Two sugars," says Winnie.

"I think we could all do with a cup," says Lettie.

We are agreeing and laughing with relief that Jenny seems to have recovered, when the back door opens and in comes Mrs. Fuller for her evening meal. "Oh my goodness!" She takes in our solicitous grouping round our friend. "What's happened here?"

"We would have come and fetched you, but there wasn't time," I say.

"If you don't mind, Mrs. Fuller, I'm not sure it's advisable for the patient —" Meg stops, having realised what we housemates have only now comprehended.

"No, no," says Mrs. Fuller, thinking she has finished speaking, "explain later. If Jenny's ill, you must look after her."

In the emergency, none of us can have noticed Priscilla slipping from the room.

We make a slow progress taking the few steps down the corridor to the former dining room, which is the Thurlow sisters' bedroom. Lettie and I are on either side of Jenny, holding an arm each. She will be in Meg's bed, made up with clean but ancient sheets and pillowslips found inside the ottoman in their room on which Meg has insisted that she will sleep, discomfort notwithstanding. Although it is only just dark, all three look exhausted so perhaps she will.

When we return to the kitchen, Mrs. Fuller is frying her fishcakes, their delicious aroma perhaps detectable to the feline sensibility, since Morris appears at the window followed by Ruskin. I let them in the back door, feeling hungry again myself. I gladly remember my untouched rhubarb tart. Mrs. Fuller and I sit down at the table, while Lettie makes more tea. Between the two of us, we manage to tell our landlady all we know.

In the silence when we have finished, she says, almost to herself, "I could do without this."

I feel intensely sorry for her. This week has been a time of freedom to move between her studio and the new Teachers' Training College, which will open in the autumn, letting ideas come to her before she starts planning and working in earnest next week on the mural in the College hall, a commission she won in competition. I understand, from what Mr. Pritchard has said to me about his writing time, how fragile the creative moment is at its inception, how easily lost. Could this distraction seriously affect her work?

"I'm glad you've told me, though," she says in her normal, strong voice. "Clearly, there's some kind of intimidation going on which must stop. In that respect only, I'm glad matters have come to a head but I must ask you, Lettie, please do not provoke any further confrontation. Allow me to deal with Priscilla."

We hear her go upstairs, knock twice then open the door and close it. As we all expected, the room must be empty.

13

Priscilla has her own front door key, so we three decide to go to bed.

"That girl in the shop was telling the truth," says Lettie, as soon as we are in our room. "Fancy Madam leading us on all this time about being a clerk. As if we'd have cared whether or not she was a nit-picker!"

I refrain from reminding Lettie that her role in this evening's events doesn't altogether bear out this assertion. "I suppose you've got to see it from her point of view," I say. "We've all been doing rather a lot of celebrating about each other's jobs. What has she to be proud of?"

Lettie snorts. "No need to take it out on Jenny. I'd dearly love to know what all that's about."

At some point after we have finished talking in whispers, and Lettie's rhythmic breathing is lulling me to sleep, I think I hear footsteps passing along the landing and a door opening, then being closed.

"I'm not going to church," says Mrs. Fuller, "I have to resolve this. No one else has to go who doesn't want to either. We'll need to help each other."

We're all breakfasting in the kitchen in our dressing gowns, with the exception of Meg, who is sitting with Jenny and, of course, Priscilla, whom we have not yet seen today. Winnie has told us that, although ostensibly recovered, Jenny is anxious but will not say why.

"We could sit with her, couldn't we Lettie?" I say, "So that you two can go to the Meeting House. You could probably do with a break."

Lettie agrees. Winnie looks relieved.

14

"I think that's a good idea, as long as Jenny is kept calm," says Mrs. Fuller, looking at Lettie. "There's no hurry but if you can manage to get her up, bring her in here. And then come and tell me. I'll speak to Priscilla in the parlour. I'm going to dress now. Then, I might as well go to the studio unless you call me first."

She must have come in when I went to the larder for a bag of flour. Now, she is sitting at the table, her smoky hair about her shoulders in a dull haze. Her face looks white.

"Hello Priscilla," I say, as evenly as possible.

"Hello, Rosy-Posy. How's Jenny?"

I can hardly contain myself. "Still upset, actually. Have you seen Mrs. Fuller, this morning?"

She ignores my question. "I'm still upset, actually, though you won't believe it, of course. That's why I went out. I was frightened."

Perhaps, she was. She looks troubled. I soften. "Would you like a cup of tea?"

"That's right, always smoothing things over." She gives a snigger. "The world can be put right with a cup of tea."

"Why are you always so hostile? I try to sympathise, to understand you but –"

"You don't understand the first thing about me, Rosy-Posy. You wouldn't know where to begin." There is a bleak vehemence in her voice which shows briefly in her face, her unnerving puce-grey eyes. She rises. "I'll go and find Mrs. Fuller." She turns at the door. "I shall say the same to her as to you now: Tell Jenny, in case I don't see her, she has nothing to fear. It wasn't her fault."

15

As intimated by this last statement, we see very little of Priscilla for the rest of the day.

"I hope I can believe her," Jenny says, when Mrs. Fuller and I relay the message to her.

Anxious not to jeopardise her recovery, none of us presses for any further explanation.

"I have made my position crystal clear to Priscilla," says Mrs. Fuller, "so stop worrying," she adds to Jenny, who is managing to eat and has colour in her cheeks again.

I leave a roast dinner for Priscilla covered with a plate, held by the pyramid of weights from the scales, in the hope that neither cat will get there first. When, after a stroll, Lettie and I return to start high tea, the dinner plate is empty and washed up, which latter suggests the cats were not involved.

I feel under-prepared for this afternoon's discussion of poetry. I thought that it would be a relief to sit, last evening, selecting my contribution, but found I could not concentrate. It was bed-time before I knew it, so I settled for William Wordsworth's To the Cuckoo, though I baulk at the line, 'Thrice welcome, darling of the Spring!' given the bird's malevolent behaviour.

Thanks to the Three Men, though, there is barely a moment when the shop does not have someone in it. In view of this, I have elected not to read today but to pass any opportunity to Mr. Pritchard.

True to his word, he has chosen Goethe. I love the sound of the language, when he reads Wanderer's Nightsong in the original German. "The poetry of every language has its own music," he says. "Goethe's German is so expressive, isn't it?" I agree. It is like a new door opening. I am grateful for the English translation, which helps me with the sense and has a beauty of its own. But I can also hear the untranslatable vehemence and longing of the original.

Jenny would like a bodice made for her just like Lettie's, which the latter is modelling in our bedroom. Jenny is of slighter build than Lettie, so that should make the task of design considerably easier for me. She removes her dress and we measure her. We go downstairs to cut a pattern on the kitchen table, whilst she sits in her dressing gown ready for us to try the newspaper against her. I am surprised how quickly we seem able to achieve this accurately, given that it is only our second attempt at such an enterprise.

When invited by Lettie, only half-joking, to place their orders, Winnie and Meg remind her that they made their own similar bodices before they came to Widdock. They are such a resourceful pair. I am relieved not to be pressed into production on a more extensive scale.

We see very little of Priscilla, leaving a plate of food for her these first three nights of the week. Although we wonder what she's up to, it seems none of us wants to talk about her, beyond remarking that she has received some letters.

As soon as I catch sight of Mr. Pritchard, my heart thumps. He is already in the shop, busily opening boxes of new books. I can tell from his stance and from his face when he bids me good morning, that last night's meeting of the Parish Council, at which he represents the Chamber of Trade, must have been a disappointment. When he is in this mood of residual anger his eyes, instead of being deep intense blue, are darkly muddy. I ache to console him. Offer him a cup of tea, Priscilla's voice taunts, but I have learnt that it is best to leave him to get over it, so I take the little wooden steps and start to tidy the shelves.

He has to summon his reserves of grace to deal with customers, but by the time he comes back from a walk at half past one his mood has blown away with the buffeting wind. Because the wind is so fierce, I decided to stay indoors and try to finish Mr. Darwin's treatise on the habits of worms, a little book given me, when I went home at Easter, by dear Dr. Jepp, who lives nearby our cottage. He it was who tended Mother in recent years and in the difficult pregnancy which ended with her death this January.

"How are you getting on with that?" Mr. Pritchard asks, as he hangs up his outdoor clothes.

"I had not appreciated how much earth the creatures move through their...digestive systems," I tell him, returning his smile. "It must be a refining process. No wonder gardeners call them friends."

He sits down opposite me. "Rose, let me apologise –"

I brush aside his regrets. "I'm only sorry...I mean I can guess it's about the meeting, but if you'd rather not –"

"Of course, I want to tell you. Why would I not? You are my greatest confidante."

I blush. "Thank you...I..." It's difficult to speak.

"Don't be embarrassed by the truth. I wouldn't speak so freely if I didn't think you'd understand."

I manage a smile at the affirmative gesture which accompanies these words, so very much a part of how he responds to life.

"In brief, they listened politely to what I had to say which, all credit to them, provoked a certain amount of interest but, with the exception of that chap Rivers, whom we see at Fabian meetings," I'm not sure whom he means, "the general consensus was that, without the intervention of 'a passing philanthropist' – those were the words used – housing the poor must join the queue, certainly behind discussion of a flood prevention scheme. This is the priority for which all the other businesses, particularly at this end of the town, have been clamouring for years. And who can blame them? So you see, they have me exactly where they want me. Hamstrung," he concludes, with a flare of his former ire. "They haven't refused the idea outright, so I can't complain. I am, to all intents and purposes, silenced. I don't know how I kept a civil tongue. I couldn't wait to leave. And I shall have to relive my humiliation when I report what happened at the next meeting of the Chamber of Trade, though you can be sure that they will have wind of it already. They have eyes and ears everywhere."

"We must not give up," I say, with conviction. "Perhaps there will be another way, though I can't think what at present."

"No, nor can I," says Mr. Pritchard, dryly.

"It's too soon, but there'll be something." Here I go again, but what else can I do? Curiously, I mean it. "If I can help in any way, I will...obviously..." I limp to a halt, feeling slightly foolish.

"Thank you, dear Rose."

We exchange a smile which seems to embody all our comradeship, but his has melancholy in it, too, it grieves me to see. Mr. Pritchard worked so hard on his report whose subject, models of sanitary housing, was called for by the Parish Council in response to his urgent social conscience as a newcomer to Widdock. Appalled by conditions in the yard behind this very shop, he soon found that it was only one of many insalubrious yards and courts in Widdock where the poor live in squalor. Whilst I spent Easter at home in the country with my father and dear sister Hilda, now his housekeeper, Mr. Pritchard went to London with his friends, the lecturer, Mr. Philpott, and a local architect, Mr. Cooper, who took equipment with him to photograph a housing estate in Tower Hamlets provided by the London County Council for their poor. In his report, Mr. Pritchard also referred to photographs of a housing scheme for factory workers at Bournville, Birmingham, and to the idea of Mr. Ebenezer Howard for what he calls a 'garden city'. All this I know from being at a rehearsal in the Coopers' lovely dining room, accompanied by Mr. Philpott and Mrs. Fuller, who plays in the same string quartet as Mrs. Cooper. The presentation was first class, we all agreed. I do hope this setback hasn't tarnished Mr. Pritchard's idealism. It is a trait that I find one of his most endearing.

I congratulate myself on getting through today, Friday, without giving anything away. Fortunately, we were busy, but walking up New Road after work this evening those images, which I have, thank goodness, kept at bay during the course of our daily duties, flash through my mind again. How I hugged him, feeling vividly his bodily presence, the texture of his hair, black as a raven's wing, as my hand reached to pat the back of his head in a gesture of comfort and consolation. The dream clearly arose from the anxiety I felt for Mr. Pritchard, while we spoke yesterday, and my heartfelt desire to help him, but the way that anxiety manifested has shocked me.

A bicycle bell tings behind me. I tug my thoughts away to Mrs. Fuller, now drawing up and hopping off to walk beside me as the road begins the upward incline.

"How are you getting on?" I ask her.

She tells me of her nervousness yet excitement at the enormity of the artistic project ahead of her. I manage to respond to most of what she says.

We join the others in the lively kitchen and, over the meal, share the highlights of our day, though my thoughts still wander. But the next thing someone says brings me right back to the here and now.

Chapter Two

I have probably been standing here, outside the shop, for only five minutes but waiting makes every one of them feel longer. I turn back from watching the bridge.

At the other end of the street, the crossing keeper is now in view closing one gate, then the other. Soon, the 'down' train will arrive and deposit its remaining, Widdock-bound passengers. I have learnt to call it this from my two brothers, Joe and Hubert, who work at the station. For a few moments after its departure, relative peace will be restored as it disappears round a wooded bend and takes a loop of track from which it will re-appear, in majesty, announcing itself with a hoot-toot as The London Train going 'up' to Liverpool Street. We hear it from the bookshop, when the door is open.

"Rose." She pats my wrist as I swing towards her. "Sorry – Mr. Gifford – wanted to chat." She's out of breath already as we trot down Holywell End. "No, no – pleased with me," she answers my concern.

High in his box, the signalman moves to his levers. As we turn into Station Road, the red arm lifts to allow the approaching train.

"Can't see them," pants Lettie.

We both glance through the railings as we pound along, scanning the platform.

"Other end, p'rhaps," I manage.

We can hear now, above the sounds of the town in general, a note which, increasing all the time, is almost a tearing noise as the great engine does its work and then, as it eases to slow down for the station, there comes the rhythmic rolling of wheels and its echo.

We run past Mr. Randle's workshop and forecourt, where his parked motor cars look like two little traps missing the horses to draw them, past one of the station flies, ready for any custom which the train might bring and, gasping for breath, into the station foyer, just as the light at the far door is blocked by the dark, thundering shape beyond, slowing to a mighty whining, clanking halt. I jib at the accompanying smell, like hard-boiled eggs which, if the wind is in the wrong direction, finds its way into the shop.

A uniformed railway official now steps forward into the doorway and faces the platform. It is my brother, Joe. We have to stand aside to let the passengers pass, a chance to regain our breath, but the minutes tick by. The last passenger leaves. We move forward at the same moment as carriages begin to slip past beyond us, the train making its loop.

"Tickets, ladies, please," says Joe, blocking our path.

"Joe – it's me, Rose," I almost shout in exasperation and to make myself heard above the commotion. "We're not boarding the train. We're not travelling, we're –"

"Platform tickets," says Joe, adjusting his peaked, braided cap, as if to emphasise his authority.

"We're seeing someone off," Lettie pleads. "She's leaving Widdock."

"Let us past, Joe, or it'll be too late."

"Nonsense. The engine will need re-fuelling, so might the tender. You've got plenty of time –"

"Here you are, girls." Suddenly, Hubert is in front of us, pushing platform tickets at us. "I recognise you, Miss, from your photograph. If I may say so, it doesn't –"

"Thank you, thank you," we both drown him out, thrusting the tickets at Joe, who punctiliously punches them and gives them back. Now we are plunging onto the platform.

"There they are!" cries Lettie. We head, pell-mell, towards the four figures, three standing together, one slightly apart, at the end of the platform where the front of the train will be. They are already looking in our direction, waiting for it to re-appear. The three look relieved, whether because we have arrived or because they can hear the train returning, it is impossible to say. The fourth figure gives nothing away.

"We thought you weren't coming," says Meg.

Lettie launches into her explanation once again, which takes until the train is back in the station. There is a moment of stillness. Then, along its length, people on the platform step forward and begin to open doors.

A porter offers to help Priscilla. "Shall I put'em both on the rack, Miss?"

"I'll keep this one next to me," says Priscilla, quickly picking up one of her valises, "thank you." She gives him a thin smile as he completes the service. He touches his cap and goes.

Priscilla rubs at her eye. "Ruddy smut," she says. For a moment she looks bleary, but she tosses her head back acknowledging an awkwardness on the part of all of us. "You don't have to wait, you know."

"Of course, we will. That's what we're here for," says Jenny.

"Anyway, it looks as if it won't be long." I nod to where two men are removing, from its position over the tank on the tender, a long sleeve on the curved end of a tall, adjustable pole, through which the engine takes on water.

"I'll say good-bye, then," says Priscilla.

We echo her, adding "Good Luck". There is, certainly, emotion in everyone's voice.

Priscilla boards the train and takes her seat. She is facing forward, so we step round and back slightly. There will not be much time for us to wave before the train has left the station. As if reading that same thought which must have prompted each of us to move, Priscilla says, "I shan't lean out, so when I'm gone —" She makes a cutting-off gesture, which coincides with a final slamming door.

The Guard steps back, regarding the length of the train. He raises the green flag and puts his whistle to his lips. He waits a moment and blows.

The engine gives a great huff, then another. A grey plume funnels and expands high overhead. Priscilla's carriage starts to slide before our eyes as we wave in an exaggerated fashion. She raises her hand once, but her gaze seems beckoned by the distance ahead of her. And then she is, as she put it, gone. The train gathers speed beside us. Now, we're looking at its back, veiled in descending smoke. And now it, too, has gone. We are left with birdsong and the resumption of normal traffic sounds as the crossing keeper opens the gates and lets through the carts which have been waiting.

We all look at each other.

"Phew," says Jenny.

Before anyone else can speak, Hubert hales us. "Rose — and friends," he says, his gaze lingering for a moment on Lettie, "it's my break. Do come to the buffet and allow me to treat you." He sweeps our protestations aside. "No, no, my pleasure."

So, we follow him into the light, pretty room with little round tables and bentwood chairs.

"I can see you're all a bit quiet, missing your friend. Perhaps a glass of pop will cheer you up."

We manage to fill the minutes before two of us have to return to work and the other three leave.

"We must have been a dull reward for his kindness."

"But he thought he knew the reason why you were subdued," says Mr. Pritchard, "so, by that token, he'll have understood."

And it's true that Hubert had been more interested in being introduced to those present than in further discussion of the absent party.

Mr. Pritchard is looking at me intently. "I think I understand. It's too soon to count your chickens, isn't it?"

Despite a Saturday afternoon's brisk commerce, the sense of numbness which affected all of us after Priscilla's departure seems to extend throughout our evening meal. Each is, no doubt, re-living that moment at this time yesterday. We'd put our spoons down and were about to clear the table when Priscilla announced, with an air of triumph, that she would be leaving, next day, for a job in London. "Query Clerk," she said and, when pressed, "Shadwell. A shipping company." So that was what those letters were about. None of us had felt encouraged to ask for amplification, nor did we remark upon the fact that she must have handed in a week's notice before she knew she'd got the job. "What time's your train?" Lettie had asked. "We must see you off." "Of course," Priscilla answered, her smile seeming to imply that she had found out an undeclared motive in words which had been spoken without guile. "You will let us know that you have arrived safely, won't you?" Mrs. Fuller had asked. "When I can," Priscilla said, and left the room to go and pack. Even Jenny had not seen her again till we gathered at the station.

Now it is almost as if we do not wish to speak of her for fear that she might appear at the window or that the kitchen door might open with a peal of derisive laughter before she enters to tell us that it was all an elaborate joke.

"I think perhaps we should spend this evening reading to ourselves," says Mrs. Fuller, giving us a purpose. "We can review whether we want to make an exception tomorrow evening and do something different." Reading would normally be our Sunday evening recreation, but we are all relieved to fill the remaining hours till bedtime in this way.

In our nightdresses, Lettie and I are just about to kneel for prayers, when we hear a cry: "Ow!" from Mrs. Fuller's room, followed by further exclamations, "Oh! Goodness!"

"What's the matter?" "Are you all right?" Lettie and I both call out together as we race out of our room. Jenny opens her door: "What's wrong?" The three of us hurry along the corridor. Lettie knocks. I call out again: "Mrs. Fuller? Are you all right?"

Our landlady opens wide her bedroom door. I recognise, in her other hand, the pincushion from her own sewing basket, the pins neatly arranged in a closely-packed diamond pattern. Their blunt heads are tiny, gleaming spots in the remaining light. She is smiling in a strange way. "Do come in and look for yourselves."

27

I take in, even as my eyes follow her gesture, a room with a bay window curtained in beautiful fabric, a hand-painted screen in glowing colours. Behind her, she has thrown back her bedclothes to reveal, nestling on the under sheet at the foot of the bed, a hairbrush and a brooch.

"Someone didn't just come back, while we were all out, in order to collect her valises. This," she says, brandishing the pincushion, "was what my toes encountered first."

"Well, well," says Lettie, "an apple pie bed."

"I suppose," I say, slowly, "it's because you're the mistress of Apple Tree House."

"How ungrateful," Meg says, the sisters having joined us, drawn by the upset.

"Her idea of a joke," says Winnie. "Typical."

"Getting her own back for my ultimatum about behaviour," says Mrs. Fuller. "The last laugh."

"I suppose that's why she left," says Jenny, quietly. "She doesn't like rules."

"She's mad," says Lettie, "biting the hand that fed her."

"Or biting the foot," says Mrs. Fuller. "But not hard, it was just a bit of jab." She picks up the brooch. "If she'd really wanted to do me harm, she could have left the pin open on this."

We are all silent. It is as if our former housemate, with her capricious temperament, is in the room beside us. I feel the need to say to Mrs. Fuller, "She checked herself when she remembered your kindness."

The others murmur, "Yes" and "that's it."

"I suppose so. I hope she remembers some kindness from every one of us," says Mrs. Fuller. Then, "I greatly regret that I disturbed you. I think we should all," she lets her gaze rest for a moment on Lettie, "go back to bed with the minimum of fuss and try to get to sleep."

…"Rose…" Under her breath. "Are you awake?"

I do not answer.

"I've been thinking… She didn't have many clothes. Why do you think she needed two valises?... Rose… You know what I reckon? In the other one, she had a pistol and a load of shot!"

I open my door to venture out and use the bathroom.

"Goodness!"

Dust motes dance in a broad shaft of unaccustomed sunlight, flooding the corridor and landing. Mrs. Fuller, who has been rising earlier since her commission to paint the mural, stands silhouetted inside what was formerly Priscilla's room.

"Good morning, Rose," she says, "I hope the shock is a pleasant one, this time."

"Indeed, it is." I pause for a moment in the transformed space beside the upstairs banister.

"Do you know," Mrs. Fuller goes on, "I think I'm not going to take in another lodger. The way things have turned out, I don't need that extra money now. I'd rather have my dressing-room back."

I have walked to the doorway and now I see, behind a chest of drawers which also serves as dressing-table and wash-stand, a door in the wall to Mrs. Fuller's room.

"I don't need to ask what you think, do I?"

I realise I must be grinning fit to burst. "It would be a great relief… just the six of us," I manage, rather incoherently.

"Yes, it would." Mrs. Fuller looks pensive, but only for a moment. "Do you think you girls could help me move this chest after breakfast? It's empty. It shouldn't be too heavy."

"Let's do it now, before we eat." This is from Lettie who, having heard Mrs. Fuller and me, has come from our room in time to catch our last exchange as, presumably, did the sisters now on the landing.

Meg calls out as they approach. "Do you need help?"

"There's not enough space for us all in the room," says Mrs. Fuller, removing the top drawers and putting them on the bed.

"You come out then, Mrs. Fuller, we can do it, can't we?" Winnie looks at Lettie and me.

Just as we are edging the chest into place further down the wall, the most exquisite sound reaches our ears. We all stare at each other, speechless, as confusion clears into astonished delight. We stand, transfixed.

None of us, I'm sure, wants to do anything which might make it stop but, although we do not speak, we must all feel as Mrs. Fuller evidently does, needing confirmation that we are not dreaming. We follow her, creeping downstairs until we are level with the parlour, whose door is open wide. There sits Jenny with the lid of the grand piano up playing, as Mrs. Fuller whispers, the most sublime Chopin Prelude, sunlight from the tall bay windows catching filaments of gold in her fair hair, a beatific smile on her delicate face.

I think I shall never forget Jenny's hands leaving the keyboard, finally, with such assured grace. And her eyes, having perhaps glimpsed eternal bliss, adjusting to the mortal world with a new authority.

"We shouldn't miss Church again, it'll be a mark against us," says Mrs. Fuller. "Luncheon's not the right time either, for reasons of digestion and because it would be unfair if Meg and Winnie had to leave before you had concluded." She refers, of course, to First Day School, at which the two Quaker sisters are teachers. "We've been patient till you felt able to open your heart to us, Jenny, we can wait a few more hours. I suggest that, as we had our quiet reading period last night, we could have an early tea and then settle down to hear all you would like to tell us. Does that suit you?"

Tea is cleared by half past five. We all sit down again around the table, Mrs. Fuller at one end, Jenny at the other. The sky is still the blue of afternoon.

"I'll start at the beginning. Get it over with," she says, "though I'm sure you will appreciate that the order and manner in which you will hear the facts from me is not," a momentary pause, "how I learned them."

Listening and completely still, we are like leaning stones.

"My mother was in service," Jenny says, her gaze on the clenched hands in her lap. "She was compromised by her employer. I was born in the workhouse."

I feel my own tiny exhalation, hear how it joins the others' to become a rustling sigh, our instinctive response.

Jenny raises her head and looks straight at Mrs. Fuller, who does not hesitate to meet the searching gaze with a gentle smile. She stretches her arms out on the table, hands open, palms up. We all follow suit. Jenny is the only one now whose hands remain in her lap. I obey an extraordinary impulse. I take Lettie's hand beside me, and the gesture is replicated all the way round the table even as I open my hand to Jenny. She takes it and Meg's on her other side. Now we are a circle, a ring.

"My grandfather relented, eventually, and allowed my mother back. The story was to be that she'd been married away from home and that her husband had died. But," this last word comes out on a high, gusting note, lacing what follows with irony, "of course, someone knew someone. Word got back.

"Grandfather would have sent both of us packing, but Grandmother pleaded with him on the basis that what was done was done. She said they should maintain their version of events. The other was, after all, only hearsay. Besides, it would look worse if they cast us out now, having taken us in. It would be seen to confirm the gossip. This last point was the one which made him change his mind and let us stay."

I cannot speak for sudden rage.

Mrs. Fuller says, "I believe I am beginning to understand. Your poor mother. And you."

"I knew none of this when I was very young. I took for granted the strictness of the household, the sense that every day should be spent in penance for sins which were always waiting to catch us out and claim us. It wasn't until I started school and found myself the subject of whispered hostility and sometimes outright jeering that I began to realise there might be something special about my own wickedness. A particular word kept being repeated. I asked my mother why. She told me I must never speak the word again and that anything anyone said about me was a lie. She said I should ignore them. I got used to living in a state of perpetual fear and misery. Eventually, the boys who pushed me in the mud and the girl

32

who snatched my apple seemed to tire of taunting me. In fact, the girl asked our teacher if I could sit next to her in class."

Jenny pauses. There is something about the way she looks, her gaze taking us all in, that brings to our lips a name, sounding like a hiss.

"That's right," says Jenny, "and the bully boys were her older brothers."

"Nice family!" Lettie says.

"They were the roughest in the village," Jenny says. "The brothers were as unkind to Priscilla as they were to anyone else. They'd pull her plaits and knock her over. Most days they came to school with nothing to eat – the family was very poor. If they did have a crust in a filthy rag, they used to guard it from each other. The father was a brute who drank his wages, the mother worn to the bone. When she wasn't seen for several days, everyone knew she was waiting for the bruises to fade. As she got older Priscilla, if she ever mentioned her mother, seemed contemptuous. I think she tried to stand up to him. Sometimes, she didn't come to school."

I wonder if the picture flashes through the others' minds of Pancake Day, and whether they, too, see another meaning in the way Priscilla said, smiling, "I'm fearless with a frying pan."

"She was bright, Priscilla. Sometimes, she would poke fun at the slower ones. She wanted me to do the same. I always thought she would turn on me again to punish my refusal. Mostly, though, school was never as bad as in those first few weeks, months. When the time came, Priscilla left abruptly. No one was quite sure where she went, not even the teacher. Miss showed me an advertisement in The Widdock Courier for a lady's companion. I applied and was

33

accepted. The maiden lady lived in a cottage at the end of St. Saviour's Lane. It was old and pretty, but very small. The front door opened straight into the living room, which was all but filled by a beautiful grand piano. She was a wonderful person, Miss Cribden. I owe so much to her."

"Ah! I think I know who you mean," cries Mrs. Fuller. "Striking to look at. She used to attend our concerts before she became infirm."

Jenny's face looks both tender and animated as she reflects: "She was the first person I could call a friend. That's how she treated me. She hadn't much money but she made it stretch to little treats: a punnet of strawberries in season, even a new piano score we both could practise. The cottage was not hers, but she left me the grand piano. She knew I'd have to sell it. Half the money I gave to my mother, half I kept in case I couldn't find a job."

She pauses. Tension is back, like the return to the room of an unwelcome guest. Lightly, I increase the pressure of my grasp on Jenny's hand in the hope it reassures.

"I thought I would never see Priscilla again. You can imagine how I felt when I came out of the interview for a secretary at the toothbrush factory, having learned I'd got the job, only to encounter Priscilla who had applied and failed, but been accepted on the factory floor. It was as if the lovely autumn day had turned to winter. Any hopes I'd had of shaking her off evaporated. She, too, had seen the vacancies at Apple Tree House. Again, I had to work hard not to feel sorry for myself by dwelling on how the pleasure of meeting you, Mrs. Fuller, and looking around this beautiful house had been spoiled. You'll recall, perhaps, how she answered for us both when you asked what our jobs were?"

34

"I'm afraid I didn't really notice," says Mrs. Fuller. "I was simply relieved that you both seemed to have reputable, steady employment but, yes, 'clerical' she said, didn't she?"

"Yes, that was to be the word, she stipulated afterwards when we were alone in the park. As far as our fellow housemates were concerned, or anyone else if the subject were to arise, her job was clerical. I pointed out that you two," she looks at Meg and Winnie, "had been described as factory workers, but that cut no ice. It was the fact of being seen to be inferior to me that rankled. I must have looked...baffled, I should think, which she read as equivocation. That's when she said, 'You will do what I'm asking, won't you? You wouldn't like your secret to come out.' I was so shocked I couldn't speak."

"I'm not surprised," I say.

"In case I was in any doubt that she knew everything, she gave me details, which I only recount to you so that you can understand how utterly horrified and overwhelmed I was."

"Go on," says Mrs. Fuller.

"It seems her relative, who came to the back door at the manor, didn't only peddle home cures and gossip. What a pity she hadn't been consulted, the woman said. She could have helped my mother with a feminine restorative. 'Lucky for you she didn't,' Priscilla said to me. I barely grasped what she meant."

"And lucky for your mother," says Winnie. "It would probably have been a concoction of pennyroyal, bitter aloes and turpentine."

"Sh...!" says Meg, the only time I have ever seen the sisters not at one.

"My word! We are having a frank discussion," says Mrs. Fuller. "No, don't apologise, anyone. It's right that we should be able to talk freely, at least within these four walls."

"There's not much more to tell you. I felt disgusted that she had no qualms in threatening me, but I couldn't run the risk of being disgraced. I might lose my job. So I went along with her bluff."

"Well, I think she was mean and wicked," says Lettie, "passing on her misfortune in life to you."

"Actually, in the end, I felt sorry for her," says Jenny.

"Well, I don't. If you think about it, she gave us all trouble – played a prank on you, Rose, with that Valentine card in your handwriting to Mr. Pritchard – " I need no reminder of that embarrassment, even though my employer wasn't taken in – "made me look a fool in the shop, gave you the apple pie bed, Mrs. Fuller. And didn't she try to trip you two up with your spelling?" Lettie looks at Meg and Winnie. "You know, when you were going for the job you've got now."

"I'm not sure she really did," Meg begins.

"Anyway, would you want to be Priscilla?" I ask.

"Let's all spend a moment in silence, wishing her well where she's gone," says Winnie.

She doesn't say, And hoping she never comes back, but the thought hangs there as Lettie gives a little snort. Still in our circle, we close our eyes. I wonder if we are also all searching our consciences. Was there anything we could have done to make things right or, at least, better? Afterwards, Lettie says, "Well, Jenny, would you like me to fetch a Bible?"

"What for?" Jenny asks.

"So, we can swear on it. To keep what you've told us secret."

"There's really no need," Jenny says.

"I agree. You have our word, doesn't she?" says Mrs. Fuller, looking round the table. "Our lips are sealed."

We raise our linked hands, repeating this.

"And now," says Mrs. Fuller, "I declare this meeting over."

We all let go. I can hear Priscilla's laughter as I ask, "Who'd like another slice of sponge and a cup of tea?"

"I can tell you," says Mrs. Munns, our cleaning lady.

Lettie and I are helping her to change the beds. This is our new, self-appointed task, freeing Mrs. Fuller from the Monday obligation so that she can go as soon as she likes to start work on the mural.

Lettie has been airing the possibilities about Priscilla's other valise.

"She had an old patchwork blanket she made herself," says Mrs. Munns. "I think she was rather proud of it. And I expect it reminded her of home."

To her credit, Lettie gives nothing away of all we know. We both simply nod and agree.

This morning, though, I am preoccupied, indeed somewhat shaken, on my own account. I have been revisited by an occurrence which I had thought was part of early childhood, a recurring nightmare. I am standing at the top of the stairs at home looking down, petrified, into the shadows where there lurks a monster. What can this signify? Can it be bound up with the fact that I am wondering how on earth, in answer to Mr. Pritchard's usual enquiry, I shall describe the weekend in order to convey to him the flavour without the meat?

In the end, I simply say, "Jenny told us her life history, which explained everything about Priscilla's part in it, but we all gave our word not to pass it on. I'm really sorry." And I am. In many ways, I'd have liked Mr. Pritchard's reasonable discussion though, of course, that could never take place on a subject touching such delicate matters.

"It's all right, Rose, that's an end to it. I understand."

Curiously, I almost feel he knows, he is so sympathetic.

We do not have time to dwell on anything further of a personal nature. No sooner do we turn the 'closed' sign, when the shop door opens and a gentleman enters bringing with him an air of urgency.

"Good Morning, Mr. Rivers," says my employer, from which I recall that this is the man who is both parish councillor and member of the Fabian Society.

It transpires that this evening's speaker is indisposed. Would Mr. Pritchard be prepared to give the Society his illustrated lecture about housing for the poor? He certainly would.

"The more people we can persuade the better," says Mr. Rivers, from which I deduce that he is, so to speak, on our side.

As soon as he has left Mr. Pritchard asks, with apologies, if we might replace our Monday afternoon poetry session with a rehearsal of his talk. "Can you bear it? By the end of this evening, you will have heard it three times."

Of course I can bear it. I could hear it countless times and not be bored.

"Oh dear," says Mrs. Fuller, with a rueful smile. "I was looking forward to giving this one a miss." She is tired, I can see, but rallies in the face of my concern. "No, I'm going. We must support our man."

Are there fewer people here than usual? Perhaps some of those who live further away, and thus not party to the new notices hurriedly put up in town, were also uninspired by the title, Eugenics, a word whose meaning I have barely begun to grasp. All the usual, local people are present, though, and this pleasant room, where on Sundays, Meg and Winnie sit with other Friends in silent contemplation, resounds with a pleasant buzz of anticipation.

I am seated at the end of a row in our customary place with Mrs. Fuller and her friends, Mrs. Cooper, Miss Robertson and Mrs. Neale, from the string quartet. Mr. Pritchard, being the speaker, is at the front standing next to a small table on which, in the absence of a lectern, he has his photographs and notes, his spectacles resting on top of them. He is chatting to Mr. Cooper and Mr. Rivers, waiting to start the meeting. My companions are using the time to catch up on each other's personal lives, so I take the rare opportunity of looking at Mr. Pritchard from a distance. I have to say, he cuts a youthful but imposing figure in dark trousers, his best jacket of midnight blue like his eyes and, against a white shirt, a dark blue and purple cravat. His thick black hair curls over his collar. He looks very stylish and full of energetic enthusiasm for his subject. Someone slides in beside me. It is Fred Rawlins, a friendly young man who started attending these meetings

39

shortly after me. He works in one of the market gardens near Greenfield, a town on the railway line nearer to London. He says good evening and, following my gaze, "Well, this is a turn up for the books, Rose, your employer."

He nods a greeting towards Mr. Pritchard, but I'm not sure the latter spots it as Mr. Rivers is calling the meeting to attention.

"I'm full of admiration," says Fred Rawlins, after the talk and subsequent debate. "Not only does he know his subject, but he manages to handle the awkward questions and give sensible answers that don't sound as if he's trying to fob the questioner off."

"Oh, he wouldn't do that," I say. "Mr. Pritchard would never lie if he didn't have an answer. He knows so much, though. I can't imagine him not giving some sort of credible response."

"What it must be to have an education such as his at your fingertips," Fred Rawlins's voice continues.

My eyes have strayed back to where Mr. Pritchard stands, talking easily with other men who have now parted to let two young women through. I can see how nervous both are, one clutching a piece of paper on which she has, presumably, noted the question she was too shy to ask in public. Mr. Pritchard inclines towards her the better to hear, against background noise, what she has to say. He smiles as she speaks, then answers her in what I can see is an encouraging way. Suddenly, I wish that I were queueing with a question for him.

"Every night when I come in from work," Fred is saying, "after I've eaten, I take out my books and read and write. I plan to send articles to the newspapers. Items of interest, that sort of thing. But I'm not yet skilled enough in the language. I know I'm deficient in expressing myself. I practise all the time, though, and I'll get there one day."

I give him my full attention. "That is very commendable," I say, "especially after a full day's work." Then, on impulse, I tell him about how Mr. Pritchard is helping to improve my education with our poetry appreciation afternoons.

"Perhaps there's scope for an amalgamation of educational interests," my neighbour smiles, as the star of the evening joins us. Our attention turns back to him with praise and mutual cordiality, but soon Fred Rawlins says he must go to catch his train and Mrs. Fuller, after congratulating Leonard once again, whispers to me that she is dropping with fatigue. We say good night.

"Did you recognise the Chairman of the Chamber of Trade?" asks Mr. Pritchard, as we walk through to begin our morning routines in the shop.

"Was he the one who asked questions about raising the money?"

"He was. Did you think I answered adequately?"

"Certainly. More than adequately. You answered everything you could and you were honest about matters which were beyond you."

"Thank you, Rose. I had hoped I was not deluding myself in feeling that it hadn't gone too badly."

41

"On the contrary. It went well. You can take Mr. Rawlins as being representative of the mood of the meeting. He was most impressed."

"I'm very gratified to hear it."

There is something about his tone, slightly ironic, slightly combative, which makes me look up sharply from my task of book-tidying. It seems to break a dream I had last night, which I suddenly recall. Messrs. Pritchard and Rawlins were at the Meeting House arguing heatedly, which ludicrous prospect might be enough to make one laugh if it did not leave an unpleasant aftertaste.

"I wasn't the only person who impressed Mr. Rawlins last night."

"Oh...?" Does Mr. Pritchard mean... what I think he means?

"You look like Bishop Amphiorax — about to drop through a hole in the ground!" says Mr. Pritchard, alluding to a scene in Geoffrey Chaucer's Troilus and Criseyde.

I am too horrified by his earlier implication to find this amusing. "Fred Rawlins is a nice young man... " I stutter, face burning, but not in that way, I want to say, except that I do not wish to lead the conversation down that route at all. "But he isn't... I'm not... interested..." I finish, lamely.

"Tell me," says Mr. Pritchard, "does your reaction apply only to Rawlins or to all men?" His expression of polite interest gives nothing away.

Now, I feel embarrassed anew but in a different, far more serious way. I cannot speak for the weight of what the answer would be.

"I see," says Mr. Pritchard, evenly. "I would just point out that men are not all the same."

42

I feel desperately weary. Oh, but they are, I want to say, in one respect. I want to say that they make complications, cause irrevocable consequences, that they are a danger. In this instant, it's January again and I am running in the icy dark, my father's stricken face before me, his terrible words in my ears, "Fetch Dr. Jepp – if only for the baby's sake." I think of the ten of us, alive. Jim and Annie who died in infancy. Lucy, who didn't see the week out. Raymond, stillborn. The one lost late in term, who would have been Paul or Paula. The five who were no more than sparks of the Divine. I want to say, but cannot trust my voice to remain steady, that I feel as if I have known this danger all my life.

It is, in spite of all my crowding thoughts, but the blink of an eyelid since Mr. Pritchard's last remark which, from a man's point of view, is perfectly logical. Of course, men are not all the same in character. Words come to me, together with a surprising sense of regret. This does not dint my determination. "I don't intend to pursue the topic. I shall never marry."

There is a very slight pause. "That's a pity," Mr. Pritchard says.

Do I detect an undertone of amusement? Or does he doubt my resolve?

All of a sudden, I feel quite cross. I turn away and start to tidy the books, rather more briskly than usual.

Chapter Three

Since the good news of Mafeking, three days ago, poles have been sprouting union flags and, in less ostentatious establishments, windows have been adorned with red, white and blue streamers. It hasn't escaped our notice that the appearance of these celebratory emblems has coincided with what might be termed, though not beyond the four walls of Apple Tree House, our own relief. As I walk to work, I recall Mr. Pritchard's comment made this day last week about Priscilla's departure. Any greater ebullience on our part still feels like tempting fate.

I find my employer in the shop holding a letter, which he puts down on the counter with an air of resignation as we greet each other. "I am invited to my cousin, Celia's, for high tea on Sunday the fourth of June to celebrate my birthday."

"Oh!" I cannot help the exclamation. "So, your birthday's in June, too, Mr. Pritchard."

"No, it's the thirtieth of May, but the Bank Holiday weekend is the obvious choice, given that she feels obliged to offer me a bed for the night. I may be a keen cyclist, but even I think that a fifty-mile round trip, with a substantial and leisurely tea in the middle, might be unfeasible in one day, though I'm tempted. You must think me very ungracious, ungrateful indeed, but Celia and I have nothing in common. She is simply doing her Christian duty out of a sense of family loyalty."

"I do understand about families," I say, thinking of Aunt Mary, Father's disapproving sister.

"For two pins, I'd make up an excuse to save me all the wasted time and energy. Who knows, my cousin might be

44

pleased to be spared the trouble of entertaining me, though I think the boys would be disappointed. They like to pick my brains, and I'm happy to extend their education. It makes a change from ping-pong."

"It sounds to me as if you have a duty – Christian or otherwise," I add, quickly, given my employer's atheistic views. "Where does your cousin live?"

"My old home town, Stortree," says Mr. Pritchard. "I shall make a pleasant day of the journey there, stop somewhere for a break – "

"You could stop at our cottage," I interrupt him, scarcely able to believe my tongue running away with me, "Markly must be the halfway point. I shall be there over Whitsun. Father's coming for me after work on Saturday, so you could take some light refreshment with us, and on Whit Monday – well, Father will want to leave early, but –"

"Whoa, Rose," Mr. Pritchard waves the hand holding his spectacles. "On Whit Monday, I shall be an arrow shot from Stortree and landing in Widdock, but on Sunday, yes, indeed, I can think of no better incentive than the thought of seeing you and your family. It will transform the trip."

I know I must be grinning like a five-year-old, but Mr. Pritchard, too, is smiling broadly at the prospect. "And speaking of transformations," he says, gently, "I've seen you, day by day, relaxing from the influence of that malign shadow and, shall I say, expanding into the light? I can't tell you how pleased I am."

My stomach lurches. His eyes are very blue, says a voice inside my head. I can't stop looking into them until his gaze widens beyond my head.

"Oh, goodness," he says, checking the clock.

In one move, I am turning the sign and opening the door before Mr. Vance's gleeful fist can wrap on the glass.

"Cutting it fine, Miss Alleyn, cutting it fine," he says with a droll smile, as I let the trio in: Messrs. Vance, Davidson and Nash. An exchange which Mr. Pritchard calls "the Saturday badinage" begins.

I return to my task, which gives me leisure to reflect. No wonder I have noticed, over the past few days, Mr. Pritchard looking at me in a manner which, although I hesitate to use the word, even qualified, was almost tender. Now, however, I fully understand this to be the expression of his heartfelt relief that I am completely unoppressed in spirits as indeed I, myself, acknowledge to be the truth of the matter. I must take this comprehension of the meaning of Mr. Pritchard's kind smiles as both timely warning and salutary lesson. Perhaps it is as a result of my lifting spirits but, ever since I stated my firm resolve never to marry I have, paradoxically, caught myself indulging in the silliest of preoccupations concerning my employer. I blush to think how I could come to dwell on the sensation when, in the course of handling coins or books, our hands chance to touch or, as in this morning's exchange about his birthday, I could allow myself to become distracted by the extraordinary depth of his blue eyes.

"Good morning, Sir, may I help you?" I am glad to turn my thoughts towards discovering, from this elderly gentleman's vague notions, the correct name of both author and title, so that I may find and present him with the book he wishes to buy.

"Rose," says Mr. Pritchard, the shop being suddenly empty, "when we spoke about my birthday and you, understandably, thought it was in June, you said, too. Is yours –?"

"Yes, the twenty-first," I say, "the longest day."

"How wonderful," says Mr. Pritchard. "I would, of course, never enquire –"

"I shall be seventeen," I say.

"Good gracious!" says Mr. Pritchard, smiting his forehead, "I always knew I was ancient in comparison but, seventeen... You see, you are so mature."

At this moment, the second post arrives. While Mr. Pritchard exchanges pleasantries with the postman, I try to place my employer's age. He does not seem as old as thirty. Could he be twenty-five, twenty-six at his imminent birthday? This would make him nine years older than me. I look at him, shyly, as he opens his correspondence. That greater age could account for his authority. I feel a sense of sadness, as if a gulf is opening between us, which is ridiculous of me, I admit, but I have always had an impression of being close conspirators not only against forces which seem set against us, but in outlook arising from our general closeness in age.

"Excellent!"

I look up from my resumption of tidying the children's shelves, which an unruly toddler disarrayed whilst his mother chatted to my employer.

"Listen to this!"

It transpires that one of the publishers, with whom Mr. Pritchard deals, has offered him not only sales of a new book, concerning Widdock, to be published at the beginning of July but, here in the town on the eve of publication, a talk by the author who will sign copies of it then and on the following morning in the shop.

"It's a pity that the whole thing couldn't be sooner, but we shall have to hope most people don't rush off on holiday in the very first days of July."

"Or, if they are about to go away, that they might want to buy a book to read on holiday."

"Quite so," says Mr. Pritchard, rubbing his hands. "Anyway, this is just the stimulus we need."

He is very energised and business-like for the rest of the day. I am, of course, glad.

There is still another good hour or more of light after we've cleared the table, so we are in Mrs. Fuller's studio, bearing armfuls of books, as her models.

"No, keep walking and chatting, as if you were going to your lectures – or coming out from one. You can stand still, from time to time, talking about what you have learnt."

As we enjoy becoming trainee teachers, who will feature in her mural, she sketches us with lightning speed.

"I don't like that Miss Whatsit, she goes too fast. I think my head's going to burst with facts," says Lettie, who is adept at acting.

When Mrs. Fuller decides to stop, we gather round. We are all surprised, I think, by the way she has drawn so freely with, often, one impression on top of another.

"But you must understand that these are just the beginning," she says, "to catch the sense of movement and to find groupings that I like and can develop."

She thanks us and invites us to look around the room at the several canvases propped on chairs and tables or against the wall. "I shan't mind what you say." She tells us in mock-exasperation, but with a good deal of pride that, "on top of everything else", she has an imminent exhibition and must choose what to include. Once again, I am struck by how rich her colours seem as the kind evening light slants across them: glowing ruby red and forest green, a blue whose depth suddenly reminds me of Mr. Pritchard's eyes.

"That's a pretty room," says Lettie, who comes to stand beside me, taking in the painting on the big easel, which shows the Coopers' dining room with Mrs. Cooper as a figure placing silver round the table. "Lovely colours."

"Like velvet." Jenny, on my other side, agrees.

"And look at how light touches objects," I say, "and how it… blooms inside the lamp."

Meg and Winnie are standing in front of three unframed landscapes. They appear nervous. Meg says, in a timid voice, "They'll be lovely when they're finished."

Mrs. Fuller gives a short laugh. "They are finished."

Both sisters look mortified.

"It's all right," says Mrs. Fuller, "I'm not offended. It would be like me trying to understand – chemical equations, but I will attempt to explain for all of you. It will be good for me, in view of the exhibition and, even more, the mural when it's seen by the public, to rehearse the exposition of my artistic credo – my vision."

She gestures that we should seat ourselves anywhere not occupied by paintings. Lettie and Jenny take an old chaise longue. Preferring not to crowd them, I sit on the stairs up to the former hayloft, whose sweetness permeates an atmosphere spiked by the scent of paint and turpentine. The sisters follow my example. They look interested and slightly more relaxed.

"You may recall that I studied at the Slade School of Art in London, where my parents lived," says Mrs. Fuller. "My professor was Sir Edward Poynter, who's now Director of the National Gallery. He was, still is I expect, a rather dyspeptic man. I shan't say that in public, but I will touch on the fact that his kind of subjects were not ones from which I could glean much inspiration – huge biblical scenes, such as Israel in Egypt, painted in a style which you would recognise, very finished. That's not a criticism of your artistic perception," she says to Winnie and Meg. "It's just a fact. I should tell you that when I entered the Slade, I was entranced by the Pre-Raphaelites."

"The Light of the World," Lettie pipes up.

"Ye...es," says Mrs. Fuller, evenly, "but less so in respect of that sort of iconography –what's in the picture – more for the decorative effect of the Pre-Raphaelites' compositions."

"Like William Morris," I say.

"That's right, and for their colour, their colour. You see they used the fresco technique of a white ground. It heightens the brightness of colour." Meg and Winnie are nodding. "What I learned from Poynter, though, was to develop my draughtsmanship, my understanding of the three dimensions. He is also a sculptor, and he taught me mural technique, for which I am profoundly grateful.

Then, one morning in the December of my first year, I decided to have a look at a gallery which had opened up in New Bond Street. Paul Durand-Ruel was a Parisian dealer who set up in London while there was war in France. The paintings I saw there and in later exhibitions completely took my breath away. What I loved was how those artists painted the effects of light – their bold brushstrokes. Those same brushstrokes which took you aback," she nods towards Meg and Winnie, "shocked me when I first saw them, but somehow the work of the artists, Camille Pissarro and Claude Monet, unknown then, stayed with me and influenced me at the deepest level.

What inspires me now is still the portrayal of light, but I have developed my abiding love of colour and I strive to simplify form to its essentials, making it, I hope, all the more powerful. It's been a lifetime's work." She gives the slightest of nods, as if to indicate a conclusion, but Lettie speaks.

"Your husband didn't mind then, you going on being an artist?"

Jenny's eyebrows rise slightly at the blunt impropriety of the question. The sisters, too, look embarrassed. Mrs. Fuller smiles, though.

"On the contrary, dear Tom was my staunchest advocate. My parents were deeply disappointed that, after I left the Slade, I didn't immediately start turning out the kind of pictures which would have made a name for me and money for them. Tom was a business associate of my father's whom I'd always liked and respected. I accepted his proposal in order to escape being married off to someone of my parents' choice. So, I gave up the London scene for Widdock, which was where Tom lived and mainly practised his accountancy. Then, I surprised myself by falling in love with him... We had darling Beatrice..."

There is a strong silence, while we all struggle to contain our emotions.

Mrs. Fuller coughs. "Really, I shouldn't be telling you all this," she says, in her normal voice.

"But we're your friends," says Lettie.

The truth of this runs, like a flame, from eye to eye.

51

"Yes, you are," says Mrs. Fuller, "and thank you for being so patient this evening."

Now, we are all speaking at once, reassuring her that it was a pleasure and that her public speech was just right. We clap, full of genuine admiration.

Jenny and Lettie start to move round the pictures again, Winnie and Meg begin a discussion with Mrs. Fuller about paint pigment, faces flushed, eyes bright, taking in what she says about the merits of one over another and offering technical comments. I stand, again, in front of the painting on the easel and marvel at how simple shapes can suggest a female figure, how that creamy dab of paint is a face which, to those who know her, is clearly that of Mrs. Cooper, and how the painting itself seems to radiate light.

"Oh, you know, pottering in the kitchen," I say, in answer to his usual Monday-morning enquiry. I keep to myself the pleasurable detail of just exactly what I was doing, and quickly ask him how he spent his Sunday.

"Bicycling," he says, as far as the north-western fringes of the county. Apparently, the author who is coming to publicise his new book on the subject of Widdock and its surroundings, has previously written about places close to the borders of Bedfordshire. "It was such a sharp, clear morning, I thought I'd go to Bartegston Hills. The views were magnificent. I could even make out Ely Cathedral. Oh, and you should have seen the wild flowers! I wish you had been there, Rose."

A new book arrived on Friday, just in time to be the focal point of a fresh window display for Saturday. Its title is Nature in Downland by William Henry Hudson. It has proved a draw already. This morning, we have been blessed with a number of customers on what would normally be our quiet day.

Thinking about the natural world I mention to Mr. Pritchard, as we are washing our cups and plates before re-opening at two o'clock that, the last time I went to the public library, I noticed a display featuring one of my childhood favourites, Bevis by Richard Jefferies, in a compendium of the two novels, Wood Magic: A Fable, in which the boy and animals commune, and the story of the adolescent boy, Bevis. I borrowed it and am enjoying re-reading it.

"Oh, yes," says Mr. Pritchard. "Have you brought it for this afternoon's reading?"

He seems so eager, I feel a pang at disappointing him. "I thought, as it was prose... "

"He can be very poetic, Jefferies. Let's see..." He scans his own bookshelves. "Ah, here we are."

The volume he places in my hands is bound in cloth the colour of mud, on which is set a stylish design of foliage, looking like bindweed, and the title, Field and Hedgerow.

"It's a series of essays," says Mr. Pritchard, "his last work, published posthumously, and I think his best prose."

My fingers curl round the book. "It looks lovely."

"Please do take it home to read when you've finished Bevis – or you want a change from it. His heart was in the right place. You'll find he makes some perceptive comments –well, I shan't spoil it for you. Oh, I've just had a thought. Would you be kind enough to write to Longmans and see whether they've got any copies left they'd be willing to let us have? As you say, the cover is attractive and the book would go well in

53

the window with the Hudson. They might profit from each other. When you've written, I might select a passage to read aloud. You've re-kindled my interest in Jefferies."

As it turns out, the effectiveness of our current sales strategy, or the desire of people to pass a pleasant half-hour or so in a bookshop, means that we have to postpone any discussion, of poetry or of prose. This, naturally, is heartening in business terms.

"I see," says Mrs. Fuller. "You use the jam as glue."

"It only needs to be a thin layer," I say.

"Otherwise the marzipan would fall off, or slide off?"

"I suppose so," I say. "I don't really know. It's just the way Mother taught us." I use the rolling pin to lift the flattened circle, as yellow as fresh butter, onto the dark surface of the cake whose heady fragrance mingles with that of apricot jam and almond paste. I gently push on the edges of the marzipan to bond it to the cake.

"And do you ice it straightaway?"

"No, no. It's got to harden." I hope my surprise was not too evident, but can it really be true that Mrs. Fuller has never made, nor iced, a dark rich fruit cake?

"Every time I've passed this week, my eye's been caught by that delightful cover," says Mrs. Fuller, who has propped her bicycle against the wall and come inside. "I should like to buy a copy of the book."

She is referring to Field and Hedgerow, a box of which the publisher sent in response to my enquiry. Both it and Nature in Downland have been selling well. "Yes, I'll take that one, too, please."

I parcel them up while Mr. Pritchard discreetly takes the money and thanks her. "Have you been working at the College today?"

She tells him that she has managed to persuade the caretaker to let her in on Saturdays as well as during the week. "I impressed on him that there is no time to lose, plus the fact that it's quiet on a Saturday afternoon. I don't have to try to think against the sound of hammering and sawing."

Mr. Pritchard says that, since it is nearly closing time, I can walk home with Mrs. Fuller. I fetch my coat and hat, and he lets us out of the shop, locking it behind us. I glance back as we walk away, and he's adjusting an open book which stands in the window. He lifts his hand and I do the same.

There is the usual Monday lull towards the end of the afternoon for which, I have to admit, I am glad. I cherish our discussions of poetry and have felt the absence of last week's almost like an ache. We sit down next to each other at the counter, keeping an eye on the street yet able to give complete attention to the subject. I always feel slightly nervous but, if it is possible to have enjoyable nerves, then these are such. Mr. Pritchard asks me to read first. I have chosen simply the first stanza of Thomas Hardy's Weathers, with all its joy of springtime. "Shall I begin?

This is the weather the cuckoo likes

And so do I;
When showers betumble the chestnut spikes,
And nestlings fly:
And the little brown nightingale bills his best."

In the following two lines, the rustic scene in spring warmth is described so exactly that, even if we didn't know it already, we would guess the poet to be a true countryman who, in the poem's final line, like the "citizens" he describes in the one before, "dreams of the south and west" although, as I point out, there's no reason why they shouldn't be imagining respite in this part of the country or its coast. Mr. Pritchard laughs, but doesn't disagree. We go on to admire not only the precise images which give us such a vivid picture, but also the poet's ability to place himself as an unobtrusive character in the poem.

In the pause, I notice that Mr. Pritchard seems a little nervous. Now I see, peeping out from beneath a copy of Nature in Downland, his own writing notebook.

"I should like to hear what you have written," I say.

"The usual reservations," he gives a self-deprecating smile, "and I'm still not sure whether –"

I dare to cut across him. "Please, read it."

"Very well. I could say – No, I'll speak about it afterwards, and of course, you must say what you like." He clears his throat:

"Flowers For A Ghost

The mist was thick along the path I followed
Beside the quiet waters of the river,
Hearing the blackbirds and the thrushes singing.

56

The light of day was slowly getting stronger.

The willows on the farther bank looked ghostly,
A darker blankness outlined on lighter.
A faint breeze stirred the dripping weeds beside me.
From time to time the eastern sky grew brighter.

A chaffinch and a wren joined in the chorus.
I heard the birds all round but could see none.
I watched my step along the slippery path,
The soaked grass waiting for the drying sun.

Out of the indefiniteness beside me
Like concentrations of the atmosphere,
Delicate white bouquets of tiny florets
Seemed to rise up, suddenly real and here.

All beyond them, everything below them
Had been made weightless, almost ceased to be.
The closely bunched blossoms leading forwards
Afloat in air were all that I could see.

As I walked on and left each one behind
The next and then the next became quite clear.
Something else rose up as I walked onwards,
Another river and another year,

A foggy morning in another May.
I gathered flowers like these with eager hand
And turned to run back to my waiting mother
Who seemed at first to have vanished from the land.

I panicked and ran faster and then saw
An outline vague at first, then growing clear,
Till breathlessly I offered her my posy
And knew that nobody could be more dear."

He reads the final line with a breath of a tremor, which sears my heart. For the moment, I cannot look up from staring at the blur of my hands, folded in my lap.

"I did think perhaps I shouldn't remind you..."

"No, no," I give a great sniff, regardless of dignity, and look straight into his eyes. "It's beautiful. Of course, I did think of – especially giving the posy, but that's the point – well part of the point. All those lovely images... I've done that, walked along by the river in the early morning. It was... wonderful – the poem, I mean. I'd like to hear it again." I fish for my handkerchief.

As if we are under a spell, no one comes to interrupt us. I relish afresh the "delicate white bouquets of tiny florets" imprinted against the darker atmosphere, and the drifting nature of the mist robbing objects of their substance, until in the last stanza there is one reassuringly solid presence.

We both know, though, that we must leave the world of the poem. Mr. Pritchard assists the transition by telling me, "While I was out taking the walk, I was simply responding to the whole experience of it. I knew I would want to write about it, but it wasn't until I came back and picked up Hudson, here," he reaches for Nature in Downland, "as part of my writing preparation, that I found the path into my poem. I began reading his passage about gazing for two or three hours at thistledown, which evokes a memory for him." He opens the book at a page marked with an envelope. "This is the nub of it. You'll see the connection:

'It was not only that the sight was beautiful, but the scene was vividly reminiscent of long-gone summer days associated in memory with the silvery thistle-down…. the sight of thousands upon thousands of balls or stars of down, reminded me of old days on horseback on the open pampa – an illimitable waste of rust-red thistles, and the sky above covered with its million floating flecks of white… But the South American thistle-down, both of the giant thistle and the cardoon with its huge flower-heads, was much larger and whiter and infinitely more abundant… These masses gleamed with a strange whiteness in the dark.'

"It's the image of the thistledown which he describes so exactly that inspired, sparked, one might say, the cow parsley memory-image with me rather than, say, the coincidence of his recollection being set in South America, which might have, but didn't, provoke a memory in me. That's the thing about reading and writing practice that keeps it interesting, one never knows what will bear fruit."

"So, it was three things together that produced your poem – the walk by the river, reading and memory?"

"Exactly. It often happens like that for me, though not every time I write. What is always the case, as you know yourself, is that reading enriches the mind."

I should like to ask him so many things, but the inevitable interruption is hovering outside the window. We contrive to look industrious.

I enter our sitting-room behind the shop and start to hang up my hat and coat. I can tell from the atmosphere that Mr. Pritchard is not his usual genial self. I recall that last night was the monthly meeting of the Chamber of Trade. Now what? I can hear him in the shop already, moving boxes of books. I go through quietly, bid him good-day, to which he responds in an abstracted fashion, and start my tidying. When the shop opens, we are both kept busy with queries and some sales. It is one o'clock before we know it.

As is often the case, a blow in the fresh air seems to restore his equilibrium. I am eating my bread and cheese, when he comes in waving a bunch of radishes.

"Oh, good, I'm glad you haven't finished yet. I thought these would add piquancy. You do like radishes?"

He looks so earnest and concerned, I can't help laughing. "I do."

"No, no, you finish your crust, I'll just rinse them."

He does so and, as he sets about topping and tailing, says, "I'm sorry I was rather preoccupied this morning."

"That's all right."

"I found I couldn't concentrate during my usual writing time, first thing. It was stupid of me, but I allowed myself to dwell on an encounter last night with Quinn-Harper."

"Oh." Anxiety steals up inside me. "May I ask...?"

"Of course, of course. Here, have a radish." He puts the plate on the little occasional table next to my armchair and starts to make tea. "It was after the meeting, which was all about plans for Widdock Day."

"Oh, yes, Lettie was saying something about that. It's the first one, isn't it? Like a fete, but including businesses."

"That's right. The idea is to see if it will attract people in from outside Widdock, as well as encouraging the townsfolk to spend their money. There's to be a parade with the brass band playing, as well as the usual stalls and beer tent on the

60

field. I'd forgotten it will be on the afternoon of Saturday the seventh of July."

"Isn't that...?"

"Exactly. The day after the talk by our historian. The afternoon following the morning on which he'll be signing his book."

"Well... isn't that perfect timing, then?"

"It is, for Pritchard's Bookshop."

"So... what's the objection?"

Mr. Pritchard twists his face so that his expression bears an uncanny resemblance to that of Mr. Quinn-Harper, his rival, if such he can be termed, a gentleman who when young, so the story goes, squandered his family's wealth. This reduced him, as he saw it, into becoming a tradesman. The first stock in his largely antiquarian bookshop was the library he had inherited. " 'You've got it all sewn up, then, Pritchard,'" says my employer in a dry, well-spoken drawl. " 'Pinched my old friend from under my nose.' I didn't know what he was talking about. Then I realised. I told him it was the publishers who had contacted me, not vice versa. I had acted in good faith."

"What did he say?"

"His friend, Bledington, chipped in before he could answer."

"He's that other nasty man who knew your father and thought you should have taken over his business, isn't he?" Just as odious as Mr. Quinn-Harper, his ally is a wealthy maltster, a trade he shared with Mr. Pritchard senior. When his son, Leonard, studied the accounts after his father's death, he could not help but see how, due to unwise investments, the business was insolvent. He ended up with just enough to buy this shop. Mr. Bledington will never know all this. "And he blamed you for starting a rival bookshop," I recall.

"Yes, but actually, he seemed rather irritated with Quinn-Harper. He said, 'Why don't you stock the blessed book in competition?' I agreed. There's nothing to stop him doing so, but he just waved his hand and muttered something which I'm still not sure I heard quite rightly. In essence, it sounded like: '...author's preference...far be it from me...' I don't think anyone else heard the exchange, or if they did, they are such gentlemen they'd pretend they hadn't."

I am trying to piece everything together. "Perhaps our author isn't such a good friend of Mr. Quinn-Harper's, after all."

"That's what I thought." Mr. Pritchard is laughing now. "He had to have the parting shot." Again, he mimics Mr. Quinn-Harper. " 'I've blown the dust off that old Jefferies book you're selling. Doing remarkably well – at my price.' He flounced off before I could tell him it was doing so remarkably well at ours, we'd removed it from the window to boost the new nature book by Hudson."

"Happy Birthday!" I suddenly feel embarrassed, presenting him with the bookmark I have made from card covered in green felt on which is appliquéd, in silk, a rose. Mrs. Fuller kindly found the pieces of fabric in her scraps bag and showed me how to suggest, by using two shades of pink, the furled and open rose petals, and how the light falls on them.

"Oh...! A rose from Rose. How exquisite!" He is holding the bookmark in both hands as if it were some rare piece of mediaeval tapestry. "Thank you so much, I shall treasure this."

We are standing so close that I catch the fresh morning scent of soap on his skin, so close that I could touch his thick, dark hair.

"You've made my day," he says, quietly.

We are looking at each other, transfixed.

For one bizarre moment, I imagine – What am I thinking? What is the matter with me? Ashamed, I step back, forgetting the little table behind me where I hurriedly placed my laden shopping bag when he came through to greet me. I feel the edge of the cake tin. We both hear the muffled clink of china wrapped in table napkins. Supposing I'd knocked the lot over! "Er...you go through to the shop, Mr. Pritchard. I'll join you," I say.

Everyone is here, straight from work, including Mrs. Fuller who has, as promised, brought a bottle of fizzy lemonade. Mr. Pritchard rushes through from where he opened it over the sink. He has it cradled in a tea-towel.

"Pretend it's champagne," says Mrs. Fuller, "if you want to," she adds in deference to Meg and Winnie, who do not drink alcohol.

Mr. Pritchard pours it into our tea cups from home and his two, all of which I have placed on his tray. This stands on the counter next to the cake.

"A toast!" cries Mrs. Fuller, when we all have a cup. "To Leonard Pritchard – and his first class bookshop!"

We repeat her words in rousing, if ragged, fashion.

"Happy Birthday!" I say, raising my cup again, and everyone echoes that.

"Thank you, thank you," says my employer, who seems quite overcome. "What an evening! I've never been surrounded by so many women!"

"You'd better make the most of it, then," says Lettie, batting her eyelashes at him.

"Oh, don't worry, I am," he says, returning her bold gaze, but then relinquishing it. "And now for this utterly splendid cake, with its beautiful decoration."

"By Jenny," I say, wanting her artistry to be acknowledged. Loosely inspired by the cover of Field and Hedgerow, she raided the larder and used angelica for leaves and crystallised violet for flowers to represent lilac blossom, writing the message (no argument about that) in perfect, pink copperplate.

"Rose made the cake," says Jenny.

"And did the marzipan and glacé icing," says Mrs. Fuller.

"Did she now?" says Mr. Pritchard, pausing, knife in hand. He sweeps me a smile, which makes me blush. "Thank you, Rose, constant helper and cake-maker extraordinaire."

"We didn't know how many candles to put on it," says Lettie. "That's why there's none."

"I doubt whether you'd have had twenty-three," says Mr. Pritchard, poised with knife.

Six years older says a voice in my head. Out loud, I say, "You must make a wish as you cut, but you mustn't tell us what it is."

"Very well." He looks directly at me as he's cutting, which arouses the strangest feeling in me. Then, Winnie and Meg are efficiently distributing slices and the room stills to 'ummms' of pleasure.

It had seemed strange to go home leaving Mr. Pritchard at the shop, but he had told me, earlier in the day, that he would be dining at the Coopers'. I was relieved he would not spend this special evening on his own. As Lettie and I conclude our prayers and climb into bed, I wonder if he has had a pleasant time.

"He's got lovely eyes, hasn't he?" says Lettie. "Rose...?"

"Yes. Very nice."

"Go on. They're more than very nice."

"You should know, you spent enough time gawping into them. When you weren't flirting, that is."

"I did that to test him... Don't you want to know why?"

I yawn, deliberately. "I want to go to sleep."

"All right, but I'll tell you one more thing. He's not interested in me."

This time I truly yawn. "Really. Can I go to sleep now?"

"Oh, you are hopeless. Hopeless. Rose...?"

I keep silent. I try to relax, try not to make five from Lettie's two and two.

How strange that the prospect of seeing each other in a different place seems so engaging. Mr. Pritchard has had the same thought, he owned. We are like two small children anticipating a party, I reflect, as I collect my shopping bag and a longer list than usual. I shall have to do some extra baking tonight in order to leave food for Mrs. Fuller to tide her over the next two days. As I walk up the hall, I see that the post has

65

been delivered. There are two letters, one from Italy for Mrs. Fuller. I am so glad, for I know she worries about her daughter. I put it on the hallstand. The other letter is for me. Hilda's rounded hand. My heart lurches. I tear open the envelope.

Dear Rose,

As you know, Father has not been well. (I did know from her last letter, but had failed to recognise the extent of his illness.) I don't suppose you had the sharp frosts we had here. He would stay out putting sacking round his seedlings. I'm sorry to say his chill came back and has gone to his chest in quite a bad way. Dr. Jepp says I'm doing all the right things, but Father must stay indoors and keep warm, so he won't be able to come to fetch you. Besides, you would do well to stay away in case it's anything more. Father's coughing his heart out and the house is full of the smell of Friar's Balsam from his inhalations. I'm really sorry, as we were looking forward to seeing you.

Father sends his love, as I do, and we both look forward to seeing you for Dot's wedding,

Hilda xx

Disappointment hits me like a fist, followed quickly by fear. Please let Father be all right. I find that I am shaking. This is what you get for being selfish. I try not to listen, try to concentrate on deep breathing. In the quiet hall, with just the ticking grandfather clock to steady my nerves, I try to come to terms with the anguish of a situation I cannot alter.

I put on my outdoor clothes and leave the house. I make myself think about revisions to my shopping list, now that I'm staying here. It forces me to remain calm. Doing the shopping will give me time to regain my composure.

He reads my face, blanked of emotion, before he reads the letter, which I've handed him without speaking.

When he looks up, it is as if our eyes devour each other's dismay.

Chapter Four

"What will you do, this evening, Rose?"

It is almost closing time, and I am waiting for Mrs. Fuller who has said that, when she leaves the college building, she will collect me.

"Oh, I shall probably finish Bevis. What about you?"

"I might go out on the bicycle somewhere – warm up for tomorrow."

It is as if the air between us carries my spontaneous thought, answering something in my employer's eyes: my unspoken invitation, though one which of course I cannot make, to spend the evening at Apple Tree House. Whilst our gaze lingers on each other, the thought seems to grow to fill the room until Mr. Pritchard nods towards the window, and I turn to see Mrs. Fuller approaching and dismounting.

"It's a pity you don't have a bicycle," says Mr. Pritchard.

My heart leaps at the way he says this, and I turn back to look at him. "I've...never really learnt..." But now, Mrs. Fuller is entering the shop and asking what it is I haven't really learnt, given that she thought I was capable of putting my hand to anything, and "Hear, hear!" says Mr. Pritchard. Blushing, I explain that we once had a bicycle, but it belonged to the boys, Ralph and Jack. My sister, Phyllis and I didn't stand a chance, especially with Ralph, who was very possessive about it. "I think he must have taken it to Sawdons with him."

Sawdons Hall is the big house where these two brothers and my sisters, Phyllis and Dot, are all in service, a fate for which I too was destined, had I not met a young man called Leonard Pritchard... I check my musings and wish my employer a safe ride and not too tedious a visit to his relatives, which sentiments Mrs. Fuller seconds, adding, "I'll look after Rose, you can be sure."

"We used to have this for breakfast, you know."

Mrs. Fuller arranges the smoked salmon on a beautiful gilt-rimmed serving plate, dividing the eight quarter-slices of buttered bread, from which I have removed the crusts, to stand as four elegant triangles at each end. I am poaching asparagus.

"Could you make the scrambled egg as well, do you think? I'll cut up this lemon to squeeze on the fish."

I assure her I could and whilst I'm doing so, she lays the table with the best silver, china and napkins. This is all part of her promise that the two of us will celebrate each other's company. Last night, we had lemon sole followed by candied fruits.

After she has told me about her day, "Always better when there is no one to come and interrupt me," she asks about mine.

I use the time I need to finish my mouthful thinking about my answer. "It's a funny thing," I tell her, "but it seemed, today, as if Mr. Pritchard and I wouldn't see each other for a long time, rather than just one more day than usual being apart." For some reason, I feel myself colouring. I race on, "I think it's just that I was imagining my time being completely occupied at home, which would have been so lovely."

"Of course," says Mrs. Fuller. She looks as if she's smiling inwardly at some kind of personal satisfaction. Then, she collects herself. "It was a shame all round. Would some Stilton help to restore you, or shall we move on to my namesakes?"

I find the cheese as slightly too strong for my taste as I found the smoked salmon too slithery, although I would never admit it and spoil Florence Fuller's delight in our "rather sophisticated supper", as she calls it. We move on to the little cakes she purchased called Florentines, which taste as good as they look; a lovely crunchy mixture of chocolate, nuts and glacé cherries.

"We could have had port with the Stilton, if I'd thought about it. I believe there's still a case of dear Tom's Sandeman's in the cellar."

"I'm glad you didn't think of it," I say.

Mrs. Fuller barks with laughter. "Quite right, Rose – and anyway, the bottles are probably covered in cobwebs and coal dust."

While we clear the table and wash up Mrs. Fuller, who insists on doing the drying, tells me that she wasn't going to mention it, (and here she looks uncharacteristically sheepish), given that this appears to be the birthday season and one more might be "de trop" but she has one on Sunday the tenth of June.

"We could have a birthday tea," I say, "with a cake, of course –"

"I don't need a cake," says Mrs. Fuller, "well, all right, a Victoria sponge sandwich, then. The point is, I thought that, if it's fine, we could take our reading matter to the park. Winnie and Meg could easily join us there after First Day School, if they would like to – and I thought Leonard might also, if you'd care to invite him on my behalf."

"What a lovely idea!" I can't stop smiling. "We could have a picnic High Tea there – cucumber sandwiches, cut very finely, like the ones Mother used to make." I can see Mrs.

Fuller wavering from her determination that there should be no fuss.

"Irresistible, I concede. Thank you, dear Rose," she says, giving my arm a little squeeze.

Then, she hangs up her tea-towel and asks if I would mind doing the putting away, as she must make use of the lengthening hours of light in her studio. Of course, I don't mind. As I return the delicate china to the dresser, it comes to me that, excluding Mr. Pritchard, who is, in any case, my employer, Mrs. Fuller is the friend I've known the longest in this town, having met her when Father brought me to start work here. I can't stop myself thinking back further to that dreadful day in January and what took place after I had been to Sawdons Hall to tell my brothers and sisters, working there, of Mother's death. As I walked homewards through the formal gardens, did the dear Lord take pity on me and fill my eyes with tears? I almost bumped into the tutor who, now his charge was well enough to go to boarding school, was leaving Sawdons and opening a bookshop in Widdock. And was it Mother who inspired me to be bold beyond belief and write to him applying for a job?

Returning the silver to its velvet-lined canteen, I muse about the richness of my life here. Bringing my thoughts fully to the present, I realise that dear Mrs. Fuller has been very kind, not only in keeping me company over a delicious meal of her own devising when, if I had not been here, she would probably have worked till light failed and dined on bread and cheese, but also in thinking of a way of including Mr. Pritchard in a birthday celebration she had never planned.

I wake to a strangely quiet room. No deep, rhythmic breathing to break the stillness. If anyone had told me, when

71

I first encountered Lettie, that I would miss "the chatterbox", as Priscilla always called her, I'd have been astonished.

Last night I sat in the kitchen, both cats wedged intricately on my lap, and finished Bevis before retiring, the sound of my whispered prayers magnified without Lettie's petitions spoken in a similar tone, fusing with mine and making a kind of comforting music, prelude to peaceful slumber.

I had thought that sleep would come quickly, uninterrupted by Lettie's routine expression of her random thoughts to me just as mine are losing their coherence but, instead, I lay awake worrying about Father's health, thinking of the two long days ahead and trying not to feel sorry for myself given that I have so much for which to be grateful. When sleep did claim me, I was troubled by dreams of moving through the empty rooms at home, then re-entering to see a figure, standing at the range, who made my heart leap and yet, as she turned towards me, being unsure that she was the one I longed to see. I must, eventually, have slept.

Now, I lie in bed in the silent room, listening to the birds outside, who sound as if they have been busy for hours, so it must be time to get up and face the day ahead.

The morning passes, without pause, in the usual Sunday way. I put in the roast, a shoulder of spring lamb which will serve for shepherd's pie tomorrow. Mrs. Fuller and I go to church for the Pentecostal service with its age-old reading about, 'a sound from heaven as of a rushing mighty wind filling the house' and the 'cloven tongues like as of fire' which sat upon each of the Apostles, giving them utterance in other tongues and confounding all who were later to hear them. But some people, the chapter from Acts goes on, thought they were drunk, until St. Peter stood up and reminded them of the prophet Joel's words, that 'your sons and daughters shall prophesy, and your young men shall see visions, and your old men shall dream dreams'.

"You'll have noticed," says Mrs. Fuller, afterwards, "that the daughters and the handmaidens are allowed to prophesy – they are simply channels, but it's the men who are vouchsafed the visions and dreams."

"I suppose the Vicar did try to include women in his sermon by saying we all have the gift of the Paraclete within us and it's our duty to go out and spread – what was it, the phos of Christ's logos? I've not come across that word before."

Mrs. Fuller looks wry. "That's right, the light of His word. Our Vicar likes to make an occasion to air his Greek from time to time."

I can imagine Mr. Pritchard commenting on the subject in the same gently mocking tone.

Over luncheon, Mrs. Fuller remarks on something which she says she noticed since my first day at Apple Tree House. "Don't look so apprehensive, I'm speaking of an accomplishment – your lack of the local accent, not that it's a strong one even in someone like Mrs. Munns."

I tell her that Mother was well spoken and taught us to be so, "though I can lapse" I say in a sing-song Widdockshire voice.

Mrs. Fuller laughs, but says, "Your mother was such a sensible woman, I can tell."

Speaking of her, it is as if I am bathed in warm sunlight. I feel the tremor of tears, but manage to control them by deflecting my thoughts. I dare to ask about Mrs. Fuller's daughter, Beatrice, of whom she has mentioned nothing since the letter which arrived from Italy the week Priscilla left.

"By now, she and little Miles should be at their villa in Ravello."

Her face has clouded. I wish I hadn't asked.

"It's a lovely place, high up above the Mediterranean. Her father and I stayed in Ravello once. There were beautiful gardens overlooking the sparkling blue sea. It was heavenly."

By hiding her anxiety about Beatrice behind a mask of nostalgia tinged with grief she, in her turn, has made a very good job of deflecting me.

I offer to clear up as I can guess that in the absence of the others, with whom she feels she must observe the conventions of Sunday, she would like to slip down to her studio.

"But what will you do?"

It is as if a voice answers for me. "I'm going for a walk." Once articulated, it seems the perfect way to spend the afternoon.

Instead of walking down New Road into the town, I turn up it. If I were to follow it north, I would quickly come upon the one-time hamlet, the row of cottages lining either side of the street in one of which lives Mrs. Munns. I do not take this road, however, which would soon give way to open country,

74

but I turn along a road branching due west. I have never before had occasion to walk along it. This makes the experience something of an adventure. As if to mark the fact, the Town Hall clock strikes three, the notes surprisingly distant from their lower vantage. I wonder if Mr. Pritchard is sitting down to his family birthday tea.

On my right, as I start to walk, are several houses in their grounds, as impressive as any of the larger ones in New Road. On my left run the long gardens of the final houses in our street, Apple Tree House included. Then comes a row of cottages, sloping down into the town but, on the other side of the road, the big houses soon give way to rough land and allotments, a pattern now echoed on my left. This road, it would appear, forms a kind of boundary to the town and, being quite high, affords a view of its western prospect. I can make out the Assembly Rooms, the Meeting House and, on a glint of river, the Old Mill housing Hallambury's factory.

Walking on I pass, after some time, a cluster of cottages around a public house. Then, after an interval, a stretch of high, brick wall and some wrought iron gates showing a glimpse of winding drive. On a plaque, situated in the wall, I read the words, "Hallambury Manor". So, this would be where Meg and Winnie's employer lives. The wall continues. On the other side of the road are smallholdings. Two white goats briefly cease their rotational chewing to stare at me from dark eyes barred with gold.

I come to a wider road, running across this one. By its orientation, I take it to be the road north which, eventually, will lead to Cambridge. At this hour of a Sunday afternoon on a holiday weekend, it is empty of traffic. On the other side is rolling parkland with, in the distance, some sort of large building, perhaps a hall like Sawdons. There seems to be no

75

sign to say that the land is private, so I cross the road and take a footpath onwards. Recalling that place makes me think of Phyllis, my favourite sister. Closest in age as children, we always played together, creating imaginary families from pebbles and cotton reels. After Mother's funeral, when I told the family of my plan to work at Pritchard's Bookshop, it was Phyllis who, with characteristic generosity of spirit, was the first to encourage me not to follow in her footsteps and those of my brothers and sisters at Sawdons, but to set out for a new and independent life. It was also just like her to do this with such wholeheartedness that she convinced me it really was what she craved even more than my companionship at the big house. My thoughts of Phyllis are always tinged with regret, for although I know that she is very good at what she does – this from the others at Sawdons, she would be far too modest to boast – truly, her sharp mind and practical capabilities are wasted being a lady's maid to two spoilt, adolescent girls. Had Phyllis been born a boy she would naturally, given her skill in woodwork, have joined Father as his apprentice. The irony of this fact cannot have escaped him when, from time to time, he utters the lament: "Six able sons, and not one of them beside me to carry on the name of Alleyn." Oh, Phyllis, I wonder whether you have any time to call your own this Sunday afternoon. If you have, may you be spending it with your tools, doing what you love.

As I walk on, swifts criss-crossing far above me, I'm thinking of the others, too, and Father, hoping he is improving under Hilda's care.

There is something about this building, now I'm closer, which tells me it is not a country house or manor. I can see a wing, which is neither orangery nor conservatory. I glimpse part of another, like it, radiating, I think from a centre – now I understand. With comprehension of function comes a chill realisation: this must be the one. I stop, everything coming back to me. I lose track of time until, faintly, I hear four chimes borne on a rising easterly wind. I turn and hurry back.

This morning, I wake early with the dawn chorus and know what I will do. Yesterday, when I returned to Apple Tree House I ate a scratch tea alone, Mrs. Fuller having already told me that she would join me for our silent reading time at sunset. I was glad, I have to admit, for my thoughts were in turmoil. I opened an anthology of poems new to me. It was as if I had been guided.

I draw back the curtain. It is a beautiful morning, the sun already up in a sky softly blue. I wash with the ewer and basin in my room and dress as quietly. Before I can change my mind and allow trepidation the upper hand, I take what I need from the drawer where I placed it, scarcely able to believe my impulsive purchase last time I went to the stationer's. It is as beautiful as ever and as inviting, if I can hold my nerve.

I put the pencil I use for writing shopping lists in my pocket, then pull the bolts on the back door. I step outside into a morning of gathering brightness. The wind has dropped and the garden is still, except for the buzzing of bees investigating snapdragons and the snip-snipping sound made by soaring, dipping swallows. Although the roses round the arbour are still tight buds, it is a pleasant place to sit, the wooden seat already warm. Sunlight bathes my face and hands. I open the lovely marbled cover, like the one on Mr. Pritchard's notebook but in softer tones. I look up towards the house, but I do not see it.

Two hours later feels like mid-morning and I haven't even had my breakfast. I am ravenous. I spend the time till luncheon writing to Hilda and preparing dinner. The sisters arrive first with Jenny, to whom they were able to give a lift. Then, Lettie comes in, 'Yoo-hoo'-ing, and everything is back to normal. I am slightly shocked to reflect that in those two hours of early morning, I gave none of my friends a thought.

"So, how was your Whitsun weekend, after all?" asks Mr. Pritchard.

I feel a curious awkwardness between my employer and myself as if, having been apart for two days, neither of us can quite believe in the other's continued existence, its confirmation, therefore, being all the more welcome. It is a ridiculous observation, so I do not share it. I do, however, tell him about Mrs. Fuller's kindness in keeping me company.

He looks pleased, but almost amused. "Don't forget your role in her life," he says.

I'm not sure exactly what he means and, feeling embarrassed, do not seek clarification, but merely smile.

"And you managed to occupy yourself?" he asks.

"Actually, yes." It is on the tip of my tongue to tell him everything, but I am suddenly overcome with shyness.

He is still looking enquiring, but it is almost as if he has guessed what I have been doing and chooses not to press me. This is, surely, another flight of fancy on my part. If this is what two days with little human contact does to me, thank goodness they are over. I move through to the shop in a business-like way, feeling Mr. Pritchard's gaze upon my back. It is a moment before he follows.

Routine re-establishes itself at Apple Tree House, which is comforting, and so it does at Pritchard's Bookshop. My employer greets the news of Mrs. Fuller's birthday party, if such it can be called, with a restraint I share. Although the opportunity for us all to socialise is an anticipated pleasure, he and I have both, I think, grown wary of too much looking forward.

And so, Sunday is upon us almost before we know it. All week, the weather has been improving. This morning, of Mrs. Fuller's birthday, dawns fair, with the promise of heat to come. Jenny plays her down the stairs with a piano arrangement of "The Ode to Joy", which I have learnt is by the German composer, Beethoven. Mrs. Fuller is delighted. She looks even more striking than she usually does, in a white lawn dress with a square neckline bordered in gold thread. We have all put on our lightest frocks, in my case Hilda's blue muslin again.

We give her the card we have bought and signed, none of us feeling equal to creating one worthy of presentation to an artist. She is genuinely pleased by its design of twining honeysuckle and roses and touched by its simple birthday good wishes. The elegant bunch of irises, not yet fully unfurled, which caught my eye yesterday in a vase out at the front of greengrocer Kate's shop, are of a velvety blue as deep as Mr. Pritchard's eyes. Mrs. Fuller is almost overcome and insists on giving each of us a little hug.

"Thank goodness we said four o'clock, not three," says Mrs. Fuller.

We have walked down New Road, hugging what shade there is. Mrs. Fuller carries a white parasol. Jenny, Lettie and I have three baskets between us containing, respectively, the sandwiches in a damp cloth; the oldest cups, wrapped in table napkins; a tin holding the sponge cake and a knife to cut it.

"What a pity I must stick to my own rules about gentlemen guests," says Mrs. Fuller, sighing. "We could have had a civilised tea in the garden."

I feel even hotter, as if I am somehow to blame for Mr. Pritchard's inclusion and the fact that he is male.

I hurry round to the back of the shop and find him outside, locking the door.

"I heard your footsteps under the arch," he says. "Yes, I know your fleet tread."

He looks cool in pale trousers and shirt, a dark blue blazer and a straw boater. "This is good of you," he says to Mrs. Fuller. "Happy Birthday – my contribution to the proceedings." He is carrying a bottle of lemonade. She laughs and thanks him.

Her spirits seem restored a little by the walk along the tow-path, mercifully in the shade of its bordering trees. They walk in front, exchanging the occasional comment, Jenny in the middle, Lettie and me at the rear. Lettie nods at the two profiles, agreeably turned towards each other. She makes a comic grimace, which I find slightly irritating and have to force a smile.

When we reach the park, we find we are not alone. Nor are we the only ones craving shade. The foot of every spreading elm plays host to humans.

"This was a bad idea," Mrs. Fuller whispers, pressed into the strip of shade afforded by a privet hedge.

"Oh, look!" cries Lettie.

There is something not quite spontaneous about her exclamation. We all follow her gaze.

"Hubert!" I say.

My brother is waving from the small island in the river, reached by a little footbridge. Behind him are Winnie and Meg, who are sitting in the shade of an oak tree, another bottle of lemonade beside them.

"We've been guarding this patch," says Winnie, as we join them.

"We bumped into each other, these ladies and I," Hubert says to Mrs. Fuller, "and I thought I'd help, but now you're all here, I'll just wish you many happy returns. Enjoy the lemonade –"

"For goodness sake, young man, you are welcome to join us," says Mrs. Fuller, "and we'll have your lemonade now. Then, I must rest."

As we settle ourselves, Lettie unwraps the cups. Miraculously, there are eight. We drink, gratefully, then Mrs. Fuller leans back against the bole of the tree, her sun hat tilted over her face. Meg and Winnie also ease themselves to use it as support, and take out their Bibles. Lettie and Hubert seem to have assumed the remaining shade against the trunk.

"Rose." Mr. Pritchard speaks softly. Already, the two sisters are nodding over their texts.

I follow his gaze and meaning: the shade afforded by a nearby spreading ash. We make ourselves comfortable and, for a long moment, neither of us speaks. It is very pleasant in this shaded warmth. As if from a long way away, we hear the voices of Lettie and Hubert, the former giving an occasional little giggle. Hubert is telling Lettie that, no, he can't say why, he just doesn't like his name to be shortened. Beyond them, we catch the odd word or a peal of laughter from the other party on the island. I feel the physical presence of Mr. Pritchard beside me, one leg stretched out, the nearer to me crooked, so that he inclines slightly my way, almost touching my spread skirt.

"Have you brought something to read?" He asks.

I am so close, I cannot help but look into his eyes. The proximity could be comic were it not rather disconcerting. I gather my thoughts and tell him that I have. I slipped the anthology underneath the cake tin.

"Good. We could read out loud." He waves towards the oak. "They won't hear us, those who aren't asleep, so there's no need to look embarrassed."

"It's not reading aloud that bothers me," I say, "but what I've been reading's rather... inappropriate."

"Really? How interesting!"

He's teasing me. I feel hot and flustered. I blurt out, "I've been studying W. E. Henley."

His attitude changes at a stroke. "He's good, isn't he? You've been reading the hospital sequence." It isn't even a question.

We elect to take turns, a stanza each before discussion. I read the opening sonnet, Enter Patient, with its evocative first line, "The morning mists still haunt the stony street".It goes on to describe the narrator entering the old hospital, led to the waiting room by "a small, strange child – so agèd yet so young! – Her little arm besplinted and beslung." He, the poet, feels his "spirits fail" at "these corridors and stairs of stone and iron, cold, naked, clean – half-workhouse and half-jail".

Mr. Pritchard reads:

"II Waiting

A square, squat room (a cellar on promotion),
Drab to the soul, drab to the very daylight;
Plasters astray in unnatural-looking tinware;
Scissors and lint and apothecary's jars.

Here, on a bench a skeleton would writhe from,
Angry and sore, I wait to be admitted:
Wait till my heart is lead upon my stomach,
While at their ease two dressers do their chores.

One has a probe – it feels to me a crowbar.
A small boy sniffs and shudders after bluestone.
A poor old tramp explains his poor old ulcers.
Life is (I think) a blunder and a shame."

We both agree that the poet's method of setting out what he sees in precise, graphic detail combined with his own heartfelt responses bears witness to the quotation from Balzac (translated by Mr. Pritchard) which he uses to head the poem: 'One couldn't say at what point a man, alone on his sickbed, becomes an individual'.

"Or stops being one," I say.

"I think you're supposed to ponder that too," says Mr. Pritchard.

"What's bluestone?" I ask him.

"I'm not entirely sure –"

83

"Copper Sulphate," says Meg, from under her hat.

"CuSO4," says Winnie, beginning to sit up. "It induces vomiting. There is another use for it —"

"Win —"

"I was going to say: but I wouldn't touch it, literally. It's highly toxic."

"What's highly toxic?" comes Lettie's voice from the other side of the tree.

By this stage, everyone is awake and Mrs. Fuller decrees cucumber sandwiches and more lemonade.

"Is that what I think it is, Rose?"

Whenever, today, the thought of this moment surfaced, I have felt a wave of sickness and quickly pushed it away. I must be mad. My mouth is completely dry, and this isn't simply because it is again hot. Never have I wished so fervently for a customer to enter but, as happens on sleepy Monday afternoons when the sun bakes the shop, no one is to be seen. We are in the cool sitting room, with both shop door and connecting door open, alert but free.

"Last weekend," I whisper, "I..." I swallow. My hands are shaking so much that the note book almost has a life of its own.

"I'll get you some water," says Mr. Pritchard, doing so. "Just bear in mind that I am entirely delighted to hear whatever it is you have to say."

He hands me the glass and I down a stale-tasting, sun-warmed draught. I take a deep breath and focus on the page, but no sooner do I speak than the words begin to blur. I push the notebook across to Mr. Pritchard and he, without hesitation, reads what I have written. As he does so, I feel a mixture of emotions: those of the piece itself, the inspiration for my writing, but I also hear the sentences for their own sake, especially the ones which, although I re-wrote them many times, are not expressed with as much elegance as I would have liked or, perhaps, do not catch the exact point of what I wanted to say. When he has finished, I stare into my hands, my cheeks flaming.

"Rose, look at me, please," he says.

I do so slowly, as he goes on speaking.

"Well done. I mean it."

"I could hear its shortcomings," I say.

"Of course. That's why reading aloud is so important. We can go through it later and test every word, but not now. I'm still taking it in. This is not the time to be critical. This, my dear Rose, is a moment of pure celebration." His big smile leaves me in no doubt he means it.

We're just crossing the cobbled market square when there is a cry behind us. The three of us turn to see Miss Robinson holding onto Mrs. Fuller's arm examining her shoe, now minus its low, pretty heel. "What a nuisance!" She shows us the offending object, as we re-trace our steps. "I can't limp round the Coopers' like a lame duck. I'll have to go home and change. Don't wait for me." She waves a dismissive arm in our direction.

"That's silly, you'll waste so much time," says Mrs. Neale. "I'm sure we're the same size." She places her foot alongside Miss Robinson's. "There! Come back to mine. It's half the distance."

The plan is readily agreed, and the three women return down the street we have just come up, Mrs. Fuller in her role as support, Mrs. Neale hurrying ahead to open her door and sort out some possibilities for inspection.

Mr. Pritchard smiles as we turn once more to cross the square. "I'm glad I shall never have that problem. I can't imagine walking with my heels off the ground."

"Nor I," I say, shortly, for my only summer footwear consists of shoes much like my boots.

Mr. Pritchard glances in their direction. "Far more practical."

I don't know why I should feel slightly annoyed by this comment.

"And they don't draw attention away from that pretty dress. Have I seen it before?"

Now, I'm feeling rather breathless. The evening is still warm after such a hot day, which is why I've chosen to wear, for once, my best summer dress of soft peach voile with a ribbon trim of a darker shade, a dress actually made by Mother for me and appropriate, I hope, for tonight's Fabian Society Summer Party.

"It suits you," says Mr. Pritchard.

"Thank you." I feel faint.

"I wonder if your admirer will be there – or should I not have mentioned him?"

I can't respond to the teasing tone, as he quickly understands. The possibility of Fred Rawlins's attendance would have worried me more today had I not had all my attention focussed on reading my work this afternoon. Now it leaps up to claim me. "I hope you're wrong about his motives." That is all I can say.

We enter the familiar street where, behind graceful black railings, neat front gardens give way to red-brick, double-fronted houses whose white-framed windows reflect the evening sunlight in their generous rectangular panes. Halfway down the street live the Coopers.

"Everything will be all right," says Mr. Pritchard, as he opens the gate and ushers me through.

At the top of the path is a notice with an arrow: 'Fabian Society, this way'. It points round the side of the house. Clearly, since it is fine, the whole event will take place in the garden.

We both arrive at the long side wall of the house together. It affords a view of a section of terrace and garden beyond. On the terrace, some kind of noticeboard has been erected. In front, looking at whatever is pinned onto it, stands Fred Rawlins. At the moment, no one else is in this oblong frame of vision.

"Slip your arm through mine," says Mr. Pritchard, "as if we were betrothed."

I gasp, but do extend my arm, which he places through his. I nestle my fingers round it. I can feel the soft velvet of his jacket through my string gloves.

"That's right," he says, pleased. "I'll let go the minute I clap eyes on anyone else, but now let's slowly walk forward..." he inclines his face to mine, "engaging in conversation in the way a couple would."

We start to walk.

"And I will tell you what a constant source of joy you are, Rose."

I can't help but giggle at his play-acting, though I'm also very aware of pleasant, if disturbing, sensations. I had never

87

supposed that walking arm in arm would be so agreeable an occupation.

"Fie, Mr. Pritchard," I say, deliberately coy.

"Leonard, please," he answers in the kind of insinuating voice a pantomime villain might use.

I have to turn away with laughter. As I do, I see Fred Rawlins look up, his glance freezing. He moves quickly out of our vision.

We have now come to the corner of the house giving onto the terrace. Before we are exposed to public gaze, Mr. Pritchard releases my hand, but with the slightest squeeze. "Well done," he says, "I'll follow you."

"Rose – how lovely you look – and Leonard, ever suave." Mrs. Cooper, resplendent in rustling silvery-blue, comes to greet us. "Do try my rum punch or fruit cup – non-alcoholic."

I choose the latter, which looks light and more refreshing. It is made from pink lemonade and garnished with floating slices of cucumber and strawberries. It tastes delicious. Mr. Cooper starts to talk to Leonard, so I accept Mrs. Cooper's invitation to follow her down onto the lawn for a "ferocious" game of croquet, the rules of which I barely know. I am aware of Fred Rawlins watching me as I go, but when I next look up, he's chatting to Mr. Pritchard, and looks reasonably relaxed, if guarded. I see him smile at something Mr. Pritchard says.

"Come on, Rose, your go," says Mrs. Cooper, and I try to aim my ball through the hoop, hoping to knock hers off course, too. "Good try. Never mind."

I notice Fred Rawlins on his own again, but the game is more fun than I thought it would be and I can't let the other players down by breaking off. When it ends, I see Mrs. Fuller and her friends on the terrace, sipping punch. I think that I will join them, but there is a crowd of people round the trestle, and the steps that end are blocked. I take a tour of the borders, which have all the flowers I love, presided over by towering delphiniums and bright lupins.

"I like those blue ones, love-in-a-mist, aren't they?" Mr. Pritchard has joined me.

"It's a bold display," I say, "with those lovely orange geums. You wouldn't think they were members of the rose family, would you?"

Mr. Pritchard is looking at me in a curious way.

"Someone has green fingers," I add, thinking of my brother, Ralph, who is a gardener at Sawdons, and of Grandpa Clark, Mother's father.

"Imogen," says Mr. Cooper, coming towards us. "This splendid array is all her doing. You're going to try my quiz, aren't you?" We follow him up the steps, the board right before us. "No prizes, just a bit of fun," he says, leaving us to it. Mr. Pritchard, who has already glanced at it, goes to re-fill our glasses.

The quiz is entitled: 'Where in Widdock?" and comprises half a dozen cunning photographs of aspects one would never notice in day-to-day life: a pretty, ornamental grille which one is sure one has seen somewhere; a bend in the river which could be anywhere, but for the shape of that building masked by trees. Now, where have I seen that?

"They've run out of the fruit cup."

Mr. Pritchard's voice, so close to my ear, makes me jump. I turn, and he offers me a glass of punch.

I take a sip. It is sweet and seems very strong. I pass it back to him.

"I see what you mean," he says, having tasted it, and with a deft movement of the wrist, he empties it discreetly over the wall onto the border below. "Don't giggle, you'll draw attention." But he's laughing himself.

Every time we try to concentrate on the quiz, we start to laugh again. "They'll think we're drunk," I say. I'm enjoying myself so much, I don't want this moment of pitting our wits together ever to end.

By the time food is announced, we think we have some answers including the line of jutting bricks on the front of our shop. "You mean the corbel table," says Mr. Pritchard.

We move towards the open French windows, as does everyone else. Mr. Cooper starts talking to Mr. Pritchard, "I'll show you," I hear the former say, and they both make their way in by the back door. I look around and meet the eyes of Fred Rawlins, as he reaches the terrace from the far steps. He does not return my smile.

"A lovely evening, isn't it?" I say, aware that my voice sounds over-bright.

"It's not my kind of thing," he says. "I don't fit in, Miss Alleyn, I've had enough." And to the group behind me, "Excuse me, please."

I am shocked. His look and formality make me feel I have hurt him deeply. I turn and see him, threading his way along the terrace. I am ashamed of how I agreed on arrival to play along with Mr. Pritchard's daredevil ruse and of how I only cared about enjoying myself. I must try to make some kind of amends. I take a step to leave the queue, but a firm hand holds my wrist.

A voice says, for only me to hear, "Let him go. It will be kinder in the long run."

I look into Mrs. Fuller's face, her sad smile, full of compassion.

"He will get over it."

90

I have to believe her.

"I'm quite tired," she says, "so I'm going home soon, after the buffet. Why don't you stay with me while we eat? We two can leave together."

Chapter Five

Mother's face is taut with fatigue beneath the soothing smile as she rouses Annie, telling her they are home. "Look, there's Rose!" She holds the smile in place as she meets my eyes, then turns back to the weary little bundle snuggled beside her.

I come out and hold Sable's head, though there's really no need. She's already dreaming of her stable and a net full of hay. Father lifts Annie and takes her through, placing her in his armchair. Then, he comes back to help Mother, guiding her foot onto the small step ready, if needs be, to take her weight. One either side of her, we walk her to her rocking chair. She settles into it with a sigh, eyes closing. The lamplight finds threads of gold in her auburn hair, rests on the fine planes of her face and accentuates how it falls away into exhausted shadows. Father looks at her for a moment, glances across at Annie and, convinced that both are asleep says, quietly, "I must see to the mare."

Mother rouses at the sound of his return. The hambone broth, which I have put to warm, fills the room with its delicious aroma. Annie wakes and, when she's ready, we bring her to the table. Her rest has done her good. She has some colour. She is eager to take the spoon and finish every drop. As she wipes the bowl with a crust, she says, "Daisy would like to learn her letters," which means she feels like playing with her rag doll. It is spoken in a tone of hope, ready to be disappointed. She knows that it is late.

"Just until bedtime," says Mother. Her gaze, resting on Annie, softens, becomes a brief smile, which Father's answers, containing every experience and emotion shared today. When her smile reaches me, it is a mask of loving kindness.

She lies back in her rocking-chair and I sit Annie next to her footstool on the rug. As I hasten to clear the dishes, I leave my little sister teaching her reluctant pupil from the four tiny books I have sewn for her, covers cut from the stiff blue of a sugar bag over pages from a sheet of Mother's notepad, all written upon by me as if they had been printed.

Father passes me on his way to make his nightly check of chickens and outbuildings. I return to the hearth, but Annie is already flagging. I take her small hand and lead her up to bed with no resistance. She is asleep before I've even finished, "Once upon a time."

Hearing my footsteps on the stairs, Mother looks up from her reflections. She meets my eyes which, try as I might to hide it, clearly contain the question on my mind all day.

"We must be brave again, Rose," she says.

My heart feels as if it has been squeezed in a vice. "What did they say at the hospital?" I whisper, clinging to the hope that I have misinterpreted her meaning.

I hear her indrawn breath. "It is cancer. 'Take her home,' the Doctor told us. 'There's nothing more we can do.'" Her face, which has been tight as a drum, crumples.

This is the fair copy of my piece of writing after we have, as Mr. Pritchard puts it, "tested every word to make sure it earns its place." I have changed how I described Father's speech, about attending to Sable, from under his breath, which sounded a little furtive, to the less obtrusive, if limper, adverb quietly and I removed a reference to the smell of the hambone broth because the word aroma does the work without tautology.

"Read it aloud now, please," says Mr. Pritchard, "and then don't look at it again for at least six months."

93

"When all its faults will glare at me," I say.

"There may be some, but let's be positive and look forward to what you next feel compelled to write."

I manage to get through it this time without succumbing to emotion.

"Well done," Mr. Pritchard says. "There is nothing further I need to know from that piece of writing. It has its own integrity. Any questions would stem from curiosity."

I am, of course, mindful of not boring him but, having disclosed this much about my family life, I am almost sorry not to tell him more.

Mine is the first birthday, amongst the housemates, to become public knowledge. I had thought Mr. Pritchard's quip, "Yours next, Rose," when we said good-bye after Mrs. Fuller's tea party, was to blame for the air of intrigue at Apple Tree House until I learned that Lettie had stored the information about the date from a chance remark I made months ago about my brother, Jack and me, sharing a birthday only a year apart, which had drawn her comment, "Goodness! Almost Irish twins!"

After stating what I should like to eat tomorrow, "Ham salad, so no one has to cook and, instead of cake, strawberries and cream, please," I ascertain the others' birthdays: Meg's and Winnie's close on either side of Christmas, Jenny's in March, passing without mention, of course, in the presence of Priscilla, and Lettie's in November, "Don't worry, I won't let you forget!"

Mrs. Fuller announces, with nods from the others, that she feels obliged to make an explanation about something which will come my way at some point tomorrow. It is a present to be shared by all of us, but I will have first use of it. Judging by the faces round the table, whatever this cryptic commodity might be, it is clearly welcome.

Lettie is greatly amused, when we go downstairs for breakfast, by my swift appraisal of the kitchen, which registers no mysterious addition to what I'd normally expect to see there. Mrs. Fuller comes in with salutations. "Winnie, Meg and Jenny wanted you to have this now, rather than wait till we are all together." She presents me with a card she herself has painted of The Apothecary's Rose, remarking, "A superb suggestion by our chemists." It is a Rosa Mundi, glorious in its opulent stripes of deepest pink and white. She has even signed the painting: F.V. Fuller and, inside, the others have, of course, written their dear messages. It is something I shall treasure. Already, I am enjoying this special day, but it's one I share. I think of dear Jack, my closest brother, going about his work as a groom at Sawdons. I hope that something he does today, or which happens to him, gives him as much joy as this.

Mr. Pritchard looks rather rueful. "None of the cards was good enough — all overblown cabbage roses — or puppies presenting bouquets. As you can imagine, the verse was execrable, so I hope you don't mind this rather plain offering instead."

He proffers a slim, rectangular shape, wrapped in tissue paper tied with raffia, under which he has secured a small piece of card. I remove it and read the inscription:

To Rose,
This longest day is yours.
May it be filled with light.

Best Birthday Wishes,

Leonard

"I'd rather have these words that mean something than a sickly-sweet greetings card," I say, with such fervour I can feel a blush rising to meet his smiling, gracious nod. I drop my gaze and untie the thin bow on the present, an elegant box bespeaking its contents. I lift the lid.

"Oh, my goodness!" It is more than I dared hope: a beautiful tortoiseshell fountain pen and a propelling pencil rest on a bed of royal blue velvet. My beaming smile meets his. "Thank you, so much... Leonard."

I cannot call him 'Mr. Pritchard' in these circumstances, but I feel myself blush afresh at the intimacy of using his Christian name. Even though we are standing in the sitting room where, my employer has suggested, we could be informal, I have kept up the practice of simply not referring to him by name. It is much easier.

"I thought you could use the pencil for your rough drafts – to start with. When you become more accustomed to writing, you may find that you always want to feel the pen in your hand."

I take the pen from its rest and hold it. I like it in every way. Its shape fits my hand. It is neither too heavy nor too light. I flex it between my writing fingers. It is as if something, some inspiration, transmits itself to me. I look up in wonder. "I... I can't wait to use it." I feel quite bashful and shy, but also thrilled, as if something exciting is about to happen.

"That's what I hoped." He is looking at me steadily.

I feel very hot now. I drop my gaze again and put the pen back, closing the box. "Thank you again." This time, I revert to my practice of not naming him.

"I've got something else for you," he says. He looks as if he is hesitating. "But I think it would be more appropriate next Monday afternoon."

I enjoy myself putting the finishing touches to a notice for a board which can stand in our window, and one for The Assembly Rooms. Both concern the author who is coming to give a talk and then sign copies of his book here, the following morning, which is Widdock Day.

It is pleasant walking through the town on this sunny afternoon, my birthday. I glance into the relative gloom beyond the ornately framed window of Gifford's, and see Lettie with a measuring tape round her neck, talking to a customer. In the park, small children are being encouraged, by their mothers or nursemaids, to feed the rather complacent ducks.

In the foyer of The Assembly Rooms is a table with a board on it, displaying the calendar of talks and meetings taking place there. I have already gained permission to add my notice to others on the table, advertising local events. I am not the only early bird when it comes to the programme of attractions on Widdock Day. Mrs. Fuller's distinctive hand is evident. The details of her exhibition are surrounded by a shimmering frame of dots and dashes which puzzle me a moment till they fuse to become – of course – our apple tree. The background to the details about her concert is different again. Washes of soft colour form striations, reminiscent of clouds in an evening sky. Her string quartet, Sonata, will be joined for the first part of the recital by Jenny. They will be playing Robert Schumann's Piano Quintet in E-flat major, Opus 44. Having heard the respective parts of it in rehearsal, I am both deeply impressed and eager to hear the whole ensemble. A door opens and closes somewhere behind me on a curt exchange of valedictions. Footsteps approach my back, then stop. Feeling unnerved, I start to turn.

"Good afternoon, Miss Alleyn." That unmistakable parched drawl.

I shudder inside. "Good afternoon, Mr. Quinn-Harper." I remember to say his name correctly, running it all together without the H.

He gestures towards my notice. "Do tell me, is that your handiwork?"

I say it is.

"Very good, very accomplished. The title of his talk should attract the widest audience. With any luck, it won't bother to read on and be disappointed."

He is referring to our speaker's Friday evening lecture, its title conveyed to us by his publishers as: 'Secret Widdock', and on the next line, 'an architectural and historical tour of the town'.

I say nothing.

His pale eyes linger on me. "Should you ever find yourself in need of employment, Miss Alleyn, I'd be obliged if you would call by my premises. Good day to you." He tips his hat and leaves me struck, like a statue, speechless with fury.

"Oh, look! Here comes Florence Fuller."

It is almost closing time. I follow Mr. Pritchard's gaze and see Mrs. Fuller wheeling her bicycle – but not her bicycle. I look again, scarcely able to believe –

"Come on! Fetch your things, Rose."

It turns out that Mrs. Fuller had long thought we should have a bicycle for general use, a sentiment with which Mr. Pritchard had agreed wholeheartedly when they exchanged a quiet word about it. My birthday was the impetus she needed to make enquiries at the bicycle shop, "And he had this one, second-hand but never been ridden, he reckons."

I put on my outdoor clothes and Mr. Pritchard locks the shop. "Just round Holywell End to start with, I should think, wouldn't you?" He asks Mrs. Fuller.

To start with... I am feeling very nervous, but excited at the same time.

"You'll be able to keep up with her once she gets the hang of it," says Mrs. Fuller, "so if you hold the back of the seat and be ready to run, I'll just hold her shoulders till she gets her balance."

"You're assuming I will get my balance," I say, breathlessly. I'm now feeling slightly sick with apprehension, but still wanting to try.

"Of course you will," says Mrs. Fuller.

"I have every confidence in you, Rose," says Mr. Pritchard, which makes it worse. Supposing I let them both down...

I sit myself on the saddle, which feels very bony even through my skirt. I clutch the handlebars still able, thank goodness, to touch the ground with the balls of my feet.

Mr. Pritchard places himself to my left and takes the back of the saddle in one hand and a handlebar in the other, both with the lightest of touches, but I am very aware of him right beside me as if shielding me. My throat feels dry. I swallow, hoping my nerves don't get the better of me. Mrs. Fuller's hands rest on my shoulders like two butterflies.

"Now try putting a foot on a pedal and pushing it down," says Mr. Pritchard.

"Which foot?"

"The one that feels it wants to go first," says Mrs. Fuller.

I put my right foot up.

"Then, as you push down with your right foot, lift your left onto the other pedal," says Mrs. Fuller. "I'm sure you don't need me to tell you that."

"It's all right," says Mr. Pritchard, close to my ear. "I've got you, Rose."

I don't answer, I'm concentrating too hard. I do as instructed. The bicycle wobbles forward. I push down on the other leg. I get my balance. Now, I'm beginning to move. Mrs. Fuller's hands leave my shoulders. Mr. Pritchard lets go of the handlebar and lengthens his gait.

And now, I'm in control, Mr. Pritchard jog-trotting beside me. I feel the movement of air on my face. I can't help laughing with the exhilaration of the moment. He lets go of the saddle. I am flying.

"Try turning," says Mr. Pritchard, still by my side.

100

We have come to the end of the shops. If I go on, I'll cross the railway tracks, something I do not wish to contemplate, so I manage to turn and head back towards Mrs. Fuller, now standing on the other side of the road from the bookshop. She waves. As I approach her, Mr. Pritchard, right alongside says, "Stop pedalling and brake, gently," which I think I am, but I find myself lurching –

He catches me as I topple sideways, Mrs. Fuller grabbing the bicycle. "Don't be startled, Rose," says Mr. Pritchard. "I would never let you fall."

Mrs. Fuller clears her throat. "I think, perhaps, we'd better be heading home. The others will be waiting."

After my birthday tea has been digested, we all take turns riding the bicycle down the garden path. Mr. Pritchard has told me that he is dining with the Coopers. I can hold the thought of his pleasant evening, while we are enjoying ours.

Meg and Winnie are tending the herbs and pelargoniums which they grow in the south-facing sun-trap by their French windows. Mrs. Fuller and Jenny are rehearsing in the parlour. Lettie and I are about to go down to the studio to see if her papier-maché chariot and horse's head have set yet – she is to be Boadicea on Gifford's float for Widdock Day – when the front doorbell rings. Who can this be on a Saturday night? We both hurry to answer it, hoping that Mrs. Fuller will be able to ignore the interruption, but she has reached the door first.

"We have gentlemen visitors, complete with bicycles," she says, as we approach.

"Would anyone like to go for a spin, we were wondering," says Mr. Cooper. "Just down to the park and back."

Behind him are Mr. Pritchard and my brother, Hubert.

"What a lovely, impromptu thought," says Mrs. Fuller, exchanging a look with Mr. Cooper. "Unfortunately, everyone's busy except for Lettie and Rose."

"Oh," says Hubert, trying not to look delighted, "well, if you two ladies would care to join us –?"

"How will that work, with only one bicycle between the two of us?" says Lettie. "If you think one of us is going to run –"

"You may borrow my bicycle," says Mrs. Fuller, with a slightly resigned air, but she is smiling.

"Lord knows how I'm going to get this lot dry," says Mrs. Munns. "Typical wash-day!"

It is as if we have returned to winter: wind and torrential rain. I hurry to the shop as fast as I can. My umbrella blows inside out twice. I have to hold the hat on my head. Even the men who are always to be found leaning on the bridge over the Blaken have thought better of it, this morning. I put my coat on a hanger and hook it on the mantelpiece. Mr. Pritchard ventures forth to pay in Saturday's takings. Soon, the sitting room smells of warm, wet wool.

We have few customers all day, which makes it all the easier to settle, without compunction, for our poetry session. It is so gloomy that Mr. Pritchard lights the lamps very low. It reminds me of occasions earlier in the year when we have sat in cosy companionship this way. Today, my employer seems more than simply eager to read and discuss. There is something charged about him.

I read first: A Scene in Summer, by Arthur Henry Hallam, which addresses his great friend Alfred, Lord Tennyson, bereft, two years later, by poor Arthur's early death. We both like the line about "a wild of leaves" above the poet's head where he sits "beneath a mossy ivied wall on a quaint bench". There's much else to praise besides.

As soon as Mr. Pritchard opens the book he has chosen I see, from the Gothic script, that the poem is in German. My eye falls on the first line: Du bist mein, ich bin dein. My heart lurches. Even I know what that means. This is a love poem.

"I'll read it through in German," says Mr. Pritchard.

"It sounds lovely," I say, when he has done so. He agrees. Although I am uncertain, I have an idea of what it might mean, which is confirmed when he translates. He doesn't need to look at the page, but gazes directly at me.

> You are mine, I am yours,
> Thereof you may be certain.
> You're locked away
> Within my heart.
> Lost is the key
> And you must ever be
> Therein.

My cheeks are flaming. I feel dizzy. Does he mean what I think he means? Surely not. I try to gather my wits. "There's no poet's name." My voice comes out in a breathy yelp.

"It's anonymous – a mediaeval Minnelied. That's what they're called, these love poems."

He is still looking at me.

My mind goes into a kind of spin. I feel the warmth of him next to me, mingling with that familiar hint of lemon. At

103

the same time, I am intensely aware of the sound of rain spattering in the gutters.

"You can probably guess why I chose it, Rose."

Yes, yes, but no, no, don't say it. I am torn. Part of me, a very deep part of me, feels as if the most thrilling thing imaginable is about to happen but, at the same time, there is another part of me which scents danger. I know I must be very careful but, as I look into his eyes, I can't remember why. I manage to whisper, "I think I understand."

Suddenly, everything falls silent, as Mr. Pritchard says, "I love you, Rose." A sunbeam enters, lighting his face, picking out the gold tooling on certain titles, making a reflection of the windows across the floor. I notice all this whilst, at the same time, feeling as if I am about to faint.

"I wondered whether... I mean, I rather thought..." I have never heard him so lost for words, "I mean I rather hoped, indeed, hope, you might feel the same way."

Of course, I do. I see it all, now. "I love you, too," I whisper. Goodness!

"Phew!" He says. He frowns slightly and, as if on cue, the sun goes in. "I realise this complicates matters, somewhat."

Why? I want to say. We get on so well. It's all lovely. There's even a rainbow just beyond the shops to bless us.

"We can't go on like this, Rose."

Even as he speaks, I realise the truth of it. My heart drops like a stone. I don't know what to say.

"We'll talk later," says Mr. Pritchard, looking towards the door, where a young lad is freeing a bunch of papers he has been holding inside the breast of his mackintosh.

He has come from the printers with a pile of fliers for Widdock Day. Clearly, he has never before tarried in a bookshop. He stands in front of the shelves, laboriously reading out several titles. He directs all sorts of questions to my employer who, of course, gives the lad an education in his answers. It's one of the things I love about Leonard Pritchard, his enthusiasm and generous spirit.

By the time the boy reluctantly leaves, it is almost time to close. Mr. Pritchard is serving a final customer, one of the commuters from the City who sometimes stray in on their way home during the last half-hour of opening.

"I don't like the look of those," says the man, fumbling in his pocket for change and nodding through the window at a mass of black clouds.

"You're right, Sir," says Mr. Pritchard. "I should go now, if I were you, Miss Alleyn."

"Oh! I haven't made the porridge!" I stop halfway up the stairs.

Lettie turns in front of me. "We can have bread and butter, can't we?"

"But everyone prefers porridge." I start to go back down.

Lettie comes, too, and joins me in the kitchen. She fetches the milk, while I spoon out the oats. "I don't know, Rose, you are forgetful this evening."

I forgot the stewed gooseberries until Mrs. Fuller asked if they were just on the dresser for decoration.

"Anybody would think you were in love."

Her words catch me in a gasp.

"You are in love. Well, well, about time you admitted it. You know he's head over heels in love with you. Has he asked you to marry him?"

"No he has not!" I put the lid on the saucepan with a clang. "He knows what my answer would be."

"Quite right," says Lettie. "But you must get him to ask. Then, you want to string him along a bit."

I say nothing. We go up to bed. Lettie rattles on until she talks herself to sleep.

I approach the bookshop with some trepidation. Did I dream yesterday's events? If I didn't, how will we behave towards each other today?

The minute I walk through to the shop, Mr. Pritchard being already in there going through papers, I can tell from his brief greeting and whole demeanour that nothing is further from his mind than thoughts of love. I recall, instantly, that last night was the last meeting of the Chamber of Trade before the summer break. I go quietly to the shelves and start to tidy them.

After a while, though, before climbing the little steps to start the next section, I turn to him. "Would it help to tell me what happened?"

He looks up and his face breaks into a smile. "Yes, it would. Then, I can forget about it. Come and sit next to me, here."

I take up my familiar position and feel warmed by everything that there is between us.

"As you can imagine, all the talk was of Widdock Day. Someone said perhaps we should have called it Widdock Weekend. 'Oh yes,' someone else pipes up, 'it sounds better.' 'I meant the advertisements for Sunday events, the church services and the brass band with their hymns in the park' says the first person. Then you can guess who chipped in. 'And the businesses who have managed to promote their Friday night events, as well those on Saturday, which I seem to recall is Widdock Day.' Quinn-Harper was looking directly at me, of course."

"What did you say?"

"I reminded him that the programme had been printed by the Parish Council, not businesses. 'In consultation,' he said, with his little smile, but the Chairman called the meeting to order and said that we can have a full discussion of next year's event after we've gauged the success of this year's."

"That was sensible."

"Yes, and I really shouldn't allow the negative to irritate me and cloud the positive. In Any Other Business, Mr. Hallambury issued us all with an invitation. I think he's rather proud of a piece of new equipment which he will be ready to show us by mid-July, and he's going to give us a guided tour of the factory. I feel privileged, being allowed a glimpse of developments in modern science."

"You might be allowed a glimpse of Meg and Winnie," I say, as the Town Hall clock strikes ten and we move to open up.

"I haven't forgotten our unfinished business, by the way, Rose," he says, as our potential first customer hovers at the window.

So, I didn't dream it.

There is a buzz in the air, with customers in most of the morning, including people attracted by my notices who use the opportunity to conjecture about Widdock Day and to take a programme or read it in the shop.

Mr. Pritchard picks one up. "What on earth's an Exemption Dog Show?"

I confess I don't know.

"New Kennel Club rules," says a gentleman in tweeds, as he leaves.

Mr. Pritchard looks none the wiser.

It is not till after I have finished my lunch and he comes into the sitting room from his customary walk that we are suddenly alone. I am having another crack at The Awkward Age by Henry James, written almost entirely in dialogue. I am flagging, but I keep my eyes on the page. My heart is racing.

"Rose..."

I hear him sit down in his armchair opposite. I raise my eyes to his – and feel weak, as if I have dissolved.

"I do love you."

I feel fluttery inside and instantly shy. "I... love you, too... Leonard," I whisper. Speaking his name seems bold, almost shocking.

"You can guess, what I'm going to say. Well, not exactly, perhaps. Really, I'm with Shelley on the subject of love between men and women. No, don't look apprehensive, I accept how things are – the status quo, I mean. The fact is, there's no one else I'd rather spend my life with than you. I know you're young and I know you've already made your views clear – abundantly so, but not in relation to me. I've got to ask the question but you don't have to give me an answer – well, not immediately."

He speaks the words. I am delirious with joy. At the same time, a mean voice says: Now you're for it.

"Well?"

We have hardly shut the bedroom door before Lettie requires amplification of the merest nod I gave her in response to her questioning look when we met at dinner.

"Yes, he asked me to marry him."

Lettie gives a little squeal of delight and kneads my arm with excitement. "Let's quickly get ready for bed, then you can tell me everything."

Prayers said, we slip between the sheets, able to talk freely as Mrs. Fuller has yet to return from rehearsing with what is now the string quintet.

"So, I don't have to give an answer straightaway, thank goodness," I conclude, after a brief summary of events.

"You'll have to get used to calling him Leonard, or you'll sound like some funny old couple from a Dickens novel," says Lettie. "Ooh, Rose, I'm so happy for you – except –"

I turn my pillowed head at the sudden downcast voice.

"I don't want you to leave Apple Tree House."

It is as if a chill fist knocks at my heart. "I don't want to leave Apple Tree House either. I don't even want to think about it."

Perhaps the Fates were listening to me. Certainly, there has been little time to call our own in the run-up to Widdock Day, a fresh delivery of programmes disappearing just as quickly as the first and bringing welcome custom. Leonard becomes, again, Mr. Pritchard as we are, of necessity, back on a business footing, almost. There is a sweet tension, but we have agreed to keep the love between us unspoken. I will give my answer when I return from the two-week summer holiday which Mr. Pritchard insists I take, culminating in Dot's wedding on the Saturday of the Bank Holiday weekend. I feel as if I would like this heightened atmosphere to last forever, but I realise that Mr. Pritchard cannot feel the same.

June slips into July on a changeable note, quashing any whims about weekend bicycling, and Mr. Pritchard has been much exercised in writing to the publishers of our guest author's new book, Widdock and its Locality, copies of which, until late this morning on the day of his talk, had not arrived. Hardly stopping for lunch, we have spent the afternoon unpacking and displaying it in the window. I rush home for a hurried high tea.

The next time I see my love will be at The Assembly Rooms for 'Secret Widdock: an architectural and historical tour of the town'.

Chapter Six

For the first time in the history of our friendship as residents of Apple Tree House, we are all six going out together. As we walk down to the town, we are joined by Mrs. Munns. Her husband, she informs us, prefers his vegetable patch to a talk about Widdock " 'which probably won't tell us anything we don't already know.' That's Munns for you."

It is a warm evening and the town is full of people many of whom, like us, are converging on the Assembly Rooms. Perhaps it is the subject of tonight's talk which prompts me to appreciate afresh this handsome building from the olden days, whose main hall has panelled walls with elegant mouldings and graceful chandeliers. As well as the faces I might expect to find at such a meeting, including the Coopers, Mrs. Neale, Miss Robertson and Messrs. Davidson, Nash and Vance, there are a large number of people unfamiliar to me but not, judging by the cheery exchange of greetings, to Mrs. Munns. These must be townsfolk drawn by the intriguing title of the talk. There is quite a different atmosphere from that of the Fabian Society at the Meeting House or of Mr. Philpott's lectures, which also took place here.

All this is a backdrop, though, to my immediate impression. At the front of the room stands Mr. Pritchard, looking tall and slim and wearing his velvet jacket of midnight blue. The sight of him jolts me to the core. I have to stop myself from rushing straight over to him, especially when he spots and acknowledges me with a smile as we take our seats near the front. Beside him stands a board displaying a street plan of Widdock. Next to this is a table bearing further papers placed ready, I imagine, to be pegged onto the board on the other side of which stands a large man, as tall as Mr. Pritchard, wearing a white carnation in his buttonhole and a lace jabot which falls over the waistcoat of his dark suit. A shock of grey hair tumbles towards fearsome brows. As if to compensate for this overshadowing, the eyes under them are slightly protuberant, a watery flint. "Do we tell them they can buy it at a discount if they come to the launch?" I hear him ask.

"I can't do that," says Mr. Pritchard. "I am bound by The Net Book Agreement."

"Oh, I forgot that's law now."

"I think we should start, Sir," says Mr. Pritchard.

He looks tense. From the corner of my eye I catch, slinking into two vacant seats nearby, Mr. Quinn-Harper and his friend, Mr. Bledington.

The room quietens in expectation. After he has been introduced by Mr. Pritchard, the author begins his talk by speaking of Widdock's origins in Roman times and earlier. The number of nodding heads suggests that this fact is not a revelation. I wonder if Mrs. Munns, seated beside me, is relieved that her husband did not come. Next, though, we learn that Widdock, as we know it, came into being in the Middle Ages.

"You may have heard of one Guy Martel," says our speaker, pronouncing the names the French way. His confident, sonorous voice has no difficulty reaching the back of the hall.

There is a barely audible murmur of recognition. This, I sense, is a polite audience keen to learn.

"He was a local knight who joined forces, around 1210, with Simon de Montfort – not the Magna Carta fellow, but his father Simon the Fourth. Guy and Simon both fought in the Albigensian Crusade in Southern France. In fact our man, Guy, made quite a name for himself in battle all over the Languedoc, the lands where the language Occitaine, or Oc, was spoken. When Guy returned home in glory, he sought to give thanks to God for His infinite mercy in sparing him. What better way could there be to do this than by following the example of the Knights Templar? He built a town and, wanting to make sure that no one forgot its founder, he named it after himself with the sobriquet he had gained from his victories in Southern France: Guy d'Oc. Over the years, the G softened and corrupted, possibly blending with the English diminutive, Will, to become –" he opens his hands to the room and we all join him in naming our dear town, "Widdock."

Perhaps having failed to absorb, from Mr. Pritchard's opening remarks, the usual etiquette regarding questions, Mrs. Munns's hand shoots up like an arrow before the speaker can draw breath to continue.

"Madam." The tone is one of indulging a tiresome child.

"That's a very interesting explanation, Mr. Buscott –"

"Truscott," the addressee interjects, clipping the final syllable as if there were no vowel, "the name's Buttleigh-Truscott."

"But we were always taught, Sir," Mrs. Munns continues, undaunted, "that the name Widdock comes from the Wide Oak." Encouraged by the gentle hiss of "yes, yes", Mrs. Munns adds, "If you walked through the park to get here, Sir, you'll have seen it."

There is a further ripple of whispered affirmatives.

"Thank you, Madam," says our speaker. "I was about to say that, of course, the Wide Oak legend has gained a great deal of popular currency over the years. Whilst it might be unusual for a tree of this genus to live as long as eight hundred years, it is not unprecedented. Certainly, the present

113

specimen could be a descendant of an original Wide Oak. Scholarly opinion regarding the name, however, favours the account I have just given you because it is based on a signed fragment in Guy's own handwriting, in which he pledges to build a villa, by which he means town, to the glory of God. I believe it would not be unreasonable, therefore, to conclude that this turned out to be Widdock."

"H'm," says Mrs. Munns under her breath, but amenable murmurs around the room suggest that some townsfolk are prepared to acknowledge Mr. Buttleigh-Truscott's argument.

He then goes on to show us, with reference to the plan pegged to the board, the streets lying behind and parallel to the High Street which follow the mediaeval pattern. This can be compared with towns such as St. Albans, he says, presenting his plan of that town beside the one of Widdock and using a pointer to identify the similarity. There are only a few nods this time in recognition of a place which, to most of us, is just a name. "Imagine, if you will, Ladies and Gentlemen, the close-packed buildings with their overhanging jetties," he says, returning our full attention to Widdock. "We may be glad that those insalubrious times are gone, but we may be uneasy, too, about what has been swept away in the name of Progress or, if you prefer it, by the hand of Mammon."

There is, broadly, a murmur of acceptance following this remark, though our speaker cannot fail to have heard a sarcastic cough from suspiciously close by me. Paradoxically, it is as if this is the spur he needs to enthuse about his subject: the importance of our historic buildings and their preservation, "not just the grand ones but those passed every day which, if one were to close one's eyes and imagine Widdock, are what imprint themselves upon the mind as being its essence – what Widdock is. Now, let us step inside The Rose and Crown and make our way upstairs to the attic. We will see," he shows us a beautiful architectural drawing, "that the roof is supported by a very fine fourteenth century king-post." Without a trace of condescension, he takes us on a tour of our town, showing us its treasures by means of more drawings and some photographs, the whole talk sprinkled with entertaining anecdotes from its history.

Judging by the response from the audience, the rival to Widdock's Roman link, in terms of celebrity, appears to be the largely-held belief that Queen Elizabeth I passed through here on her way to the royal hunting grounds, The Queen's Head being named in commemoration of her fleeting visit. "Finally, does anyone here know what Dr. Johnson had to say on the subject of Widdock?" Our speaker surveys the room.

There is an anticipatory pause. Mr. Davidson raises his hand. "I can't recite the quotation verbatim, but the tone wasn't entirely complimentary, was it?" His doleful voice booms out to a murmur of mild affront.

"Ah," says Mr. Buttleigh-Truscott, "you'll have to buy my book to find out!" With this, he thanks us and says he'll take one or two questions. Yes, he has a whole section in the book on the subject of pargetting. No, not all modern developments are bad. The pumping station at Water Meads is an example of good design in the service of practicality.

"In your and its locations," says a gruff voice not far from me, "do you extend as far as Stortree?"

I realise that the speaker is Mr. Bledington, friend of Mr. Quinn-Harper.

"I do, indeed, Sir," says our speaker. "You may also wish to know that my first publication in this series featured

Stortree. It is my home town. I'm sure Pritchard's Bookshop will have copies."

Mr. Pritchard nods and, whilst confirming this fact, I see him catch the speaker's glance up at the clock above the entrance. He thanks him in sincere tones, gives the details of the launch and reiterates his thanks. The applause is loud, even from Mrs Munns.

Before anyone can detain him further, Mr. Buttleigh-Truscott gathers his papers into a portfolio.

Both men move towards the door, Mr. Pritchard saying, "I've booked a table at The Railway Hotel."

Our eyes meet.

"What's the a la carte like these days, Pritchard? I could eat a horse."

My love drags his gaze back to the speaker and they leave the room.

"Any relation to Edward Alleyn?"

Anticipating the likelihood of this question, Mr. Pritchard has already told me the curious tale of the sixteenth-century actor who, one night when he was playing Faust, or Doctor Faustus as he is in Christopher Marlowe's play, believed the Devil to have been incarnate amongst the cast. In shocked contrition for what the actor took to be sinful pride in his own performance, Alleyn used his wealth to found educational establishments which, apparently, still exist.

My reply is hardly unexpected. "Oh well...I wonder may I crave an indulgence of you, Miss Alleyn – if your employer has no objection?"

I turn immediately to Mr. Pritchard. Our eyes meet for an instant before he looks directly back at Mr. Buttleigh-Truscott. "Go ahead and ask her," he says, evenly.

"I woke, this morning, rather later than intended and didn't have time to purchase a white carnation for my buttonhole."

I am smiling before he finishes his request.

Mr. Pritchard looks relieved. "Allow me."

As I take the cash from him, our fingers touch. I feel like skipping across the road to Kate's.

I have placed a flash bearing the word 'Today!' across the corner of my notice in the window. No one yet has entered. It is only just gone ten o'clock, though.

"Oh dear, they're not exactly flocking in their droves, the hoi polloi of Widdock," says our author, seated with a small stack of his books at the rather fine table and chair Mr. Pritchard has borrowed from the Coopers.

I feel a spark of irritation. The street looks busy, a good sign, though mainly it is true with women carrying laden baskets. "I expect everyone's been to market and is going home with their goods before setting out again," I say, keeping my voice from betraying any emotion.

Almost at once the shop is suddenly full of people, several of whom we don't know. Mr. Pritchard chats easily, inviting them to spend as long as they like looking round the shelves. "If you have any questions, don't hesitate to ask me or my assistant, Miss Alleyn."

"I've found the Johnson quote," Mr. Nash tells his friends as he stands in the queue behind Messrs. Davidson and

Vance, who are enjoying a congenial colloquy with our author whilst I wrap signed copies of his book for them.

"Go on, then," says Mr. Vance.

"Here, you do it," Mr. Nash passes the book to Mr. Davidson, "you've got the voice for it."

Mr. Davidson declaims, in what I take to be Dr. Johnson's manner, "'There is nothing about Widdock to provoke a man.'"

They all burst out laughing, Mr. Pritchard and the author included.

At points during the morning, all our dear friends who can come in. I look up from taking money and become aware that Mr. Hallambury is here, a quiet presence just as powerful as that of our flamboyant author. "I enjoyed your talk, Sir," he says.

Once I'm sure the ink is dry, I take the book he has bought and wrap it.

"Your master's busy, Miss," says a gruff voice in front of me. "Can you tell me where to find the book on Stortree?"

I look up in the knowledge that this is Mr. Bledington without his friend this time, Mr. Quinn-Harper being, presumably, at his own bookshop. The man gives the merest nod of thanks, goes to the shelf and locates the volume. To give him his due, he soon becomes engrossed in it.

Mr. Hallambury takes his purchase, thanking me, "and Pritchard, well done. Oh, and don't forget, gentlemen," he says at the door, his glance embracing both my employer and Mr. Bledington, who has raised his head at the words of praise, "I look forward to seeing you both at The Old Mill on the eighteenth."

Mr. Pritchard says he's looking forward to it, too. Mr. Bledington returns his gaze to the page.

"Well, I'm glad he's gone," says Mr. Pritchard, having escorted our author to the station.

I agree. Everything went as smoothly as it could and sales were as good as could be expected in a town like ours during the beginning of the holiday season. This I had pointed out to Mr. Buttleigh-Truscott, but he still seemed a little disappointed.

I dismiss him from my mind as we join the other shopkeepers in Holywell End, who are standing outside their premises, along with other townsfolk, waiting for the parade to start. It is a warm afternoon and I am thankful I chose to wear the trusty blue muslin.

The floats have been allowed to assemble in the extensive grounds of the Training College. They will cross the railway tracks at the strategic time and process up Holywell End, along the High Street and down to the Park. Already, the onlookers are enough to call a crowd. A number of men, armed with pints of beer, stand watching, while children get hot and over-excited. Tired mothers, giving in to pleas, join the queue in front of a colourful handcart on Bridgefoot. This bears a mounted churn from which the vendor scoops into small tart-cases and puff-pastry horns a white, frozen ball, magical but treacherous. Dabbing at sticky trails down little fingers, or at tears when the treat is accidentally dropped, how those poor mothers must wish that Mr. Hallambury had not been so generous with the Manor's ice well and his chef's time and expertise.

There is a terrible din and commotion coming from Station Road. I see Joe and Hubert, their colleagues and some of the shopkeepers from the end of our street, all waving their arms. The front of a motor car appears with Mr. Randle, the motor-workshop owner, seated at the driving wheel dressed in motoring hat, gloves and goggles. The machine is kicking up an enormous quantity of dust from the dry surface of the road.

"Stay here," says Mr. Pritchard, as he joins other shopkeepers, running towards the menace.

After their remonstrations, the car makes a laborious turn and moves out of sight again. From the return of relative silence, I assume it to be back on its forecourt. I am reminded of the time when both my brothers tried to frighten me from taking up my job in Widdock with tales of dangerous motor cars. These are the only ones I've ever seen, driven once a week up to the turnpike on the London road and back.

Mr. Pritchard is shaking his head. "He thought he'd join the end of the parade, if you please. Can you imagine that thing going through the High Street?"

"And frightening the horses pulling the floats," I say.

As if on cue, we hear the sound of the brass band, playing Polly Oliver. An excited hush falls on the crowd... And here is Hallambury's float featuring a number of young women from the factory floor dosing the bundles of cloth cradled in their arms with Hallambury's infant food whilst, on another part of the float, fit young people take part in on the spot gymnastics... And here is the float from the toothbrush factory imaginatively decked out as a desert island with cardboard and crepe paper palm trees. The import of a large notice, 'Don't Forget Your Denticlean Toothbrush' is illustrated by a band of children, supposedly in skins or grass skirts, exaggeratedly cleaning their teeth... And now, here is Gifford's float with Boadicea standing behind her chariot holding the reins of her papier-maché horse's head. Both the horse and the chariot afford me pleasure in our handiwork, guided by Mrs. Fuller, "No, not flat areas of paint. Make it look three dimensional – like this. They're effectively stage properties." Lettie looks superb, her wild black hair unrestrained, save by a circlet. She wears an eau de nil evening dress in raw silk with the simple lines of a kirtle, whose elbow-length sleeves are slit to reveal, whenever the warm breeze blows, a tantalising glimpse of bare arm. Around the sides of the float runs the slogan: Gifford's – glad to dress the most demanding client! Gifford's – making every customer a queen! Hubert reluctantly waves as the float turns into the High Street and he has to go back to the railway station.

There are all the usual stalls, of course, and there are donkey rides, a roundabout and swing boats. I spot Meg and Winnie in one. The other three are occupied by couples. Shrieks and laughter drift across to me. It is almost uncomfortably hot now and there is a limit to the number of bran tubs on which I want to waste my money. I cross the park, passing the Wide Oak, and enter the cool of the Assembly Rooms. The door to a side room stands enticingly open: 'Painting Exhibition'. I catch Mrs. Fuller handing over stewardship to Mrs. Cooper before going home to rest for this evening's concert. We both look in the little book of sales. She has done well. I feel time passing, though, and I do not want to abuse Mr. Pritchard's kindness in letting me out to sample Widdock Day. I view the paintings rather more hurriedly than I would have chosen but, even so, they make an impression – their vibrancy of colour and bold form – which stays with me as I hurry back along the High Street.

Here we all are again in the main hall of the Assembly Rooms. My love is seated next to me. I bask in his appreciation, am inanely glad to be wearing my best summer dress, the one I wore when we pretended to be a couple at the Fabian Society summer party. Jenny is looking beautiful at the piano, her pale hair flattered by dove grey. Her slender fingers move deftly over the keyboard, producing sounds of such power and grace it seems a miracle. The older women are resplendent in lovely silks, lawn and voile, their muscular bowing arms moving with vigour or with infinite delicacy, creating blissful cadences, the whole ensemble sending a sublime music soaring to the heavens.

If we had thought Mrs. Fuller's birthday hot, we were wrong. This is hot. The sun is already high and burning when we return from church. We throw the back door open, pull the curtains and eat our Sunday roast in gloom. Mrs. Fuller goes to lie upon her bed. At her invitation, Jenny, also exhausted from last night's concert, takes the spare bed in her dressing room. After clearing up, we others follow their example, making our way to the only other east-facing room, the cool parlour, where we sink into the comfortable cushions of the armchairs and sofa, and drift into oblivion.

I wake, sensing another day already bright. In my nightdress, I take my blue muslin down to the scullery and wash it, ready to peg it out when I am dressed in my new, sprigged, summer frock, a purchase from the market.

We are busy this Monday morning, including further sales of Mr. Buttleigh-Truscott's book. In the afternoon, custom slacks to nothing. The shop is an oven. We place ourselves in the sitting room with all the doors wide open. Mr. Pritchard starts to read aloud a poem he has written. I jerk awake, full of fuddled apologies. He shushes me to sleep.

I get home to find my dress on the line is bone dry and stiff, almost as if it had been starched.

There is no trace of roasting barley, these days, as I step outside the door. Every one of the maltings is closed down for the summer because of the risk of fire presented by those great floors of germinating grain. Now that Widdock Day is over, the town has an empty feeling. All the able-bodied men, and their female counterparts, have transferred to the brickfields.

Mr. Pritchard reads out, from his paper, that the temperature is set to climb still higher today, Tuesday, and tomorrow. We discuss covering the books in the window during the afternoon hours of searing heat to protect their covers from possible bleaching. Before we open, while there is still a trace of freshness in the morning, I go to Giffords. "You're lucky I had this left," says Lettie, pulling off the end of a roll of tough, natural linen. "It's what everyone's after to make blinds."

There are scarcely any customers. Almost everyone has conducted their essential business early and then gone home to shelter from the heat.

The afternoon is unendurable, even in the sitting room where Mr. Pritchard has let the fire go out and made a jug of lemonade. I hear him moving between the two rooms. I sit quietly, trying to focus on the same wretched order.

Today, Wednesday, Hallambury's have changed their hours because members of the workforce have been fainting in the heat. Meg and Winnie will leave the factory at one o'clock and go back again from four till seven. Mr. Hallambury has promised his employees that, if it can be done, he will have electricity in his premises by next summer, "which means," says Meg, "electric fans," says Winnie. They are excited by the prospect, but it does not help them now.

"The siesta idea is sensible," says Mr. Pritchard, who has moved his mattress to a position under the stairs. "You may as well go home at one o'clock. Come back at four, if it's cooled down. I'm going to lock the shop, draw the curtains and take off all my clothes for a couple of hours. I suggest you do the same – at home, I mean."

Now, I feel even hotter.

There are three more working days this week, days which normally I would cherish. If I had the energy, I would be angry about the torpor which this terrible heat induces. The toothbrush factory has followed Hallambury's lead and changed its hours, too. I start work at nine o'clock, following our own ad hoc, heatwave hours. It is unbearably hot, already, and sultry. I can feel an unpleasant dampness at my hairline. I start to tidy the shelves, but the slightest movement is a penance.

"This reminds me of summer in Buenos Aires," says Mr. Pritchard, fanning himself with a large piece of cardboard.

No wonder he seems much more able than I am to continue working despite the heat.

We have no customers all morning but, as one o'clock approaches, the skies suddenly darken. I am about to say that I don't think I'll get home before it rains, when the shop is lit up briefly and then, one, two, three miles away, we hear the rumble of thunder.

"Look, Rose! Look!"

I hardly need to. That great forked brilliance has left its after-image, even when I'm looking down, trying to eat my sandwich in peace, even when I close my eyes.

"Phew! Right overhead."

The sky is rent from top to bottom like a piece of cloth. The whole building shakes.

I wish my love would come away from that window.

A fierce, drumming squall follows the thunderstorm. The temperature drops.

We go through to the shop. Mr. Pritchard turns the sign and opens the door. A sweet, rain-washed fragrance gushes in, but the wind is too strong to leave the door ajar. I start unpacking books and finding their corresponding orders. My employer works on his accounts. It is quiet except for distant mutterings, subdued flashes on the skyline like a lamp lit and then extinguished.

Mr. Pritchard closes his ledger. "I've been thinking about your piece of writing, Rose. No, not in a critical way, not at all. I know I said I didn't need to be curious because it stands alone, and that's true, but I just want to see if I have understood... certain things. Do you mind me asking a couple of questions about the subject matter?"

"My family, you mean? Of course not." I've stopped working and I'm standing facing him, my back to the window and its sullen gleams. I realise I'm feeling tense.

"Your family and you," he says, gently. "Will you come and sit next to me?"

I cross the room and take the stool beside him. He turns to face me.

"When, in the piece, your mother says, 'we must be brave again, Rose,' I assume you had already lost a brother or sister."

"My brother Jim died before he was six." I hear how flat my voice sounds, as if I didn't care.

"I'm sorry."

I can't look at him. I stare out of the window at the deserted street, occasionally lit up by lightning.

"I have to ask – and then I'll stop – in the writing, it sounds as if your mother was heavily preg–"

"She lost the baby," I blurt out, "like the five miscarriages and the stillbirth and Lucy, who lived a week."

"Steady on, Rose."

But I can't stop now. "Shall I tell you something else?" My voice sounds hard, unrecognisable.

126

"All right, but please don't shout. I'm on your side."

I try to be calm. "When I was born I was small and very poorly. The midwife told my father she thought I'd be going back to the angels. He ran for the doctor – not the young one we have now, the previous old man. He came and examined me and said nothing except that he'd call back later. When he did, my mother was feeding me. 'Oh,' he said, as if remarking on the weather, 'I didn't expect her still to be alive.' His casual manner," I know I'm grinding the words out but I can't help myself, "made my mother furious – and determined. She thinks – thought –" I gulp, "that's what kept me alive, her determination."

"And your anger," says Mr. Pritchard.

"I'm not angry." My voice sounds high and silly, choked. I take several deep breaths.

"Please look at me, Rose. I want to apologise – no, you've no need to protest – for putting you through that, but thank you. I now think I understand why you feel as you do about marriage in general terms. Clearly, there's a serious conversation to be had between us. I'd like to say one thing now, then not another word. I hope you can take it in. Here it is: That was the past. This is the twentieth century. I would make sure nothing like that ever happened to you. I love you."

"I love you." I smile in a watery way.

I say that I don't need to go home early and rest after the emotional exertion. As it is cooler, I'd rather be active and get on with work. Mr. Pritchard looks relieved. It is almost like the old days only, I think, better.

The heat is back, worse than ever. It is Saturday afternoon, normally our busiest day, and we haven't had one customer since noon.

"This is a disaster," says Mr. Pritchard. "The weather forecast says no change for the next two days at least. That's as far as the meteorologists are prepared to go, but you know all the pundits and seaweed soothsayers predict it's set fair till the end of the month. I think," he runs a hand through his hair, "if your father wants to collect you sooner than next weekend, he may as well."

We stand, staring at each other. There is a terrible logic in what he says. I know, too, that sales of the new book, which should have given our profits a boost, have been affected. Another thought occurs to me. "I shouldn't mind working for nothing."

"Don't be ridiculous, dear Rose. I wouldn't dream of taking advantage of you in such a way. I feel bad enough about your holiday."

I, on the other hand, am overwhelmed with being paid a small amount whilst not at work. Mrs. Fuller, too, has been magnanimous in asking for only a token sum from us all as a retainer for the fortnight when the factories close down and Lettie has time away. Mrs. Munns will not need to come in as often, but she is pleased because she is working with her husband on the brickfields.

When I get home I discuss Mr. Pritchard's suggestion with the others. If I were to catch the post on Monday, I could be gone by the middle of the week. "But how do you feel about the cooking?"

"We'll cope, won't we, girls?" says Mrs. Fuller. "Besides, it's really only a couple of days before the rest of you are away."

"And no one wants to eat a thing except salad," says Lettie, with which the others all agree.

I'm at the shop at eight o'clock. This morning, Wednesday, Mr. Pritchard goes to Hallambury's for his tour of the factory. This evening, I shall leave Widdock. Father will come when the heat is less intense, which means that I can eat first with the others.

Mr. Pritchard looks smart and cool in his light summer trousers, blazer and straw boater. My heart melts and, once again, fills with conflicting emotions over going away.

"I hope you find the morning interesting – and enjoyable," I say.

I watch him walk off with purpose. As he reaches Bridgefoot, he turns and waves. I wave back, and then he takes the towpath and disappears from view.

As it's so early, and relatively cool, I decide to do some much-neglected dusting. Soon, I am coughing. I rush through to the sitting room for a drink of water.

When I come back to the shop, my heart leaps to see the tall, dark-haired figure with his back to me. What has brought him back so soon? I cannot conceal my delight.

"Well, there's a lovely smile."

The 'lovely smile' freezes on my lips. How could I have mistaken this person for Mr. Pritchard? Where my employer is tall and lithe, this man is inches shorter and stockier in every way. Where Mr. Pritchard's eyes are deepest blue these, which turn their gaze on me as if they could see straight through me, are the palest imaginable. I try to gather my wits. "May I help you, Sir?"

"Undoubtedly. And you are, Miss?"

I do not give him the benefit of my name. "My employer will be back soon if —"

"A nice emporium your employer's got here." His voice, though not uneducated, has an undertow of London. He walks over to a shelf and gazes at it, scanning the titles.

"I read a book once. I wonder if you purvey it: The Secrets of a Gentleman's Servant, written down by a friend."

I feel a pulse of anger. This stranger hopes to make sport with my presumed naivety. I look him directly in the eye. "We don't stock that kind of book here, Sir."

He chuckles, moving to the door. "That's not what I heard."

What does he mean? Is this some misguided reference to the talk on Widdock's secrets? It doesn't make sense. "I suggest you try the station bookstall," I manage.

He laughs again and leaves.

"They really are pioneers in surgical equipment, Rose. I had no idea. I thought it was all pills and potions. And Mr. Hallambury's talk was very encouraging. Being one of the Society of Friends, he has what could be called a social conscience..."

How can I sully my love's enthusiasm by telling him of the unsavoury visitor? I want to leave him on the sweetest note.

This time, it is me walking up towards Bridgefoot. I return his wave, my heart torn in two.

Chapter Seven

I have come to the conclusion that I am not in favour of indoor lavatories. The less said about that subject the better. On the other hand, what could be more congenial than this modest structure, placed discreetly at the end of the outbuildings, where one may sit in cool half-dark, listening to bees in the sweet-scented honeysuckle, on a comfortable oak seat made by Father and polished by all our bottoms?

Yesterday, the first back in my old home, I heard Father leave the house at six o'clock. He, like the businesses in Widdock, has adapted his working hours to accommodate the heatwave, returning home to eat and sleep and only going back to his workshop later for the lightest tasks. After that, the green shade of his runner beans and fruit bushes is a haven until sunset. We ate a proper dinner at one o'clock over which I mentioned to him and Hilda that this is what they do in foreign countries where it is intensely hot. They make this the main meal of the day followed by a siesta. "I wouldn't know," said Father, in a tone which implied: nor want to. Hilda gave me a sharp look only for an instant, but I really must remember not to seem as if I think myself superior...

I tip a scoopful of wood shavings from the sack down the pan and go outside into the blinding brightness and the heat like a wall. The water runs weakly from the butt, so I take only enough to cover the bottom of the bowl which sits on a ledge next to it. The water is warm to the touch, as is the block of carbolic soap. I rinse the bowl, replace it and make my way back to the orchard where I have left the book I propose to read.

Hilda, wearing her spectacles, is propped against the old walnut tree in its shade with her workbasket beside her. She is carefully picking, with scissors, at something cotton in her lap. This turns out to be a pillowcase, worn to a gauze where the head has rested. I see that she is removing the undamaged lace appliqué which trims the hem. She glances up at my approach, her fond smile directing mine across to the sight of Father, fast asleep in a deckchair under the Bramley. She returns to her task and I make myself comfortable next to her against the broad trunk.

I have decided to read the history of Widdock by Mr. Buttleigh-Truscott. Rather than starting at the beginning, however, I cannot resist turning to the index to see if Markly is mentioned in the chapter concerning the towns and villages surrounding Widdock. There is one reference. In a state of anticipation, which would be eager were it not so hot, I find the page. My gaze falls on the opening words: 'Little more than a village, these days, Markly...' Little more than a village! How dare he?! I slam the book shut, causing an enquiring look from Hilda. I explain my involuntary action.

"Stupid man," she says. "Here," she leans across the space between us, passing me what were Mother's scissors and the matching pillowcase, "you can do something useful instead."

While Hilda puts her chickens to bed and Father waters his vegetables, I sit as Mother used to like to, on the bench by the front door in the cool of a hot summer's evening, enjoying the deep fragrance of the old rose climber and listening to the zinging of swifts forever wheeling as the sky turns softly from peach to lavender. I can still see to read and have, of course, been drawn back to Mr. Buttleigh-Truscott's estimation of Markly to see what else he has to say besides bemoaning the fact that it has suffered a dramatic loss of population during the years of agricultural depression. "Markly retains a character both unassuming yet charming and," he says, "quintessentially South Anglian". I suppose I forgive him his earlier blunder.

I've always known our church was old, mediaeval. When Hilda and I went down, this morning, to buy our Friday fish, I viewed it with new respect.

Now, with both my sister and father asleep in the orchard, I have returned with the book to look at it properly and inform myself. I screw my eyes up and put a hand to shade the blinding page.

'Church of St. Mark, late fourteenth century. Modestly pleasing. Flint patched with roughcast and rendering, tower with lead spire'.

Sunlight gleams from the smooth surfaces of grey and ochre flints, and bleaches plaster to startling white. I step inside, letting the door close softly behind me. Here it is cooler, this end of the church shielded from the sun by the bell tower. I smell the greenness of fresh-cut flowers and the scent of beeswax polish mingling with sun-warmed candle wax, old prayer books and the dust of summer, though there is not a speck to be seen. The lady helpers have been in this morning, buffing the lectern eagle's brass feathers to a shine.

In two tall vases flanking the aisle, cottage garden favourites have been arranged. I slip into a pew. The scent of stocks and sweet peas winds about my prayers. I open my eyes upon a stand of deepest delphiniums, the blue of Leonard's eyes.

I have been trying not to think about him every other moment, wondering how he is. We have agreed we shall refrain from writing "pointless letters, 'I hope you are well'. Much better for you to write something you can read back to me when you return. And I'll read to you, my love. We can have a literary celebration." My love... I treasure those words. I see the sense in the arrangement. All the same, I do hope he is well.

I pick up my book and open it.

'Inside, whitewashed to the roof beams. Large East window of four lights, contemporary glazing in side windows, all with original flowing tracery of the Decorated period which latter has, perhaps, saved it from infelicitous re-modelling.'

There's no mistaking the whitewashed walls. 'Flowing tracery' must refer to the delicate patterns of the carved stone in the windows' pointed arches. Something is bothering me about that capital 'D' in Decorated. There is something I should remember. Why did it save the church from a misfortune...?

While I've been musing, the church door has quietly opened and someone else has sat down at the back, a man, I think, judging by the sound of his weight on the pew. After a moment, I hear him rise and approach, at which I rise too and turn to meet his greeting.

"Good afternoon, Miss, I hope I don't disturb you."

"Not at all."

He is a young man, about the age of Mr. Pritchard, with curly brown hair, brown eyes and sideboards. By his cassock, I take him to be the new Curate, mentioned by Hilda in her summary of local news. Extending his hand, "Gerald Armstrong," he confirms my supposition about him. "How do you do?"

I introduce myself, noticing his interest in the book in my other hand.

"Ah... Rose Alleyn, of course," he says, "I see the family resemblance to your sister."

He is simply being gallant.

"She said you were bookish."

She would.

"What are you reading, if I may ask?"

I show him the description of the church, but now I am eager to discuss it, for I have recalled Mr. Philpott's lecture on John Ruskin, as I explain. "'Decorated' is one of the descriptions of the Gothic form of architecture, isn't it? He talks about it in 'The Stones of Venice.'"

"Indeed, so. Augustus Welby Pugin was another proponent of Gothic."

"Ah, yes... Ruskin didn't like him, did he? And yet they had similar architectural principles."

"True, but the people Ruskin really came to loathe were those who re-worked existing mediaeval churches, stripping away the layers of building work which they believed didn't fit with the true architecture of the church. They held that the Decorated style – the middle Gothic period – was the purest. That explains this passage." He jabs a finger at my book. "St. Mark's escaped."

"Of course. And the two other styles, were...?"

"Early English – very plain and the final phase of Gothic, Perpendicular. Have you ever been to a cathedral, Miss Alleyn? No…? Then, that is a treat in store. It is as if they were walled in glass."

I sense that our exchange is over, that Mr. Armstrong has things to do, so I thank him and move to leave.

"It has been delightful to make your acquaintance," he says. "Do give my regards to your family."

I step outside into almost unbearable heat, but feel exalted by intelligent conversation. My only regret is that Mr. Pritchard is not here to share it. I think of the sweltering shop and wonder if any customers have been in. My heart goes out to him. I cannot deny I miss him.

When I reach home, Hilda is inside pouring lemonade. "Where have you been?" she says. "You could have made those pillowcases into rags for me."

I tell her of my adventure. "I didn't think you'd want to go down there in the heat." She says nothing, but I have somehow vexed her. "I met the Curate, Gerald Armstrong."

"I know who he is," she says. "I'm going to lie down on the bed."

I call up the stairs after her. "If you tell me where the pillowcases are –"

"I've done them."

I sit down in Mother's rocking chair, suddenly overcome with weariness.

Lightning sends its brilliance into the room as we are turning in for the night. Thunder mutters. We run outside with buckets and basins. Later, when all is calm and we are

137

drifting into sleep, we hear rain drumming on the roof, rattling against the windows when the squally wind whips it.

I wake with the dawn. No one else stirs. The house is hot from the range, kept in low, and the air stale from lack of ventilation, the windows being closed, of course, during the thunderstorm.

I take a certain pleasure in exercising my old skills. I know every creaky floorboard in this room, exactly where to place my feet on the stairs.

I ease the bolts back and open the front door without making a sound. Sweet, rain-fresh air greets me. I take a deep breath to fill my lungs. I can smell the wet leaves, spicy and pungent, of Mother's geraniums, really called pelargoniums, in pots on either side of the path. From the garden come the scents of lavender, rose, wet grass and earth.

I step outside, the air still deliciously cool, though warming enough already for me to feel no chill in my loose summer nightdress, which ends at mid-calf. Damp grass caresses my bare feet. As I walk to the fence and gaze at our field, the sun breaks fully over the rim of the world. It shines on the coats of the horses. Sable is in her perennial glossy black, sleek with summer, but Iolo has shed his rough white winter coat for one of a rich, burnished russet. He ambles gently over to greet me. Sable raises her head, then returns to her cropping. Iolo walks to stand by the old crab apple tree. He looks at me and a thought passes between us. He dips his head, then lifts it, a confirmation.

Before I can argue myself out of it, I go quickly and fetch his bridle. He is still standing as he was. I climb onto the

138

lowest, sturdy branch of this tree which has seen all our childish play over the years. I slip the bridle over his head. With the reins and a chunk of mane in my nearside hand, resting on his neck, I use the branch as a springboard and, Iolo being at least two hands shorter than Sable, I can pull myself bodily over his back. I ease into position and sit up straight, glad that there's no one here to have witnessed such an indecorous mounting.

Iolo starts walking towards Oak Meadow. Without the barrier of a saddle, I feel the lithe, living warmth of him, a direct connection between us. I sense his confidence in us both. I let out the reins, so that I'm not gripping his mouth. I manage to open and shut the gate without falling off and now we are in pastureland, with clover red and white, daisies and vivid blue self-heal. Although the birds are not singing with the gusto of spring, all around us they are in concert: warblers, heard but not seen; the bright flash of a yellowhammer with its distinctive "A-little-bit-of-bread-and-no-chee-ee-se" and the bird which announces its own name, "chiff-chaff." In the distance under the oak, cows make a patchwork of black and white.

Iolo quickens. I know what he wants. I shorten my reins and we're plunging off into a canter across the expanse, the breeze of our movement cool on my face, lifting soft hair at my temples. In the next field, the corn has already been cut, dried and stored. Leaving the sun-hardened path, barely softened by last evening's downpour, we fly across stubble and reach, on the far side, a path through a beech wood, which could be enchanted, where trees frame our passage but no bramble snags nor branch makes me swerve, where our hoof-beats are muffled by mast and we find ourselves reaching the river, taking the bridle-path sheltered by willow and ash. We slow to a trot, go to a fast walk, and now we are ambling into the end of our field and up to the top. We stop by the garden gate in the fence and I slide from my height down to earth. I rock as the ground seems to rush up to claim me again as a two-legged creature. I throw my arms round the warm neck and bury my head in the sweet, soft fragrance of horse. As I thank him, I think that in all of that time we did not meet a soul, nor – and it comes to me as a slight shock – was I thinking about my love.

I wake again at dawn. It is far too hot already to want to repeat my rapturous ride on Iolo and, besides, I do not trust my knowledge of ground conditions, with the baked earth so hard, to run the risk of hurting his feet. In the pearly darkness, I reach for my notebook, but torpor envelops me and I slip back into a fitful sleep… I am in the bookshop. Mr. Pritchard wants me to come over to where he is standing, so that he can show me something in a book. I am behind the counter. I cannot move because, I realise with horror, my lower half is unclothed. "Rose," says Mr. Pritchard. His note of irritation wakes me with a jerk. Hilda murmurs, but goes on breathing with regularity. I take a sip of water and try to calm my own pounding heartbeats. Breathe in…breathe out…breathe in…breathe out…

I have never been this warm in Church. Through the east window, strong sunlight gives the pictured figures depth, the glowing reds and blues of their robes reminding me of Mrs. Fuller's paintings, their vibrant tones.

It becomes clear that, this Sunday, the curate will be preacher. We have already been reminded, by way of the Collect and the reading from St. John, Chapter 20, verses 11–18, that today, 22 July, is the Feast of Mary Magdalene. Mr. Armstrong commences by saying that, in preparation for this sermon, he has studied every biblical appearance of the saint, returning to the original Greek as a cross-reference, and he feels confident in the assertion that contrary to popular belief, there is no clear evidence concerning her occupation prior to her meeting with Our Lord. The true picture which emerges is that of a strong woman – her name, Magdala, meaning 'tower'– who is present during His ministry, there at the Crucifixion and, most importantly, it is she who sees Him first when He is risen, mistaking Him for the gardener but, as soon as He speaks her name, she knows Him. "Rabboni", she says, Teacher. There are many stories which have grown up by word of mouth and in supplementary texts, the curate tells us, which are just as persuasive as the most well-known one. There is, for instance, a strongly-held belief that Mary herself became a teacher and that the Apostles may have learned from her how to spread the Word. The point for us all to absorb – women and men alike – is that, whatever we have done and been, and whatever stories people tell about us, our past lives are over. It is what we do now in the name of Our Lord that's important. Whatever the setbacks on the True Path, we should be resolute, our own Tower of Strength. "On this Feast Day of Saint Mary Magdalene, may we be filled with her grace. In the name of the Father, the Son and the Holy Ghost."

We all mumble, "Amen."

When the service is over and we disperse into the churchyard, I overhear, "We all know who that Mary was, whatever he says." "Of course we do. There was no need to drag it all up like that." One of the older matrons adds, "He'll be preaching about Votes for Women next, as if we haven't got enough to do without all that bother."

The Vicar, with a skill borne of long practice, slices through his congregation in the direction of his Sunday roast, but the Curate hesitates as if hoping for a kind word.

Hilda steps forward. "A very inspiring sermon, Mr. Armstrong," she says.

"I'm glad you thought so. Thank you for telling me, Miss Alleyn," he replies.

I have seen that dazed, adoring smile on more than one young man's face when encountering my sister. The surprise is how, before the Verger draws him away, Hilda smiles back at him.

The heat is even worse now, but the washing is drying in no time, so that's an undeniable advantage.

We meet the Curate while we're in town this morning finishing our shopping. He asks me if I have discovered any more interesting facts about Markly. I tell him that the mill, or a mill, was mentioned in the Domesday Book, but I keep my answer brief, the question being a courtesy. He says that, after the Bank Holiday, he intends to start his own Bible-study group for younger members of the congregation.

"You may count on my attendance," says Hilda.

We comment about the continuing heat, then go our separate ways.

"If you join a Bible-study group," I say to Hilda, "won't you have to wear your spectacles?"

She gives me an ungrateful look. Then, her brow clears. "I shall ask beforehand what the passage is to be and learn it by heart. It'll be like you and your poetry with Mr. Pritchard."

I wonder for the hundredth time how he's getting on. My love, I say the words to myself. How is he coping? Will Mr. Pritchard – Leonard – open the shop as usual or is the town now so silent and empty, that he will decide it isn't worth it, and take himself off to seek a shady spot by the river, where he can sit and read and dream? And if he does so, will his daydreams...

"You've gone quiet," says Hilda.

"I'm just thinking about everyone back in Widdock," I say, which is more or less true.

"Ooh, it must be even hotter there – horrible!" says my sister.

I tell her that today, Monday, all the factories will be closed for their fortnight's summer holiday, which is a mercy for the poor workers in these conditions.

"Good," she says. "When we get back, you can pick a lettuce for me. That bit of veal and ham pie from yesterday smelt all right, so we'll have that."

We are up with the birds, or not long after. Noiselessly, we wash and put on the lightest muslin dresses, mine the sprigged one from the market, Hilda's in a pale but vibrant shade of blue, like harebells. Our feet hardly touch the treads as we slip downstairs. Father's regular breathing, audible through his bedroom door, is uninterrupted.

The range is reduced to within an inch of its life, but the room feels close even though it's not yet seven o'clock. Hilda gingerly slides the latches on both front and back doors, propping them open to catch what draught there might be. I move the kettle onto the hotplate for tea, but we put on our pinafores and carry out the cleaning and tidying jobs while we still can do so in relative comfort, and before we have our breakfast.

We sit on the bench at the front to eat our porridge, wreathed in the scent of Mother's rose, whose yellow blooms fall in cascades around us. It is almost too warm already. This sunshine which bathes us will later be our scourge.

Whoever lives in this cottage has gleaning rights to the cornfield between us and the Jepps. In recognition of the farmer's good will about this fact, Mother would contribute to the fare provided by his wife and those of the hands. At elevenses, dinner time and tea-time, she would cross the spinney between our lane and the field, carrying a stoppered pitcher of tea. Each of us sisters has taken our turn at being bearer of the milk or of the freshly-made lemonade, knowing we must not slop the contents of the jug. On a few occasions, when Mother was too poorly, Phyllis and I took not only the drinks, but her place working the field, backs bent, eyes fixed on the stubble for those ears of corn detached by the reaper's rotating blades. In the olden days, she told us, the fields at harvest time would be full of men with scythes, joined at dinnertime by their womenfolk bearing a spread. Even by my childhood, though, the numbers had dwindled. Our cornfield can be covered in less than a day by one man and two horses with the reaper-binder.

In this summer of great heat, the corn harvest has followed hard on that of hay. Yesterday, as we cleared away our tea things, the blackbird's song, falling into soft stillness, was punctuated by the distant shouts of the harvesters. In golden light and slanting shadows, Hilda and I took our pails to collect water from the pump that we are allowed to use in the yard at Dr. Jepp's. Through the trees, as we approached our lane, we saw the team in the cornfield, men with pitchforks tossing the stooked sheaves up to the loaders on the wagon. We offered no refreshment that late in the evening. The field, which is small and stands alone on the other side of the road from most of the rest, is last on their circuit. They would have wanted to get back to the rickyard before nightfall, there still being skilled work to do in finishing the stack. After that, no doubt, their chosen beverage would be beer.

This morning we bring down our spurned eiderdown and counterpane to air on the line. Then we can fold both away till we need them. "That'll make the weather change," says Father as he leaves for early work, walking down through the orchard to take the river footpath under tree cover.

As we step back from levelling the weight of the eiderdown and pegging it, we glimpse what we expected, the arrival of the hand with the horse-drawn rake, which we will follow.

"I'll clear up here," says Hilda, meaning Father's breakfast bowl and cup. She nods in the direction of the field. "I'll join you."

I put on one of the hemp aprons. I tie the skirt to the waistband making a big bag, open at each end, so I can add to it from left or right, but tight enough not to be in danger of scattering any ears already gathered. I fill a bottle with our homemade lemonade, for the hand might prefer that refreshing drink to the tea which, by the time I've finished this task, is brewed and ready to be poured into the stoppered jug. I find a bung which fits a smaller bottle, so I can carry milk safely, too, then take four enamel mugs in case another hand should come to help. I place all in a cloth bag, which I hope to store under an obliging clump of mossy tree roots or cool leaves. I tie on a wide-brimmed straw sunhat whose laces are the two halves of a voile scarf, already ancient, like the hat, when Mother sewed them into it. Now, they are worn to a tissue of muted colours, but the fabric is still tough enough to do the job, and the tails long and thick enough when doubled round my neck to protect the back of it, should the gleeful sun find a gap between the collar of my dress and the sunhat's brim.

I cross the spinney and find a shady hollow for the bag of drinks. As I straighten and walk out onto the field edge, the horse pulling the rake is close by, coming towards me. I look up at the man perched on the seat. He is looking down at me. Despite the shadow cast by the peak of his cap, there is something about his face I recognise.

"Whoa," he says, quietly to the horse. Then, he jumps down, "Good morning to you, Rose – I mean, Miss Alleyn. It is you, isn't it?"

He looks ready to break out in a wide smile, which he does as, smiling, I place him, "Bert Welland. Good morning to you. And please, go on calling me Rose," I add, to reassure him that we are on a level footing. Of all the lads from farmsteads near and far who, when they weren't needed on the land, came to our village school, Bert was the one with manners. Never scornful as others were of us girls, he always had a kind word for everyone. Rather than losing him status with his friends, however, this affability, combined no doubt

146

with his strong physique and a lack of concern bordering on fearlessness, seemed to gain him their respect.

"I haven't seen you here these last four years or more," Bert is saying, "I thought you must have married and moved away."

"I worked as a housemaid in the town when I left school," I tell him, "so I couldn't come gleaning." I decide not to burden him with unnecessary detail: how those people left Markly, but I didn't want to go with them, and how I could have worked at Sawdons. "Then," I say, "I got a job in Widdock." The image of my love rushes into my mind, and I have to hope I'm not blushing.

"Oh, well done," says Bert, his brown eyes full of selfless pleasure in a way I do remember. "And they're decent folk, your new master and mistress?"

Of course – he thinks I'm still in service. Now I really am blushing. "I work in…" I hesitate, "a shop."

"And that's better, I expect. What sort of shop?"

Wondering how this will be received I tell him, "A bookshop," adding quickly, "and what of you?"

But he is not to be deflected. He's nodding and smiling. "That doesn't surprise me. I always used to like it when you read out in class. I tell you – what with you being clever and the way you speak, I thought at first you must be one of the gentry."

"Goodness!" My hand flies to my mouth. I'm astounded.

"You've got the right job there and no mistake, Rose."

"So have you, haven't you?" He is, after all, a tenant farmer's son, I think.

"Farming's all I…" He begins, but his eyes have strayed to the spinney and, as we both turn, widen in appreciation of the approaching vision in ethereal blue.

147

I make the introductions.

"I do remember you," says Hilda. "I always thought you were a nice little boy."

We all laugh, and Bert looks bashful. "I don't know about that," he says.

"Well, I've met someone who must think you're very nice. She told me you're betrothed."

Bert smiles with shy pride. "You've met my Milly, then."

"Yes, at market," says Hilda.

We both offer our best wishes for their future life together, for which Bert thanks us. "She'll be down here by and by."

"Well, we'd better get on then," says Hilda, "or she'll tell us off for idle chit-chat."

Bert laughs and shakes his head, "No, no, she's placid, my Milly," but he agrees that though it was very good to make our reacquaintance, he must get on. So doing, he climbs up onto his seat and slaps the horse's back with the reins, "Walk on."

We bend to our task, the sun already hot on our own backs.

The moment that horse and rake have progressed with their owner out of earshot, Hilda says, "Placid, my foot, that Milly Brown. She hasn't changed a bit from what she was aged seven. All that simpering. Remember the way she used to widen her eyes and look all innocent to get what she wanted? As soon as I saw those yellow corkscrew curls bobbing up and down at the fish stall and heard that voice trying to wheedle a penny off a piece of cod, I knew it was her."

I glance up but, thankfully, there is no indication that Bert has heard Hilda's outburst. I don't know what to say. I find myself disturbed. Before I offer any comment, I think about observing Milly Brown in school and in the playground. The truth, I have to admit, may be very close to how Hilda sees it. Hoping I'm wrong, I say, "She was friendly to you, though – I mean, when you met her at the market?"

Hilda snorts. "She heard my name and remembered me, but she wasn't being friendly. She just wanted to talk, so she could show off her ring and make me jealous that she'd caught Bert Welland."

"Oh, dear."

"Ah, well," says Hilda. And then, "Funny, the way things turn out."

I say no more, and we get on with our labour. I'm feeling both saddened and slightly light-headed, which may be due to the intense heat. We break for a lemonade, and Hilda declares that she's had enough of gleaning in these conditions. I'm relieved on more than one account. As we walk back through the cool spinney, I'm weak with fatigue, and could easily burst out laughing or crying. A deep wave of longing shakes me to the core.

Chapter Eight

The insufferable heat continues. In between tasks which cannot be avoided and meals which must be eaten we do nothing more strenuous than just existing. When evening brings relief, we wander out into the garden. Hilda cuts stems from her sweet peas, a tumbling profusion of colour, to scent the house with sweetness. As I move along a row of bean poles with my basket, I hear Father's rustling hands engaged like mine picking and uncovering ever more tapering runners. Above our heads, the promise of plenty still to come is signified by scarlet petals against a honey sky. In the fading light, flowers which had been bleached under the fierce eye of the sun have now regained their colour. The white blooms of roses and of privet are imbued with a magical intensity rivalling the sweetness of their scent, drawing bees and butterflies. Gnats dance. Swallows swoop. They flash away to our outbuildings. We hear the excited chatter of their fledglings as they approach. Soon these young will take their first flights from the nest. Summer, though it may deceive us, is turning to face its end.

"Tell me I'm not imaging things," says Father, at another close of day. "It wasn't quite as hot, was it?"

We agree.

"They say it's over," I tell him, news we'd gathered from our last trip into town.

It is noticeably cooler in Church. Contributing to the chilly atmosphere is the presiding presence of the Vicar who, this week, has re-assumed the role of preacher. He gives a testimonial to the life of Samuel Wilberforce, whose day of remembrance this is. If anyone can make a rousing and noble subject lose its lustre, it is our Vicar. I try hard to concentrate but my thoughts stray in an inevitable direction. I sense Hilda's disquiet beside me.

When we leave, at last, her eyes search and find another pair in a similar pursuit. I feel a pang of envy. I resolve to learn a psalm this afternoon to try and make up for my lapses.

Now the days seem to pass quickly, heading towards Dot's wedding. A shower of rain has softened the ground a little. Iolo and I go out once more. He is a good companion, but the occasion doesn't have quite the magic of that first ride. I find I am too self-conscious in case of meeting someone, clad as I am, only in my nightdress. He seems to understand, as we simply make a circuit of Oak Meadow. On his back and feeling a slight breeze stirring as we trot, I experience something I haven't felt all month – a shiver.

I make two entries in my notebook, which I am glad of, firstly because something has moved me enough to want to write about it, and secondly because I can look forward joyfully to sharing the results with Mr. Pritchard – with Leonard.

I have nearly finished the book on Widdock. In the chapter about literary connections, I have found the reference to Dr. Johnson. I try to imagine what sort of man he was, always making emphatic utterances as if he knew they would be treasured for posterity. What confidence! I have also found a word, in that chapter, which I do not understand. I search for it in our battered family dictionary, but it does not appear there. It looks foreign, possibly Spanish. What a pity Mr. Pritchard isn't here to ask. I wonder whether Dr. Johnson put it in his dictionary. If I have a moment tomorrow between pressing Father's best suit and getting together with Hilda to sort out our own attire, I wonder if I might prevail on Dr. Jepp, or even go down to town and look for the Curate to ask him. This time Hilda could come with me.

We do nothing of the sort. The day is appalling, sheets of rain driven by a vicious, gusting wind. Only because we won't want to do it tomorrow, the wedding day, Hilda and I run down to the town and back for essential food. We hear that forecasts are better for the next day or so, thank goodness, but fingers are wagging: there's more like this on the way. Father, with a sack over his head as he comes stamping in to eat, confirms they're saying it's bound to worsen for the Bank Holiday. He will take me back to Widdock on Sunday.

"Do you want to come, Hilda?" He asks.

"I shall be going to church," says Hilda, sailing through to the scullery.

Father and I exchange a look which says that neither of us would have thought Mr. Armstrong was Hilda's type.

"It just goes to show," Father murmurs.

"You look a picture, Hilda," says Father, and so she does. She is wearing a dress of turquoise organza with little pearl buttons on bodice and cuffs. "And you look lovely, too, Rose," he adds.

"Yes, you do," says Hilda, with feeling. "That colour suits you."

I am wearing my best dress. We have clean string gloves and have trimmed our straw hats with wild roses. Father looks smart in his best suit. He puts on his hat. We are set to go.

We are, of course, on the tradesmen's road, approaching Sawdons from the rear.

"Ugh... this place," says Hilda, as the Hall comes into sight.

She doesn't speak about her time there, when Master Greville, heir to Sawdons, made her life a misery in his lustful pursuit of her. In the tragedy of Mother's death, the one blessing was that Hilda came home to keep house for Father. I wonder what courage she has had to summon to be part of Dot's wedding day.

"At least we can escape," I say, thinking of Phyllis, who can't. I am longing to see her.

And here she is, dear Phyllis, stylish in a silk dress of lavender pencil stripes on an ecru ground, bodice like a trim little single-breasted jacket with lapels and a row of raised buttons down the front.

"You look wonderful," I say, in answer to her compliment to me, as we stand beaming at each other. "What a dress!"

"Miss Caroline's cast off," says Phyllis. "She's grown plump. When she forced herself into it, I thought the buttons were going to ping off and it would burst open."

"Don't you wish it had?"

"I only wish you'd seen her. She looked like the caterpillar in Alice."

We're both giggling and even Hilda has to smile, as we stand waiting in the sunlight which warms the cobbled courtyard.

Here comes Ralph in his best suit. This is such an unusual departure from his usual gardening clothes that Father jokes, "Who is this young dandy? I don't recognise him." We exchange enquiries about health and well-being as Ralph steps forward to pin, into Father's buttonhole, a creamy-white rose to match the one he is wearing. Others like it lie in a trug, stems on moistened cloth, for Jack who, after stabling Iolo, will be putting on his best, and for Joe and Hubert, when they arrive. Father straightens his shoulders and decides it is time to find the housekeeper's room, Dot's for the afternoon, where she'll be waiting in her wedding dress.

Hilda asks Phyllis, "Are you going to Switzerland?" My mind flashes back. On that day, both terrible and sublime, when I first met Leonard Pritchard here in the gardens, his young charge, Master Hector, had been playing tag with his sisters. Both of them, their tutor informed me, were impatient with the school room. I see his image vividly, and hear how he spoke the following words, "They can't wait to be sent to Switzerland for finishing."

"Do you think they'd bother to tell me till the last minute?" Phyllis says, wryly.

"They like you, though, don't they, the misses?" Hilda says.

"As much as they like any one of us," says Phyllis, in much the same tone as her earlier response. "But what they like and what their mother wants are two different matters."

"Oh, I see," says Hilda. "She might have decided to keep you..."

Ralph touches my arm, drawing me away to one side out of earshot. "I've got something to tell you." He's trying not to look too eager. "You know that article on dahlia propagation I sent to The Gardener's Chronicle?" This, he had mentioned to me in a quiet moment on our own when all the family met at home on Easter afternoon, a precious two hours' dispensation from their duties here. Now, Ralph can't keep the grin from his face. "They published it in the next issue!"

"Oh, Ralph, I'm so pleased." I'm grinning, too. "It's what you wanted, isn't it – to write about gardening as well as doing it? And now you have. Well done!" Though all my brothers have achieved much, according to their lights, it comes to me that Ralph, besides having green fingers, has always been the most literary one.

"It's a start," he says, trying to sound modest.

"But now you've got your foot in the door there –"

"Exactly," he says, excitedly. "They said they'd welcome more from me."

"Both feet in the door, then."

"It's what you have to do to get on in gardening – publish articles, which is good because I enjoy the work – research, I mean. And another thing –"

But I'm not to learn what the other thing might be because our attention is diverted on two fronts. Jack, in his suit, comes to join us just as the sound of hooves and wheels, echoing under the arch, heralds the arrival of Hubert, with Joe and his betrothed in a horse and trap driven by the son of the man who runs the station fly. Jack whistles for the boy, who hastens from the stables to take the horse's head. Once the passengers have alighted he will, on Jack's instruction, provide refreshment for both horse and coachman. The latter, thanking Jack, gets out and holds the door for Joe, who comes next in order to help Catherine. I recognise her from a glimpse I caught one Sunday, when she and Joe were standing chatting outside the church which they attend. Today she is wearing a white dress sprigged with flowers of a delft blue, which matches her eyes as she shyly glances up at what must seem a rank of Alleyns. Swept up under her wide-brimmed hat, her auburn hair shines. Phyllis and I need do no more than glance without expression at each other to know that we are thinking about her complexion, so like Mother's and Hilda's, and wondering how the latter will react, for we can be sure she will herself have noticed the resemblance. But Hilda steps forward graciously with a smile and, being the eldest of those of us assembled, starts the introductions. We each clasp Catherine's hand and try to put her at her ease, and the dimpling smile returned to us relieves not only my own concern for her, but clearly that of Joe who, as he stands beside her, looks so proud but anxious that we all should take to her, which we do. So now he can relax and smile, too.

Although I'm longing for a chance to be with Phyllis, I notice Hubert hanging back, so I go to join him. I half-expect to see Lettie with him, and guess that he's probably thinking in the same wistful vein. I wish Leonard were here, too. We exchange a smile which feels almost complicit.

A group of servants, some of whom have added decorative embellishments – flowers or buttonholes – to their dress, come out and tell us it is time to go. They fall in behind our family group. Phyllis walks the other side of Hubert, as the little party makes its way out of the courtyard onto the path, across a short stretch of parkland, to the chapel where the bridegroom, George Landers, will be waiting. We walk down to the pews at the front on a cloud of the sweetest scents: two tall vases of white stephanotis and roses. "Grown by George in his own garden," Ralph answers my praise. "All the wedding flowers were." I follow his brief glance across the aisle to where a besuited man of middling years, with a handsome, weathered face, sits clasping and unclasping his muscular hands, as he chats to his best man, the deputy Head Gardener.

Now there's a subtle change. Muted, expectant chat ceases. As one we all stand, facing forwards. And here's my proud Father, with Dot on his arm. She is not in some practical colour for subsequent use but in white slipper-satin, her face veiled. As she draws level with her groom, the look on his face says what I am thinking: she is perfect. When they become man and wife and he lifts back her veil, his restrained joy makes it hard for eyes to stay dry.

Outside – goodness – there's a photographer! While we stand and chat, he poses the couple against the church porch. Used to concealing her cheek, blemished by a dark birthmark, Dot naturally turns her profile to the camera and gazes into her husband's eyes. Then, we all line up, blinking into the sun, after which a radiant Dot ensures her cascade of blush-white roses and myrtle lands in the hands of Catherine, not too modest to reach out and catch it firmly from the token throw. We walk back and exclaim at the splendid spread of sandwiches, pikelets and scones, the tea-cups ready, a beer keg for those men who may or who dare. If alcohol's smelt on a footman's breath, he will pay for it with his job. We all stand waiting.

Tables covered by snowy cloths are arranged in a T shape, with a long one for the servants and a short 'Top Table' across it to which, amid cheers and applause, Dot and George make their way. Father follows. On his arm is an older lady, whom he gallantly helps to her place next to George before he takes his next to Dot. I hadn't absorbed who she was when family and servants stood in groups outside the chapel, whilst Dot and George were being photographed, nor when we lined up in strong sunshine for our turn. Now I understand.

When we were all at home on Easter Sunday afternoon, before Father drove those in service back to Sawdons, Dot told us of her forthcoming wedding. Afterwards, out of earshot of the men Hilda, surprised that Upstairs had agreed to servants marrying, asked her how she would cope, "if anything happens." A Head Gardener was not a servant, Dot had said. Men in his position were encouraged to take a wife. She went on to explain that George's sister would continue helping to keep house for him, an arrangement which allows Dot to keep a job she loves. It also allows Upstairs to keep a cook they would be sorry to lose as a result of their own rules.

We are all standing in a hush now as, at his end of the table, the Butler says grace. The lady, George's sister, looks down at her hands upon which her slight weight is resting. Then, as we all sit, her brother helps her into her seat. I'm still looking on when she raises her face, with a tired smile for all of us gathered. My heart gives a lurch at the whiteness beyond natural pallor. Just like Annie. I try to dismiss the thought, quickly composing my face to look serene, but in glancing away catch Dot's eyes. What I read there before she, too, masks her true feelings, is fear.

158

Conversation and eating begin. I have Phyllis on one side and Jack on the other, an ideal arrangement. It's soon clear that Hilda, on Phyllis's other side, is keen to catch up on Sawdons gossip now that she cannot be touched by it. I turn gladly to Jack.

"You look well, Rose," he says. His dear smile would lift the dullest spirits.

I tell him I am in good health. "And what about you?" Under the tablecloth, my fingers are crossed. When I returned to Markly at Easter, Jack came home early on his way to another big house, beyond Widdock, where he was to learn how to drive and maintain motor cars, a prospect which depressed him, given his love of horses. I was shocked to hear the extent of his unhappiness. Alone in confidence, a trust which he and I have always shared, he unburdened himself in such a way that I realised, though he didn't spell it out, that my not having gone to work at Sawdons contributed largely to his melancholia. Mortified, I even contemplated his suggestion of applying for a new job here, cataloguing the library. The idea filled me with profound despondency, for though I would have had the company of dearest Phyllis as well as Jack, and the work would be of interest, probably, I thought I had evaded the tendrils of this place when taking up my new life in Widdock. But during our time together at Easter, Jack's mood changed, so I did nothing. As it turned out, he took to the work with motors.

He breaks into a grin. "Life couldn't be better. There's been an almighty rumpus upstairs. Master Greville sent for a motor car. His father knew nothing until it arrived."

"Goodness!"

"Young Master's sitting behind the wheel, all togged up. I'm supposed to be teaching him. Then, the Squire appears in

159

a towering rage and tells the salesman to take it back. Gives Greville a dressing down – usual theme – spending money they haven't got."

"Oh. Were you sorry – about the car?"

"A bit, but then – you will not believe this, Rose, the Squire decides to show him who's boss. Orders two spanking new cobs as a carriage pair, to drive as a pass-time. At which point, Greville storms off to London. Hasn't come back."

"But it's good for you, though, isn't it, tending the horses?"

"Oh yes – apart from the fact that Madam is livid with both of her men and that rubs off on me if she sees me."

"It's not your fault." These scones are so light, they're bound to be Dot's, delicious with strawberry jam and thick cream. Whilst eating, I dare to raise the other topic from when we last met. "What happened about that job in their library?"

Phyllis is free now and, overhearing, leans to join in. "They found some young relative fallen on even harder times than them – by their standards. So he does it for nothing but bed and board."

"Is he someone to talk to?"

"He won't speak to me," says Phyllis, with a sharp laugh. "Not that I care. I can tell you, Rose, he isn't a patch on Leonard."

I open my mouth to ask how Phyllis really is, but someone taps on a glass and Father, with a good deal of huffing and puffing, gets to his feet and launches into his speech. Having had two glasses of beer, he becomes sentimental, eulogising his "little ray of sunshine." When, his gaze resting on the sprigs of rosemary entwined in the table decoration, he speaks of "the person here in spirit" it is, for the second time today, almost impossible to hold back tears. As we in the family know, this is her birthday month, which she loved for its late, vibrant garden flowers.

After speeches by the bridegroom and the best man, both of them touching and gently humorous, the couple cut the resplendent cake made by the bride. We raise a toast with whatever's to hand, and the party begins to break up. The newly-weds are allowed the night off, but everyone else must attend to their duties. Dot, looking lovely and confident after all the fine words in her praise, comes to speak to Hilda and me. She is followed by Father, who begins to look restless.

"It's a pity you couldn't have had your wedding next weekend," Hilda says, "when they're all in Scotland."

"They'd be afraid we would burn the place down," says Phyllis.

"Besides, I'm going with them," says Dot, with pride. "I'm to teach their cook patisserie."

"What's she going to teach you," says Father, in a rather loud voice, "how to make porridge?" He laughs at his own joke. It turns into a hiccup.

"I'm sure that Mrs. McFarlane will have plenty of Scottish dishes I shall be only too willing to learn," says Dot, apparently unconcerned about being apart from her new husband.

Phyllis and I walk outside into the late afternoon sunshine. "Oh, Phyll, why do we never have enough time for a proper talk? Things aren't too bad, are they?"

We walk under the courtyard arch and stand looking out at the parkland where, in the distance, cattle graze.

"I'm all right. I'm used to it. And I'm going to Scotland next week, so that'll be different. But what about you? How's the house? And how's Leonard Pritchard?"

"The house is lovely." I tell her how harmonious it is now that the one awkward person has left.

"I'm envious," she says. "No, I'm not really, I'm glad for you."

I tell her about Widdock Day.

"And Leonard? ... Rose?"

I take a deep breath. "Actually, we're in love. He's asked me to marry him."

"Oh... Rose..." The look frozen on Phyllis's face combines horrified shock with deep disappointment."You haven't said 'yes', have you?"

"I... haven't said anything yet."

"Thank goodness for that. Rose – just think about what you'd be losing – in terms of freedom, I mean."

I'm feeling awful now, wishing I'd never spoken. "We've talked about – you know –that sort of thing, and he says he'll..." I'm blushing furiously.

Phyllis waves a dismissive arm. "I don't just mean babies – although all that's bad enough, as you well know from what happened to Mother!"

I want to tell her about my outburst to Leonard, but she's in full flow.

"Do you really think that, if you marry him, you'll still be working in the bookshop?"

"He hasn't said I can't."

"Who's going to do his cooking, his washing, his cleaning?" She's striking these off on her fingers.

"He does his own cooking –"

"At the moment," Phyllis interrupts, "because he has to."

"I do the cooking at Apple Tree House and I work in the bookshop, and Mrs. Munns, our cleaner, does his washing, so perhaps –"

"Perhaps nothing! Even if you begin to make a profit from the Training College custom, think about it, Rose. He's not going to pay a cook or a washerwoman or a cleaner, when he's got a wife who can do all the skivvying."

I start walking quickly away towards the chapel, my chest heaving.

"Oh Rose!" Phyllis is hastening after me. "I didn't mean to make you cry. I was so proud of you, though, managing not to get dragged into drudgery. Please, please, don't throw it all away."

I'm batting my eyes with my handkerchief. I let her catch up with me. "It's all right, Phyll. I know you've got my best interests at heart. I've been deluding myself, thinking it would all somehow work out, but it can't, can it? There's no way out of it."

"Let some other woman do his chores, if that's what he wants. Try to get over him, romantically, and then you can keep him as a good friend."

I attempt a smile. We briefly hug each other, but it feels conspicuous here.

By the time we walk back under the arch, I'm breathing normally. Iolo is harnessed. "Oh, there you are," says Father.

Jack gives me a searching look, but I smile as we grasp hands and say good-bye.

The three of us bid farewell to the rest of our family including the newly-weds, themselves about to depart for George's house, Dot's new home.

Phyllis reaches up to the cart and I take her hand. "Courage!" she whispers.

"And you," I say.

Father gets up and Jack helps Hilda. We're off. As we turn through the archway, I look towards Phyllis and Jack. Both lift a hand and I lift mine.

We're all tired, but from time to time Father and Hilda make the odd comment, going over the moments of this great day. I try to join in, but feel as if my heart is gripped in a vice.

"Cheer up, Rose," says Hilda kindly. "You'll be home for Christmas before you know it. We'll be bound to see them on Boxing Day."

Chapter Nine

I could stay at the bookshop and make myself get over Leonard "romantically", as Phyllis says. I feel sick at the thought, with a kind of fear.

I could leave the bookshop – another sickening wrench – and take up Lettie's suggested side-line as full-time work. Giffords have agreed a trial of my bodice to be made up by us in the three standard sizes. These models would serve as guides to be adjusted when the customer's pattern was cut to fit her measurements. If the line proved popular there would be work here to be had. The thought settles over my spirit like autumnal dampness.

I could leave Widdock altogether. Unthinkable. Besides, where could I go? I love my old home whose heart is still beating, thanks to Hilda's tender care, but I know I cannot go back there. It has changed in the most fundamental way, and so have I. Cambridge? London? I feel sick with fear again.

These are the rats which chased their tails round and round my brain as I lay awake in the dark, next to Hilda's gently slumbering form. In fresh air and morning sunshine, with the rhythmic trundling of the cart, I fall into a deep sleep against the reassuring block of Father, rousing only as we enter Widdock.

In my drowsy state, I am overcome by a surge of conflicting emotions. It feels like meeting an old friend not seen for years, but also as if I am about to part from such a friend. I cannot bear it. I fumble for my handkerchief hoping that Father will not notice, or if he does will not comment. Fortunately he is occupied with taking his place amongst Sunday morning traps on their way to church.

The house can barely be seen behind its namesake tree, now bearing trusses of ripening Pippins. Father loops the reins loosely round an obliging branch and gives Iolo his nosebag, while I get down from the cart with my valise. Mrs. Fuller is probably at church and the others are unlikely to have returned today, so I produce my own door-key, seldom used. As soon as I step inside, my nostrils tell me that the chimneys have been swept.

"Coo-ee," I flute, but as anticipated no one answers. I walk down the hall to let Father in, as requested, at the back door.

In the scullery I fill a bucket of water which Father takes for Iolo. The kitchen feels dusky, the sun not quite round as far as the side window. The kettle is still warm, so I set it on the hob and place two cups from the dresser on their saucers. As I do so, the first ray of sun to reach the window glints on the silver teaspoon in the sugar bowl and falls on this week's Widdock Courier, folded into four. I shake it out, skating over the intrusive front page advertisements, reading the main headline: All Set for Bank Holiday Bonanza. The kettle is boiling. I can hear Father's footsteps clanging down the side alley. I am about to put the paper down when my eye is caught by a headline further down the page: Judge Opposes Controversial Book. (See letters page.) I am intrigued. With some reluctance, I re-fold the paper and put it back.

I place Father's tea on the table and look in the biscuit barrel. "Oh, sorry." I show him its emptiness.

After tea we take a stroll in the garden and Father admires our vegetable patch, but I can sense his anxiety. "I don't want to leave the horse and, you know, I should be getting back."

I do know. He is ill at ease when dealing with a situation outside his routine. I do not press him.

Iolo is waiting, head up and ears pricked at our footsteps. Father pats his neck. "He's a good old boy."

"It must make a difference not having to share him – except with Jack," I say, thinking immediately of my brother and hoping he is faring well today.

Father climbs up and we say good-bye. I wave as the cart disappears from view.

The house feels as empty as the biscuit tin. I refresh the tea pot with hot water, pour myself a cup and sit down at the table with the newspaper. In my absence, could the public library have acquired new 'controversial' stock? I turn to the letters page.

Dear Sir,

With reference to Mr. Cutler's letter (Widdock Courier 27th July) concerning Widdock: An Architectural and Historical Guide by Roger Buttleigh-Truscott, I deem it my duty to pursue a point touched upon, though not developed, in that letter.

My wife comes from an old Widdock family, the Beaumarises. Despite the demands of running a substantial domestic staff, she also takes a keen amateur interest in local history. I had, therefore, requested a copy of the above volume to be sent to the house and had intended to present it to her as a birthday gift.

I invite gentlemen readers, especially those who are husbands and fathers, to imagine my consternation when, sampling the contents at leisure, the offending sentence seized my attention by dint of its colourful word for a tawdry and shameful business, rendered no less so by its connection to the historical figure named in the book, an anecdote which would, in my opinion, have been best left unrecorded. I need hardly add that the thought of my wife, my four daughters or, indeed, any of the maidservants who can read, coming across such material fairly sickened me.

I returned the book straightway with a letter voicing my disapprobation in the strongest possible terms and I would urge Mr. Pritchard to remove it from his shelves before more harm is done.

One cannot help but observe that such a book would not have crossed the threshold of Mr. Quinn-Harper's premises. Is this a further sign of the new century's moral degradation?

I am yours truly,

Rear-Admiral Jocelyn Hyde, J.P.

Bardingfordbury

Somehow, I know what this is about.

"Oh, Rose..."

I am still sitting, numbed and staring, when Mrs. Fuller returns from church.

"If I'd guessed you were coming back today, I'd have hidden the paper and broken it to you gently." She comes round to my side of the table and hugs my shoulders. I catch a trace of her floral scent, a comfort.

"Poor Leonard," I whisper. "I wish I had been here."

"Well, you are now," she says, removing her outdoor clothes and hanging them up. "He'll appreciate that."

"It's to do with that word, isn't? The Spanish-sounding one."

Mrs. Fuller pauses. "Bordello, yes. And you don't know what it means? No, you wouldn't. I'd better tell you. It's a brothel."

I clap my hand over my mouth, speechless. Thank goodness I didn't ask Dr. Jepp about it or worse, the Curate.

"It was something to do with Samuel Pepys coming to Widdock, wasn't it?" says Mrs. Fuller.

I can quote the phrase, I've pondered it for what feels like ages: " 'Samuel Pepys frequently enjoyed visiting Widdock's bordellos.' "

Mrs. Fuller makes us each a cheese sandwich, having planned to eat dinner in the evening, a casserole to be brought by Mrs. Munns. I can hardly finish my round. Afterwards, in answer to my inquiry, she hands me last week's paper, folded at the letters page. "I'll read it again after you," she says, putting the kettle back on the hob.

Dear Sir,

I feel I must draw to the attention of your readership the fact that there is, upon the shelves of Pritchard's Bookshop, a volume which purports to be a history of this fine town, but which casts aspersions on its character in the vilest possible manner. (I refer to the chapter: Literary Connections.)

It is to my eternal regret that I purchased a copy of Mr. Buttleigh-Truscott's Widdock: An Architectural and Historical Guide and, thinking to relax in my garden with both liquid and intellectual refreshment, the experience was anything but relaxing!

That the fair name of Widdock should be besmirched is an insult to all Widdockites, not only I, who call upon my fellow townsmen to censure this immoral book and its purveyor, Pritchard's Bookshop.

Yours,
C. Cutler
Widdock Moor

While I am reading, Mrs. Munns arrives with the casserole and some personal laundry of Mrs. Fuller's. She takes in the scene at once and moves about the kitchen quietly. Mrs. Fuller re-reads the letter.

"H'm! Semi-literate, whoever he is," she says, throwing the paper down on the table.

"I'm surprised the Editor didn't correct it," I say.

"Perhaps it's part of his policy not to. Let the readership draw its own conclusions."

"It'll have done that all right," says Mrs. Munns. "He's a fine one, this what's-his-name, Cutler, to be talking about immorality."

"Do you know something about the man, then?" asks Mrs. Fuller.

"No, but as soon as I read 'Widdock Moor'– well, you know what they say about folks out that way. They keep themselves to themselves."

"Really, Mrs. Munns!" says Mrs. Fuller, frowning and eyeing me. "I'm shocked to hear you repeat that sort of nonsense."

My head is reeling.

"All I meant was that this Cutler's six penn'orth would have been easily forgotten if His Nibs hadn't pitched in," says Mrs. Munns, "but I'm sorry I upset you. It won't happen again."

Mrs. Fuller looks as if she thinks it probably will, but she gives a curt smile and nod of acceptance.

Wanting to avoid likely bad weather tomorrow, just as my father did, the others arrive during the afternoon. They come out to the garden, where I am sitting in a deckchair trying to make sense of what I've learned and to sort out my feelings. As I tell them what has happened, their dear faces become lined with concern. The sisters and Jenny go inside to read the letters and scrub potatoes, so we can eke out Mrs. Munns's casserole between us. Lettie flops down on the grass beside me.

"I bet you wish you were with him right now."

I nod. It's true. Everything that Phyllis said has flown out of the window in the face of a fierce impulse to defend my love from unjust criticism. I feel as if I would marry him right now, if by doing so I could somehow show his critics that he is a good-hearted man of honourable intent.

I hear the wind in the chimney, rain slapping against the window. I hear Mrs. Fuller moving quietly. The Bank Holiday represents the perfect opportunity for her to go to the Training College, while no one else is there, and paint her finished mural with boat varnish, a large tub of which stands by the front door. She has ordered a fly from the station for nine o'clock. It would be so easy to go with her, alighting at the shop. But perhaps he wouldn't be pleased by my surprise return a day early and out of hours. Besides, I have something I must do today. The urgency of the enterprise wakens me fully. I make no noise getting washed and dressed. As I pad downstairs, I hear the fly pull up, a dark blur through the stained glass, and see Mrs. Fuller's diminishing back view. I am thankful to find the kitchen empty. The longer I have alone with my thoughts, the better.

As I guessed, it takes all day, what with interruptions, not that I mind in the main. Sometimes, I need to step back from the jumble of sentences, scratched through and re-written. So, I'm glad to help Lettie lay out the cloth, pin on her paper pattern and get her started with the cutting out. Once we've set the tension and tested the stitches on a piece of rag, the whir of the machine as Lettie works is soothing, seeming to allow my hand to answer to my brain more fluently. The others, sitting reading, offer comments to the two of us when needed. While the rain tips down outside, the kettle simmers and we are cosy.

Today, thank goodness, it is fine. I walk briskly down to town with Lettie. As I leave her at Gifford's, she wishes me, once more, "Good luck," as did all my house-mates before we went to bed last night, spoken with a sincerity all the more heartfelt because, after long discussion, we agreed that their participation in any action might jeopardise their jobs, whereas I have nothing to lose.

I head across town and am soon outside 'one of the most impressive buildings in Widdock,' according to Mr. Buttleigh-Truscott having, I recall, 'an order of grand Corinthian pilasters in rubbed brick and graceful carved stone capitals'. On one side of its elegant doorway are solicitors' chambers. On the other are the offices of The Widdock Courier. As the Town

Hall clock strikes nine, I mount the steps to the front door, which stands slightly ajar, as does the door inside on the left from which issues the noise of clacking keys and a general buzz of busy people. Today is the deadline for any copy to be placed in this Friday's paper before it is, as I understand they say, 'put to bed'.

Entering the room on the left, I am confronted by a counter, the main function of which seems to be to separate the staff from the public. At one of the desks nearest me sits a young woman typewriter, head down, fingers flashing. At another desk, a young man with a notebook wedged open beside him, laboriously strikes the keys of his own machine. At the back of the room are two older men, one of whom I think I recognise as a fleeting customer at the bookshop. They are discussing final adjustments to the paper. No one acknowledges me. The big hand, on the wall clock, inches towards ten past the hour. The man whom I take to be the Editor, slaps his hand down on his desk, "Yes, yes, dispense with the giant marrow. The escaped puma's far better." He looks up and sees me.

Before I can lose my nerve, I say, "I have a letter for you, Sir." I proffer the envelope.

The other man turns to his boss, "Would you like me to – ?"

"No, it's all right," the Editor says, coming towards me as he speaks. He takes the envelope and rips it open, scanning the few words which took me so long to compose more quickly than I can repeat them here, though I know them by heart:

Dear Sir,

I should like to speak up for Pritchard's Bookshop, which reflects the good character of its owner. It is a place which welcomes anyone and everyone who seeks self-improvement, intelligent discussion and spiritual refreshment in an enlightened atmosphere.

In my opinion, Pritchard's Bookshop is a benefit which complements the admirable town of Widdock and, as such, should be cherished.

Yours truly,

Rose Alleyn (Miss)

Apple Tree House

Still holding the letter, he rubs his stubble in a contemplative way. My cheeks are burning. "You work there – the bookshop – don't you, Miss Alleyn? I thought so. You did well not to get involved in the mudslinging. He ought to be very pleased with this encomium, your Mr. Pritchard. The trouble is," he sighs, "I can't publish it. People are bound to think he's put you up to it. They might even think..." His eyes have softened. "You see, I'm concerned for you, my dear, and your reputation."

This is not a dissimilar conclusion from the one to which we all came in relation to the involvement of the others. I can understand the Editor's depressing logic, even if most of me doesn't care.

"There's no point in you drawing unnecessary fire and I," he straightens his shoulders, "wouldn't want you on my conscience, besides," he hands my letter back to me and calls out to his sub-editor, "haven't we already got one from Apple Tree House?"

"Yes." The other man roots around on his desk. "A Mrs. Florence Fuller."

Once again, my head is reeling. Dear Mrs. Fuller has said nothing of writing to the newspaper which, given the Bank Holiday, she must have done as soon as she read the latest letter in Friday's Courier. Either she did not want to make me feel that I, too, should write or, her mind focussed on her mural, she simply dismissed the task when completed.

Any sense of elation, inspired by my dear friend's act of kindness, wears off as I queue in every shop – for I have a long list. In our absence, that same dear friend has lived on air. I wonder whether I should have accepted, with such meekness, what the Editor said with regard to my letter. Still, his is the final decision. As I criss-cross the High Street, these considerations take second place to a growing anxiety about Leonard's state of mind. I am now much later than my usual shopping time. I come out of the butcher's in East Street, one of Mr. Buttleigh-Truscott's mediaeval alleys. As I turn to cross the High Street, I have to wait while Hallambury's massive land train, powered by a steam traction-engine, trundles through on its four-hour journey to their London depot, the minutes leaching away with every clanking truck.

I hasten past the men lolling on the bridge, into the baker's, then the greengrocer's, unable to stay longer than to exchange greetings with Kate and thank her for her concern. I cross the road as the clock strikes ten and my love is turning the sign to 'Open'. His concentrating face looks drawn, a study of resigned despondency, which tugs at my heart. As he stares out, he catches sight of my wave. His expression transforms to such a relieved, joyful smile, tears prick my eyes as I rush under the arch and through the back door at the same time as he comes from the shop.

"Rose…"

"Leonard…"

We are transfixed.

"I thought, perhaps… I mean, I assume you know–"

I cut across him. "I don't care about those letters. I will always stand by you. In fact," my voice wobbles. I take a deep breath. "I'd like to give you an answer to –"

He holds up a hand. "Well don't, not yet. Feeling sorry for someone is no basis for a marriage, believe me."

"I'm not saying it because I feel sorry for you – I mean, I do, but – I love you… Leonard."

"I love you, too, Rose," he steps across the room and gently takes my hands, "but I can't go and speak to your father with all this… notoriety hanging about me. I don't imagine he would be very willing to bless our union."

It's perfectly true. Being in the public gaze, especially in a situation such as this, is just the kind of thing of which he would strongly disapprove. I say nothing. I want to go on holding Leonard's hands, whose heat I can feel through my summer gloves, but the part of me which isn't overwhelmed by his physical presence recognises that, although he is keeping his tone light, he is really quite concerned. I must not present him with a cause for further anxiety.

"I'm very heartened by what you've said, Rose, but you do understand, don't you?"

I nod, fiercely. "Yes." It comes out rather hoarse.

"Good." He gives my hands a little squeeze, then releases them. "There's work to do. The last part of the order for the Training College library needs checking. I've requested

176

transport for a quarter past one, while we're closed. The librarian's expecting us."

Work is the perfect antidote to tension and anxiety. Seated in our sitting room, I am tallying the order form with textbooks on subjects as varied as music, political economy and writing. I have to exercise an act of will not to start reading them, particularly the last. Leonard, who has already checked a substantial quantity of books today, has said that he will serve at counter while he works. I hear the shop door opening steadily all morning and, predominantly, the bass tones of male customers.

Olly Bates, whose son we saw at Dot's wedding, runs one of the station flies. He helps load the crates of books onto the floor inside. There is just room for the two of us. While we are waiting at the crossing for the 'down' train to pass us and re-pass us as the 'up' train, I comment on the fact that business seems to have been brisk.

"It has." Leonard looks surprisingly displeased. "I regret to say that the publicity has attracted – how can I put it? – a rather unsavoury type of customer. That's why I suggested you should work in the sitting room – not that they'd have approached you!" He gives a wry laugh.

"You mean..." I am trying to work out the implications, "some men just buy the book to read the sentence with the Spanish word in it?!"

"I'm afraid so. Let's hope they go on and read the rest of the book. The word's not Spanish, by the way, it's Old French: bordel, a small farm. You may as well know."

"In case it comes in handy in polite conversation," I say, and we both burst out laughing.

Now we are on the move, bumping over the railway tracks and turning west under an avenue of horse chestnuts. I realise I have never walked this way before. To our right is the glint of the Blaken, the town on the other side of it and Hallambury's old mill premises in the westerly distance. To our left rises the gently-wooded south side of Widdock, the favoured location where Joe's betrothed lives with her prosperous family. Before the hill gains any height, we have turned into the driveway of the Training College. On a pleasant site, framed by trees and surrounded by lawns, gardens and tennis courts, there is a well-proportioned central building. This is flanked by harmonious classrooms and a residential block, all built of the local brick with white-framed windows, which give the group a welcoming aspect. That sense of ease, I find as we enter, is sustained inside. After I have been introduced to the friendly librarian, and both men start to unload the books, I take in the airy room with its plentiful windows, the large, inviting table and chairs in the middle, the oak shelving whose beauty comes from simplicity of ornamentation arising from function. How Father would approve! The library is almost complete. Here, in the literature section, are titles I know such as Milton's Paradise Lost. There are others which are less familiar to me, books by Dryden and Pope and Dr. Johnson's many other works besides the popular Rasselas. Seated at this comfortable table, inhaling the scent of polished wood, leather binding and fresh paper, one could work very agreeably, I think.

"Would you be able to come in at nine o'clock tomorrow morning, Rose?"

Try to stop me.

When I arrive, two brand new bookshelves have been delivered to take a representative selection of college textbooks for those students who have the means to purchase their own copies. More books can, of course, be ordered through us. The shelves stand back to back and dominate the space between a wall and the counter. In one way it feels odd, yet in another it confirms the identity of this bookshop. I spend the day as before, trying not to be tempted by the books' contents, as I know Leonard is anxious to place the books on the shelves ahead of the beginning of term to make them available to any eager or conscientious student.

"Rose! The most wonderful news!"

For a moment I am confused, muddling today, Thursday, with tomorrow and thinking that someone has written a letter to the paper of outstanding praise for Pritchard's Bookshop.

"Mr. Hallambury has sold a sizeable parcel of land to the Parish Council to build houses for the poor."

Of course, there was a Parish Council meeting last night. "I'm delighted. I hope someone appreciates your part in it all."

He waves this aside. "I think he was planning to do it anyway. He's the real benefactor. I get the impression he practically gave the land away so that the Council could afford it."

I hardly dare enter the shop today. Leonard will, already, have been out and bought, with his daily papers, this week's copy of The Widdock Courier.

I can tell, instantly, by his determination to look cheerful, that there has been further correspondence. The paper is lying, as if tossed down, on the floor by his armchair.

"Right! Let's get to work!" he says, rubbing his hands, and we go on as before.

"If you really want to," he says, at one o'clock. "I'm going out for a breath of fresh air."

In case I can't face it afterwards, I eat my bread and cheese first. I open the paper. The letters page is dominated by further discussion of the wretched book and, by connection, Pritchard's Bookshop. Mrs. Fuller's letter is brief, for reasons she explained to me when I told her about my conversation at the Courier offices. "I'm so sorry, Rose, it all just came at the wrong time." It turns out that of all appalling things, the king of Italy was assassinated at the end of July. "You can imagine how worried I am," she went on, "if this act speaks for a general state of civil unrest there." I could. My mind flew to Mr. Philpott and his family, somewhere in Italy. "I hope to goodness Beatrice and Miles are still in the villa at Ravello. That's where I've written." Given all this anguish, it is a miracle that she wrote to the Courier at all.

Her letter simply, but effectively, asks the question: what sort of society do we want to live in – one where books are censored? The Coopers have also written in similar terms and saying that Pritchard's is precisely the place where constructive discussion of contemporary issues can take place. The bookshop should be encouraged to flourish.

It is hardly surprising, however, that two landowners have followed the Rear-Admiral's lead with further trumpeting on the subject of moral degeneration. They, too, call for Mr. Pritchard to remove the "offending volume from his shelves". They also speak highly of Quinn-Harper's Bookshop.

Leonard returns as I am about to read the final contribution on the subject. A glance shows him where I am on the page. "What a damn silly way to start a letter!" He says.

It is from the vicar of St. Saviour's, the same man who gave us the Pentecostal sermon about the phos of Christ's logos. After referring to previous correspondence, he opens, "Prima facie, I can see no reason to shoot the messenger, as it were." In other words, I gather he is not against Leonard, but he does go on to quote, for his benefit, Galatians 6:5, 'For every man shall bear his own burden', in light of which, "given the imperative to uphold public morality" he concludes, "if Mr. Pritchard were minded to withdraw the book, one would applaud his discretion."

"So, two for, two against and one hedging his bets," says my love, with asperity.

"Well, you know who I think's behind these letters," says Lettie, after dinner, as we finish work on the first bodice.

"It's probably who I think, too."

We both speak as one.

181

Fortunately, I am still coming in a little early. I find him sitting in his armchair, white-faced. All this pressure on the nerves is bound to have an effect. I feel immediately contrite, and I apologise for my part in his indisposition. Last night, bone tired though all three of us were feeling, we dragged along to this season's first Fabian Society meeting, Leonard wanting to thank the Coopers for their letter and Mrs. Fuller showing support for him, which describes the mood of the majority towards him. I noticed instantly, to my relief, the absence of Fred Rawlins. Perhaps he did not care for the topic, the postponed lecture on Eugenics. Nor, as it turned out, did most other people. During the evening, I had felt a growing anger, in two minds whether to speak out or not, but as so many others were voicing shocked disapproval, I kept silent. Walking home, I gave vent to my emotion. "If I understood him correctly, he would have done away with my brother, Jim, at birth – or earlier, in some unspeakable way." Both Mrs. Fuller and Leonard were as concerned at how the debate had affected me as they were disturbed by the proposition.

And now, poor Leonard has a terrible headache and is sitting quietly. I ask if there's anything I can do. "Not really, just be your dear, caring self, Rose. I've taken Citrate of Caffeine. That usually works to clear my head. Oh, there is something – would you mind going for my newspaper?"

I refrain from suggesting that the last thing he needs is to be squinting at print. I take the coins and leave.

As if I needed a reminder, today, Tuesday, is the deadline for this week's Widdock Courier. As I approach the newsagent's, who should I see with The Times under his arm turning back towards his shop? I hasten to purchase Mr. Pritchard's Manchester Guardian.

I catch up just as Mr. Quinn-Harper is unlocking his shop door. He turns at my footsteps. "Ah, Miss Alleyn, I wondered if – or rather, when, you would come to see me." He opens the door and ushers me inside. The smell of old paper, mould and dust assails me. It is not unlike a church smell but without the scent of beeswax. There are piles of books everywhere. He starts to lift one from a rickety chair.

"Please don't bother, Mr. Quinn-Harper, I'm not staying," I say.

"As you wish. The offer of employment is, of course, still open."

"How dare you!" I am fired, perhaps, with the residue of last night's anger on top of what I'm feeling now. I regain control. "As if I would leave Mr. Pritchard! You know very well why I am here."

"My dear Miss Alleyn," he spreads his hands, "I don't know what you think I can do about the unfortunate situation in which Pritchard finds himself. I have no authority over the Press."

"I'm not talking about manipulating the Press," I say.

"Then what...? Oh, I see..." He gives a dry little laugh. "You think I am somehow implicated because he is my business rival. That I have coerced all these disparate people to write indignant letters. And that I've paid them to mention me favourably. Is that what you think? Would that I had that kind of omnipotence. I'm not even acquainted with any of them."

"But you're one of them," I say.

"Please listen to me, Miss Alleyn. I may, from time to time, have expressed my displeasure at your employer's irksome behaviour, but I wish him no lasting ill. You do believe me, don't you?"

"And you said you did?!"
"I could see he was telling the truth."
"H'm!"
We are pinning the pattern on the fabric for the second bodice.

"So, who could it have been behind those letters?"
I sigh. "I don't think anyone was behind them. I think we have just to accept that there are some people like us and a lot of others not like us at all. They've a right to their opinion, too."
Lettie sniffs.

We try to live as normal. Leonard and I set up the new bookshelves, which look both imposing and tempting with their display of brand new books covering an array of subjects. I disappear behind the shelves when any dubious-looking men enter the shop. In the evenings, Lettie and I continue working on the bodice. We have all tried sitting in the garden, but this season's crop of wasps make it a penance rather than a pleasure. Thus, Wednesday and Thursday pass.

"Good morning, Messrs. Alleyn," says Leonard.

"It's Rose we've come to speak to," says my brother, Joe, Hubert behind him, looking sheepish.

"I'll leave you —" Leonard begins.

"No, please don't," I say, lightly and to Joe, in an innocuous tone, "Can I help you with anything in particular, or are you just browsing?"

"This shop's getting too much of a bad name," says Joe. "Have you seen this week's Courier?"

I have, of course.

"We don't think you ought to be working here, do we, Hubert?"

"Mmn..." says Hubert, avoiding my eye.

"That's very kind of you to worry on my behalf, but I can assure you I'm thick-skinned. I can weather it," I say, deliberately misreading his meaning. I can feel the dull pulse and heat of anger, but I must not let this show.

"That's not what we meant, is it, Hubert?" Hubert doesn't answer. "Our family is being dragged into the mud because of you."

"Let me just say that your sister is free to leave the minute she asks," says Leonard.

"And let me just say," I respond, before Joe can answer, "I'm sorry if the parents of your betrothed are making life difficult for you, but I'm afraid I'm not prepared to hand in my notice to please you or them."

"Thank you for your support, Miss Alleyn," says my employer. "It's greatly appreciated."

"They haven't actually said anything yet, have they, Joe?" says Hubert, suddenly.

"No, but the way this is going on, they soon —"

"I've been thinking, Joe," says Hubert, "Rose ought to make up her own mind."

185

There is a charged silence.

"Thank you, Hubert," I say.

"Well, she'd better do some serious thinking – and you, too," says Joe to Hubert. He moves to the door. "Reputation," he says, looking at all of us, as he exits.

"I don't know how to thank you," says Leonard, grasping hands individually with Messrs. Davidson, Nash and Vance. They clap him on the back: "Matter of principle," booms Mr. Davidson, and, "Hear! Hear!" cry the other two.

A letter which they have written and undersigned appeared in yesterday's Courier. I was surprised and, I have to admit, rather gratified at the striking similarity to my unpublished one. They speak of Pritchard's bookshop being a welcome new resource for the educationally-minded and a haven for intellectual discussion in which freedom of speech plays a fundamental part.

Notification about the Parish Council's purchase of land for housing the needy has also appeared in the paper. A letter from Mr. Hallambury draws attention to this welcome state of affairs, praising 'Mr. Leonard Pritchard' as being 'a gentleman of the highest probity, whose vision and purity of purpose have inspired us all.'

A counterblast comes in the form of a letter from the Bishop, who says that he has refrained from commenting hitherto, but clearly must intervene to give moral guidance to those who have been 'so duped, by The One who works through a human mouthpiece to further his malign hegemony, that they are no longer able to distinguish right from wrong. They become lax and tolerant. By their failure to repudiate and cast out works of evil, they allow evil to flourish. Be warned, people of Widdock. The Scriptures are stark in their clarity upon the subject: "Wherefore by their fruits ye shall know them" (Matthew 7: 20).' There is only one course of action open to those of right mind, and that is to censure both book and premises.' The Bishop concludes with the hope that this will draw a line under the "disgraceful" matter.

"Two for, one against," I say, trying to look on the bright side.

"But the one against will carry a lot of weight with many local people," says Leonard.

We are busy in our usual Saturday way. This is good for morale, but second post brings a letter which, when we are closed for luncheon and he opens it, makes my love groan. "It's the Chamber of Trade. The Chairman feels obliged to tell me that they will be holding an extra-ordinary general meeting about me on Monday evening."

"Oh, Leonard..." I place my hand on his arm. I'm not sure whether he notices. He looks devastated. "Can they expel you? Would it close you down?"

"Undoubtedly and I don't know. Those are the answers to your two questions." He pats my hand, but flings the letter down. I step backwards from the violent movement.

"I had better tell you – I met the Principal of the Training College this morning when I went for my paper. He says he doesn't give a fig for all this – they're open-minded and not a church set-up – but if I go on being in the news, the parents of students might start questioning the College's involvement with me. He hopes they won't have to revoke their contract."

Chapter Ten

"Now you may," says Ralph. "Now, it's ready."

So, I open wide my paper bag and run my fingers carefully up the seed-packed spire of the tall mullein as far as I can. The seed cases yield to the touch without coercion, which is what Ralph meant by their being ready. They plop and patter into my bag like summer rain.

"Good girl," says my grandfather.

He comes to stand on the path behind me and leans over to the tops of the spires I cannot reach. His fingers, dipping and closing, dipping and closing, remind me of a bird alighting, pecking and darting away. The scent of the lavender border, against which we both are brushing, mingles with the trace of old woolly cloth and pipe tobacco which signifies Grandpa Clarke, Mother's father.

We make a good team, working in this fashion, and have soon gathered all the seeds from the stand of mullein, which I love for its cheerful yellow flowers, when Summer is past its peak, and for its felted, blue-green leaves – 'glaucous' Grandpa has told me is the word for them –which feel soft to the touch.

When we have finished, Grandpa folds the top of the bag over twice and puts it in his jacket pocket. Later, he will apportion the seeds to their small packets. I shall be allowed to write upon them in my neatest hand, copying his script to the letter, Verbascum phoeniceum.

"Look at your fine asters, Rose," says Grandpa.

He is being generous. It is true that they are flowering, but they sprawl in an unruly clump. Ralph's Michaelmas daisies, in comparison, are vigorous, straight-stemmed plants turning their blue faces to the sun as if they know they are on display. My brother is currently dead-heading his splendid dahlias using Grandpa's secateurs because, although only eight, he can be trusted with them.

We all look up at the cheerful cry from the back door. It is Mother, accompanied by Dot and Hilda. They have been blackberrying. My sisters' mouths are stained dark with juice. Grandma now steps outside, bearing a tray which she sets down on the old wooden table. There is a jug of apple juice and ten assorted little glasses. Mother follows with another tray on which sit ten similarly diverse little bowls containing blackberries. Running footsteps around the side of the cottage herald Jack. He is preceded by Gyp, loping along, ears flapping, tail wagging. They have been playing outside Father's workshop. And here comes Father, holding Phyllis's hand. In the other, she grasps the little boat-like wooden shape which she has been whittling. We all make ourselves comfortable under the apple tree, Mother in a deckchair, the rest of us on rugs, while Grandma distributes the bowls and glasses. I cannot think of any more pleasant way to spend a bright autumnal afternoon.

I close my writing book, profoundly glad that I decided to conclude my account at this point in order to counterbalance the sorrowful subject of the last piece which I shared with Leonard, Annie's fatal illness. It is Monday afternoon, and he has asked me to bring the work in to cheer him and divert his mind from this evening's extra-ordinary meeting of the Chamber of Trade at which he will be the topic under discussion.

After thanking me and making some kind and helpful remarks, he says, "So, I suppose that's how Ralph came to be employed at Sawdons. Everything he learnt from your grandfather must have stood him in very good stead."

"It did."

This is true. There is no need, at this inappropriate moment, for me to tell him how Grandpa, whose job was in an office at the Gas Company, whose joy was his garden, had started a modest business selling seeds through the post. It was always thought that Ralph, when he left school, would be his assistant and even I, in my turn, might help. Within months of that afternoon, Grandpa's kindly heart had given up the task of taking him into his seventies and Grandma had moved to the alms-houses. Ralph, bereft, immediately offered to tend the courtyard garden there and was soon helping with individual plots in front of the little cottages. Of the ten souls present on that afternoon I described, four have gone ahead.

There is no further opportunity for discussion. Our notoriety still brings us custom. Just before we close I ask Leonard, quietly, about his plans for the evening. The thought of him alone and brooding has been playing on my mind.

"I'm invited to the Coopers'," he mouths back and even more quietly, "Thank you, Rose." Then, as the Town Hall clock strikes six and the three men present show no sign of leaving, he says, in his normal voice, "Time for you to go home, Miss Alleyn."

As I close the door between the shop and the sitting room I look through at him, but his tone has stimulated our customers and he is engaged in serving them.

We try to carry on as normal at Apple Tree House, Meg and Winnie tending their pot plants, Mrs. Fuller and Jenny rehearsing, Lettie and I working on the bodice, but we are all living under a cloud of concern for Leonard.

He is waiting in hat and coat. "I've been summoned." He shows me a letter. "The Chairman must have written it straight after the meeting last night and posted it himself. It was on the mat when I came down this morning. No, it gives nothing away."

"I'll be thinking of you, of course," I say.

He nods, his smile grateful but distracted. Then, he's gone.

I start to tidy the shelves, but it's impossible to concentrate for wondering how he's getting on. I am gazing out of the window when the parcel post arrives with, unsurprisingly, a consignment of books. I untie the string and push back the brown paper. Glimpsing the title on the spine, I recoil. This is adding insult to injury. I go back to tidying, but it's set me thinking... Although infamy has attracted, it has also repelled. Sales of the book have been steady, rather than soaring. Thus, I don't recall either of us ordering further copies. Our orders ledger confirms my supposition. Sitting at the counter, looking at the barely-broached parcel, I almost fancy that what's inside has a sprite-life of its own.

I pull myself together. In view of all the circumstances, I can't just leave it there for Leonard to find when he returns. There are no customers at the moment. It's my duty to deal with it. I pull back the paper and am confronted by a brief letter from the publishers, apologising for the "printing error on page 124. Would you please replace the copies you have on your shelves with these and return them to us? Postage will be refunded."

I am intrigued. I can guess where that page falls. I turn to it and find the section about literary notabilities of the Elizabethan and Stuart era who graced the town with their presence. I read: 'Indeed, Samuel Pepys was a regular visitor to Widdock'. I read it again, unable to believe the blank space which indicates the paragraph's end. The apostrophe and 's', which had followed the word 'Widdock', together with that scandalous French word to which they appertained have disappeared.

I am still sitting, bemused, when Leonard returns, looking grim.

"They want to support me, but someone tabled a motion that I must remove the book. It passed by one vote." He points an angry finger. "I had to leave with the matter unresolved. I could see the Chairman was disappointed. He'd written the draft of a letter, ready to go to The Courier, commending my discretion etc. etc. But if I agreed to this – directive, where would it end? Rose," his eyes rake mine, "I can't do it. I can't act as a petty censor."

"All the fuss is only about that particular sentence, isn't it?" I ask, with care.

"Of course!" He answers in a wild, exasperated voice.

"Then, let me show you something – something that isn't there."

Leonard has left this weekend's copy of The Courier open on the letters page from which I deduce, together with his demeanour, that the deadline must have been met following his gallop round to The Chairman of the Chamber of Trade on Tuesday straight after my disclosure. The Chairman has written that 'readers will no doubt be relieved to learn, concerning Widdock: An Architectural and Historical Guide ...' and goes on to paraphrase the publishers' letter, stating that the corrected text is available at Pritchard's Bookshop. He continues with a glowing testimony, saying how impressed he was with Mr. Pritchard from the first time he met him because it was clear then, as it is still, that he wants the best for Widdock and its townsfolk. The Chairman concludes with the hope that Mr. Pritchard may be allowed the tranquillity to go on developing his ideas towards the betterment of Widdock. I read Leonard's thanks, succinct but sincere, to those who wrote to the paper in support of him. He says no more than this. There is also a letter whose address is the University of Bologna, Italy. It is, of course, from Mr. Philpott, referring to recent correspondence in The Widdock Courier, which he has sent out to him, and speaking about upholding freedom of speech, and the importance of having a local forum where unconstrained discussion can take place.

"Bologna in late August must be idyllic," says Leonard. "No wonder he's staying on there."

"Oh... for good?" I ask.

Things seem to have settled down in Italy, as far as we can tell from the few lines penned by Mrs. Fuller's daughter, still in Ravello.

"No, no, just for the Michaelmas term. I had a letter while you were away. Didn't I tell you?"

He hadn't, but it's hardly surprising that it slipped his mind, given everything else preying upon it.

"He says he'll start his Widdock lecture programme a week earlier in January than he did this year and run it on past Easter."

"What's the topic?" I ask.

"Well, he's been travelling all over Europe this summer, so it's International Affairs. It sounds fascinating."

"Perhaps it's as well the course isn't starting in September," I say. "If we're very busy, it would be a pity to miss lectures because we're too tired to attend." I dare to say this because another good thing which has happened is that the Training College has settled the bill from Pritchard's Bookshop for the books provided to furnish their library. With the cheque came a letter of endorsement. The fear of losing their custom and that of their students has vanished.

"Yes, we might be used to being busier by January." We both hear ten o'clock chiming. "But we won't be busy today if we don't turn the sign over," says my employer and love, with a lightness I haven't seen since my return to Widdock.

In case we might relax, however, second post brings a letter which makes him give a quizzical, smiling grimace. One customer follows another, though, and it is not until we close at one o'clock and are both in our sitting room that he is able to tell me: "I've had a letter from old Bledington. He says he will soon be in possession of something of value to us both. He says he can't attend the Chamber of Trade meeting on Monday and suggests we meet on Tuesday."

"I thought he didn't like you."

"Certainly, when I first came to Widdock, he was abrasive with me about not taking over my father's business," says

194

Leonard, accepting a cup of tea and sitting down, "but he was actually the one who, a couple of times, tried to restrain Quinn-Harper's waspishness."

"Do you trust him?" I feel uneasy on his behalf.

"I don't know, but I might as well find out what this cryptic note's all about. He suggests noon at The Crooked Billet. I think his company owns it."

"I don't know it – well, I wouldn't."

"It's the other end of town on a cut next to one of his maltings. You don't mind running the shop while I'm out do you, Rose?"

"Of course not."

We exchange a smile, deep but fleeting, as if neither of us dares hope that we might be entering a more peaceful situation, one where we could begin to reconsider that question which, if not burning, has been all the while smouldering.

I can hear their voices below me, Lettie's the most excitable in a rising intonation, then the rich notes of Mrs. Fuller's, perhaps answering a question. As I dry my hands, I savour both the comfort of these familiar sounds and the anticipation of joining my friends.

"We've been discussing your predecessor," says Mrs. Fuller, as soon as we've all greeted each other. She looks delighted.

My predecessor... Of course, Bella, the cook who eloped on the day I arrived in Widdock. Oh...

"It's all right, Rose," says Lettie, "she doesn't want her old job back."

"Indeed not," says Mrs. Fuller, "she's done very well for herself. Who has the post-card?"

"We do," says Winnie. "They've got electric trams."

"Look," says Meg, passing it across to me.

The table's laid, the fish floured and everyone seems to want me to read it, so I turn over the photograph of The Promenade at Blackpool and read the large hand, extending right across the card.

Dear Mrs. Fuller,

We have had a very good Season. I am training to be a Chef in a big Hotel. My Husband works on the Trams. I hope the Enclosed will meet some of the Cost of a new Mrs. B.

With Heartfelt Thanks,

Bella Ibbot (Mrs.)

"She really needn't have sent a money-order," says Mrs. Fuller, as I hand the card back. "I'm just pleased to have helped her and glad she seems to be happy."

"A pity there's no address," says Lettie.

"She doesn't want to be traceable," says Mrs. Fuller, "by his kinsmen or hers."

We have to remind Lettie, who came to the house a week later, about the two feuding families, Hobbs and Ibbot, from which Bella and her true love came.

Then, Jenny says, quietly, "You know who we haven't heard from..."

I pause, a plaice fillet suspended over the pan. Lettie turns from the bobbing broccoli, the sisters from slicing and buttering.

Mrs. Fuller assumes her full height. "We won't hear from Priscilla now. So, you can all stop looking like that."

Once the words are spoken, we all feel certain that what Mrs. Fuller says is true.

He looks so smart in dark blue jacket, trousers and tie, all reminding me, as if I needed reminding, that his eyes are such an astonishing shade of blue. His black hair against a white shirt completes the picture of elegance.

Last night's Chamber of Trade meeting was clearly a triumph, although he will not dwell on it, with even Mr. Quinn-Harper making a pleasant comment about him. "I'm glad to say, they were eager to get down to business and discuss the success of Widdock Day, with a view to its continuance."

He has also, before I arrived this morning, sent off three poems to a publisher: the one about skating; the misty morning walk and another which he was going to read to me yesterday, but there was no free time to do so.

We hear the clock strike the three-quarters. "I'd better go. It'll be a good ten minutes' walk, and I'd rather be early." He puts on his hat.

The shop seems very quiet when he has gone. It is not a particularly pleasant day, rather dull and cool. Perhaps this has deterred people from venturing further than they need. I become absorbed in next month's Bookseller magazine, reading about a lovely book written and illustrated by a lady gardener. The door opens and shuts. I look up – in horror.

A man has entered. He is throwing books off the shelf nearest him.

I leap off the stool. "What are you doing?" My blood is fire. Everything pounds. I am made of rage.

"What's it look like?" he says, with a nasty smile.

I start round the counter towards him, but stop dead. No. It is as if something holds my arms preventing my legs from moving forward. That would be what he wants. Now, I'm beginning to feel afraid as well as angry, but I won't let him see it. I haven't glanced at the back door, but he must have read my thought.

"I'll get there first – little thing like you," he says.

It's true. I've stupidly increased the space to the door, but if I'd moved the other way, the new shelves would have blocked the view of him. I shiver. I don't know what to do. Why doesn't someone come to the door and see what's happening? I force myself to breathe deeply and stand my ground. While he's over there, he's not here. I'm feeling sick and light-headed, dying to rush to the books on the floor, their covers like the wings of wounded birds, but my fear of him and repulsion is the greater.

"Why are you doing this?" I ask him, hoping he can't hear my voice shaking. I try to look firm.

He pauses and turns to face me. "I have it on good authority that your employer needs to be taught a lesson."

I feel both intensely weary and full of renewed anger. Once more, I master my voice. I look into his eyes – and recognise him as the man who came in before my holiday and made the lewd remark. "If it's to do with that wretched book, Mr. Pritchard didn't write it. Read The Courier and you'll find –"

"I'm well acquainted with The Courier, thank you. Listen, Miss. Personally, I don't care what books he sells. He can purvey all kinds of pornography as far as I'm concerned." He gives a dismissive gesture. "It's not what he's done to me." He turns as if to resume his destructive action.

Purvey. "You're C. Cutler, aren't you?"

"I might be."

"If you didn't write that letter for yourself, you wrote on behalf of someone else. To stir up trouble."

"Very good," he gives his nasty laugh again and turns back to the shelf.

I'm beginning to make some very swift deductions. "Would you please stop that?" I hear my own voice sounding calm and authoritative. How can it? "You see, I'm finding your violence very painful."

He turns back to me. "The last thing I want is violence between us. I rather hoped you'd have understood that by now. All you've got to do is be nice to me."

This must be a dream. No, a nightmare.

"You be nice and then nothing worse will happen to this place."

My throat is bone dry. I can't speak.

"Oh, come on. You and him must be −" He makes an obscene gesture. "All we've got to do is pop out the back, eh?""

In the blank white shell of my brain, a voice speaks.

I force myself back from shock, make myself appear relaxed, keep looking at him, but gently. Then, I repeat the words I heard in my head trying, trying to sound light, conversational. "Are you ambitious, Mr. Cutler?"

"What's that got to do with the price of fish?"

He sounds defensive, but it may be surprise.

"I just wondered. That letter you wrote −"

"It was good, wasn't it?"

I think, please God, something has changed. He shifts his bodyweight and he's still listening.

"It certainly made its point." I try to look encouraging.

199

"I showed them. Anyone who didn't think I was up to it, that is."

I take a deep breath. My heart is hammering. I cannot believe what I am about to suggest. "I could help you to improve your written English even more. That would show the person in question – or anyone else. It would help you pursue your career."

For a moment, he seems to be looking inward, thrilled at the prospect. Then, he narrows his eyes. "How? Where? When? What do you charge?"

"How is easy. By suggesting what you could read and by giving you some exercises, which I could go through with you. For about half an hour a week. The location would have to be a public place –"

"Not too public," he cuts in, "I don't want to look like an idiot."

"Of course not, but you understand…"

"I understand." He looks uncomfortable, but at the same time not wanting to lose face. "I'm sorry…" He gestures towards the books. "Do you want me to –?"

"No, it's all right. I know where they go."

"What about when? I have Saturday afternoons off."

"Saturdays are our busiest time – unless," I'm thinking fast, "let me speak to Mr. Pritchard."

He nods.

"Oh, and I shan't charge you anything on condition you promise me, Mr. Cutler, there are to be no further incidents like today, whatever Mr. Bledington says."

"Blow him. I promise. This is all about me, Charlie C., and my future. I'll come back on Saturday and see what you've arranged. Good-bye, Miss Alleyn."

200

I stand motionless by the counter, blood thumping in my ears. Then I go to salvage the books.

I'm just returning the last one to the shelf, when Leonard appears, running, and bursts in, hatless, white-faced and wild-eyed. "Rose! How could I have been such a fool – leaving you on your own?" He is gasping for breath.

"I'm all right. He's gone."

"Who has? Are you sure you're not harmed?"

It's nearly one clock, so we shut up shop and go through to the back. He puts the kettle on and I start to tell him what happened, but find I'm shaking and can't speak.

"I'd like to hold you and comfort you, but I'm not sure – I mean – "

I walk up to him and he opens his arms. We stand holding each other until we both stop shaking.

While we drink our tea with two sugars, I manage to tell him everything.

"What I'd like to do to him – and his master," he says.

"Well, please don't," I say.

"And you thought of this plan, really, to protect me?"

"And myself and the bookshop." I give him a wan smile, "That was my first thought, but I think we can take Cutler at his word. It's clear he's fed up with doing Bledington's dirty work. He wants to be able to make something worthwhile of himself."

"Nevertheless, I should go down on my knees before you."

"There's really no need." The thought of Cutler is repellent but, having offered, I'm prepared to put up with him.

201

"He can come in here at half-past five on Saturdays. I shall ask Mrs. Kemble from the yard to sit with you. Wedge the door open and I'll keep an eye on you, too."

I ask him to tell me about the meeting with Bledington.

"It was a bit of a rough place, even in the saloon. I was just ordering a half when he arrived. He congratulated me on the way things had turned out. I said that was an end of it as far as I was concerned. Then, he started waffling about how he had built up his business from nothing. I wasn't sure exactly what the particular relevance was supposed to be for me, although there was a general point, I suppose. After he'd been speaking for about ten minutes or more, I tried to broach the subject of the thing of mutual value, the reason we were meeting, but he brushed me aside, 'All in good time.' I was about to say that, really, I didn't have all that much time, when someone he knew passed by as he was leaving and touched Bledington on the shoulder. 'Very sorry to hear about the Hallambury land. These bloody do-gooders, eh, Bledington?'"

"You mean the land sold to the Parish Council for housing the poor?"

"Precisely, so. Apparently, Bledington had been about to buy that parcel of land from Mr. Hallambury and build another malting. I was taking that in, just as you are now, but Bledington, as soon as his friend was out of earshot, let me have it in no uncertain terms: 'I'd worked very hard, very hard but then I have to say, Pritchard, you came walking in and, at a stroke, the deal fell through. And now you've got them all dancing to your tune. But let me tell you, Pritchard, you have to take these things on the chin. These misfortunes come along.' He had a peculiar look on his face. I should have realised then, I should have realised, but I was so keen to clear

202

my name, I didn't think – I never dreamt that you might be in danger.

I told Bledington I didn't know any of this. Not that it would have stopped me – I didn't say that to him. I said I was sorry that he seemed to see me in such a bad light. That was a mistake. He started on about my father and the 'tidy little business' I could have taken over from him. That's when I felt I had to tell him the exact state of my father's financial affairs which, I made clear to him, I would not otherwise have revealed. I said that all I have is the bookshop. This obviously came as quite a shock. I could see that he did believe me, albeit reluctantly. Before he could start again, I asked him if he remembered my mother. That seemed to jolt him. 'Of course', he said, 'charming. A real lady'. I told him that I had had a very good relationship with my mother all her life. How heartbroken she would be that someone thought of me as a ne'er-do-well and wanted me to fail. 'Would your mother not feel the same, if you were in my place?' I asked him, which was a risk. He might have had a terrible relationship with his mother. But he didn't. I could see my words working on him. Then, he began to look perturbed. 'I think you'd better get back to your shop, Pritchard, as quickly as you can.' I realised I'd fallen for a trap – that you were the thing, oh God…I've never run so fast. To think – the person I care for above all else! I love you, Rose."

"I love you, Leonard."

We gaze into each other's eyes.

Eventually, he says, "Would you like me to take you home?"

"No, thank you, I'd rather stay here with you. It must be nearly two o'clock. Let's open up and carry on as normal."

It takes the rest of the week, with nothing untoward happening, to regain a sense of normality but, by Friday evening, we are sufficiently recovered to join Mrs. Fuller at the Training College. The Board of Governors has acceded to her request that the hall might be open for an hour, so that the public may see her mural without the hindrance of all the chairs which will be put out tomorrow for the official Opening and the Welcome to Scholars.

The Apple Tree House-mates are joined by Mrs. Munns and we pick up dear Leonard, who never looks anything less than smart, however he might be feeling inside. Tonight he seems calm and cheerful.

We are not the only interested townsfolk. As we walk through the vestibule and down a corridor I recognise, ahead of us, the editor of The Courier, some of the Fabians and, as we enter the hall, there are Mr. and Mrs. Cooper, chatting to Mrs. Fuller, who came down ahead of time.

Against a backdrop of the college, its grounds, and Widdock melting away into the distance, there we are, the five of us, our images taken from the sketches Mrs. Fuller made of us all those weeks, months ago. We have been transformed into archetypal figures, simplified into elegant shapes and rich, glowing colours, Mrs. Fuller's hallmark.

"Oh, that's very clever," says Mrs. Munns. "You meant those figures over there to look unfinished, a bit like ghosts."

"I didn't run out of time, if that's what you're thinking," says Mrs. Fuller. "They're supposed to represent students of the future. That's why they're in outline only."

"And wearing shorter skirts and look – trousers!" says Lettie. "Or they could be men, I suppose."

"They are what you imagine," says Mrs. Fuller.

"That's what I thought," says Mrs. Munns.

"We are very privileged to be here," says Leonard. "This is a major work."

"Ah, good," says Mrs. Cooper, nudging her husband and discreetly directing Leonard's attention to the door. A tall, distinguished stranger has just entered the room and gazes about him, nodding an affirmation to himself. "That'll be him."

I have grown wary of newspapers, but Leonard's pleasure is so visible that I overcome my reticence and take up his copy of today's Manchester Guardian to read their art critic's praise for 'Slade School-trained Mrs. Florence Fuller, hiding her light in the shires'. He describes the mural, with particular reference to its 'bold, economic forms and vibrant colours' and he likes the 'ethereal, androgynous figures of future students sketched in grisaille. It is an impressive work, forging a dynamic way forward. I urge anyone interested in modern art to make an appointment with the College and take the train to Widdock to view it.' Well, well... He must have telegraphed it through straightaway, such was his admiration.

"We just thought, the Coopers and I, there would be nothing to lose by issuing an invitation. It paid off, didn't it?"

There is a distinct mood of elation in the shop this morning, augmented by the appearance of Messrs. Davidson, Nash and Vance. It has at least as much to do with what we have come through at Pritchard's Bookshop and their support for us as it has with last night's viewing, at which they were also present.

Shortly after mid-day we are visited by Mr. Cutler, whom one might describe as a reformed character now that he is obliged to us. He looks very nervous and neat in a way which could never be described as stylish.

Leonard manages to speak to him civilly, thank goodness, without emotion, telling him when he may return for tuition. He nods and says 'thank you, Sir,' several times. Apart from a passing resemblance in hair colour, he really looks nothing like Leonard. I am disgusted with myself that I once mistook this person for my love. After he has gone, we exchange a look of toleration under pressure. For me, the rest of the day is overshadowed by the thought of his return.

"No, I will not accept any money," says Mrs. Kemble. "You've been a good friend to us in the yard, Mr. Pritchard. You know we're first on the list for the new houses. This is our way of repaying you."

She seats herself in my armchair, her baby swaddled against her chest and gets her needles out of the bag carrying her knitting. I push the footstool under her feet.

"Thank you, dear, lovely," she says.

I hear my student arrive in the shop. Leonard shows him through.

"How d'you do, Charlie Cutler – haven't seen you for a while," says Mrs. Kemble. "I'm here to make sure you behave yourself."

I am overcome with relief by the fact that they are acquainted and rejoice in her forthright manner. I sit Mr.

Cutler, as I must call him, in Leonard's chair and I perch on the little steps I use for the highest shelves. This gives me a height advantage without having to stand like a school-ma'am.

I suggest that we have a look at some grammar exercises, asking my student to identify the subject of a sentence and the predicate.

"Easy," he says, pointing these out correctly, which is what I had hoped so that he should feel confident to progress.

"Every sentence must have a finite verb, which is –"

"A doing word – the action," he interrupts.

"Good." We look at some examples.

Then, I produce his letter to the Courier, with its long, muddled phrases. This is a risk. I see him glance across at Mrs. Kemble to see if she has understood and is amused, but she seems entranced by the clicking of her needles. We untangle the letter, me sitting just to the side of the student. He re-writes it so that it is grammatical.

"Try not to strain for an impressive word," I say, "but strive for the right word."

He writes this down in his little notebook.

We just have time to read through a book review, passed to me by Leonard because it is written in the kind of plain but lucid language which we both admire. "He always writes well, this gentleman," I say, "so look out for the name, Edward Thomas, and see what other books he reviews – and read the ones he likes."

Both our guests have gone.

"Good God!" Leonard props the back door open. I can't blame him. He is smiling, though, thank goodness.

I, myself, feel tired out and slightly sick from the sour-milk smell of baby, the rank, oiled yarn of Mrs. Kemble's knitting and the overwhelming odour of my student's bay rum pomade. I suppose I shall get used to it.

Chapter Eleven

"Goedenmiddag, missen Rose," each of the two young women greets me as she enters the shop.

"Goedenmiddag, missen Maria, missen Geertruida."

So cheerful and friendly are these sisters that I have fallen into first name terms with them. Besides, soon after meeting them, when they came in with their reading lists and then returned to collect their ordered books, it began to feel faintly silly, in salutation, to repeat their shared surname, missen De Vries, missen De Vries.

There are strong links between this part of the country, with its tradition of market gardening, and Holland's bulb fields. These are nieces of Jan De Vries, a local nurseryman, originally from Holland, but with an expanding business here. ("You mean, he's their Dutch Uncle?" Lettie giggles.) It makes sense that they should learn to improve their English at the same time as becoming teachers, so that they can return home and teach the language to their pupils, many of whom will enter into horticulture and are likely either to come here or have commerce with their English counterparts. Maria and Geertruida's arrival in Widdock has not gone unnoticed, as testified by The Courier, one letter speaking of 'a welcome addition to our splendid new Training College under the auspices of The British and Foreign School Society, which thus appropriately justifies its old and honourable title.' Another, as heartfelt if less eloquent, whilst initially bemoaning the absence of Dutch bonnets and clogs, concludes on the affirmative note that 'they are like two sunbeams'. This is true. With their butter-blonde hair, blue eyes and wide smiles, they brighten any day.

At five o'clock the students have an hour's recreation before dinner. When these two look in and there are, as today, no customers who might be disturbed – as distinct from those who take a positive pleasure from joining in – Leonard has a short lesson in Dutch.

"Ik been al naar Zuid Amerika. Ik heb niet naar de Nederland geweest, maar ik zal gaan er op een dag, hoop ik."

I can guess what this means: I have been to South America. I have not been to Holland – the Netherlands, mar ik zal gaan er… but I shall go there op een dag, hoop ik… one day, hope I – their inverted word order.

"Erg goed," says Geertruida. Maria agrees. They say this all the time. He is very good.

"…als het Duits en toch als Engels," says Leonard, not for the first time and which, therefore, I know means: like German and yet like English.

Looking back, it seems as if one moment the shop was relatively empty, the next full of lively young women, keen to improve their own education in order to pass on their learning, more effectively, to their charges. This atmosphere of intellectual stimulus and enquiry is one in which, of course, Leonard thrives. Although many of the student teachers are friendly and approach me for advice, many more like to speak to him and benefit from his greater knowledge. We no longer close at one o'clock, but take an hour separately, because the College breaks between noon and half-past two for luncheon, recreation and for the trainees to work in laundry and kitchen. This is, of course, on a rota system, so there are nearly always some of them in our shop.

The fact that we have been busy since before the start of term has greatly aided our recovery from being the target of Mr. Bledington's hostility and the focus upon Pritchard's

Bookshop which it inspired, all now, thank goodness, well and truly over. We have scarcely had time to register the resultant easing of anxiety as the days have gone by.

"Dank u," says Leonard, prudently concluding his lesson as the door opens to admit the chimes of the three-quarter hour and a smart gentleman from the city, who has stepped off the evening train. "Good evening, Sir. May I help you?"

As the customer produces, unfolds, then squints at a piece of paper, Leonard mouths to me, "You can go, Rose."

I come out of the archway from the yard just as the De Vries sisters are leaving the front of the shop, followed by the gentleman clutching his wrapped purchase. I glance back through the glass of the nearest window, but the lamp beyond it dims followed by that on the other side of the room. I cannot see Leonard, but know that next he will be locking the door and turning the sign to 'closed'. I hesitate, feeling as if I should go back and say a proper good-bye, but I must get home and help with dinner.

"We ought to have had some kind of celebration," says Lettie, after we've all finished eating and before we clear the dishes.

"Let's wait till the first sale," says Mrs. Fuller. "Then we can think about celebrating."

Her ten most striking paintings have, today, gone to London under expert porterage from an influential gallery in Pall Mall where they are to be displayed. Word apparently travels fast in the art world, and days after the favourable review of the mural which appeared in The Manchester Guardian Mrs. Fuller received a letter from the gallery owner

211

requesting a viewing not only of the mural but of all her work. This astonishing and wonderful turn of events completely overcame the sense of disappointment the rest of us felt, though the artist herself remained remarkably stoic, when the opening of the Training College and consequent coverage of her mural had been forced to play second fiddle, on The Courier's front page dated 7th September, to the outbreak of bubonic plague in Glasgow and discussion of 'Widdock's response should this deadly disease make its insidious progress south'.

"But you must feel excited," Lettie persists, "or do you miss your pictures?"

"I..." Mrs. Fuller shrugs, "I'm excited about the work I'm doing now. The finished paintings can stand on their –"

The sound of the knocker interrupts her. We all look at each other.

"Is anyone expecting a guest?" Mrs. Fuller asks, rising.

We, too, are mystified. She opens the kitchen door. In the darkening shadows beyond the hallway, a figure is discernible through the stained glass of the front door. By the hat and general stature, it would appear to be a woman. Looking relieved, Mrs. Fuller turns up the lamp nearest her and starts down the hall with a business-like gait.

Then she gives a little cry and breaks into a stumbling trot. We follow, somewhat alarmed, but all stop by the stairs as she throws the door open.

"Beatrice!"

"Mother..." The young woman gasps.

Instant, pricking tears rush to my eyes. I take a shaky breath. Lettie's hand gives mine an unobtrusive squeeze.

Mrs. Fuller, arm round her daughter's shoulders, is sweeping her over the threshold together with a small boy of about two or three years old, who holds his mother's hand.

"And you must be Miles!" Mrs. Fuller drops down to the level of the little boy, who regards his grandmother with dark, solemn eyes. "Hello, Miles...Emilio."

At the sound of his name in a language to which he is probably more used, Miles gives the flicker of a grave smile.

"I'm sorry – there wasn't time to write," Beatrice is saying, "I just had to get away."

"That doesn't matter. You poor loves," says Mrs. Fuller, regaining her full height and patting her daughter's free hand, "Has the situation worsened in –"

Beatrice interrupts with a short bark of a laugh, not unlike her mother's. "It's got nothing to do with politics."

"Well, it's wonderful to have you both here, safe and sound," says Mrs. Fuller. "Take off your hats and coats."

"Where do you want this, Ladies?" Olly Bates appears, his son behind him holding the other end of a trunk.

"Upstairs, along the landing to the front, please," says Mrs. Fuller.

The men begin to heave the trunk up.

"Goodness, I haven't introduced you all," says Mrs. Fuller mainly, I think, as an attempt to cover the audible grunts and cusses of the men as they try not to chip the paintwork or dislodge pictures with their shoulders, and struggle to negotiate the bend at the top. The formalities over, she asks us to escort Beatrice and Miles to the kitchen for refreshment. "I'll be with you in a moment," she says, and we leave her, no doubt wishing to settle the bill discreetly.

"Thank you, I'd love a cup of tea," says Beatrice, flopping into the armchair and pulling her son onto her lap, where he curls against her. She must be about Dot's age and is as arresting in looks, though differently so, as her mother. Height and fine bones they share but Beatrice has an abundance of thick flaxen hair, straining to spring from its pins, which magnificently sets off her melting dark eyes now trained on us as she pleads, "and could Miles have a drop of milk, if you have some to spare?"

While the sisters make tea and Jenny fetches milk and a glass, Lettie and I start to clear the dirty crockery and leave it in soak for Mrs. Munns to finish tomorrow morning, our gesture towards helping her without diminishing her role. What a turn up says the glance we give each other. By the time we return, the travellers are seated at the table, Miles on cushions, enjoying their sustenance. Mrs. Fuller is back, asking Meg and Winnie to help her go through the ottoman for clean sheets, together with spare pillows to make a bed for her grandson. They leave the room.

"I can't tell you how welcome that was," says Beatrice, pushing her cup away. "Do you know, we were still in France first thing this morning?"

We ask about her journey.

"Frightful. Rome to Milan to Paris to Calais. Can you imagine – staying the night in Paris and not walking down the Champs Elysees or strolling by the Seine at dusk?" She nods towards her son as explanation.

Fortunately, Mrs. Fuller reappears before we need reply. "Meg and Winnie are making up your beds, Bea."

"You are all too kind," says Beatrice, looking overcome. She rises and reaches for her empty tea-cup, as if to transport it to the scullery, but Jenny takes it from her and swiftly returns.

As one, we move to the door. "We'll just... er..." says Lettie, opening it.

"Give you some privacy," says Jenny, following her out.

Mrs. Fuller looks slightly rueful that we feel obliged to leave what is our sitting room, but grateful, as I say, "It's all right, we'll go in Meg and Winnie's." I pull the door closed.

We stand in the hallway, waiting by the sisters' room. We can hear them finishing their task upstairs, about to leave the little front bedroom. We can also hear, distinctly through the kitchen door, Beatrice's voice. "You do understand, don't you Mother? I had to leave after the way he treated me?"

"I do, of course I do, but that's the kind of behaviour you get in those circles."

"But I couldn't stay after that."

We three look at each other agog.

"I agree, but he's used to rubbing shoulders with the aristocracy. They'd expect you to turn a blind eye."

"Is she here for good, then?"

Unusually for these days and especially on a Saturday, we haven't been quite so pressed by work to be done before opening. I have, therefore, taken the opportunity to relay an edited account of last night's events to Leonard, before we go through to the shop and he becomes Mr. Pritchard. I do not mention what we overheard, nor the ensuing discussion which took place in Meg and Winnie's room, in charged whispers, during the very short space of time before the kitchen door opened and we fell abruptly silent as the travellers made their weary way upstairs, "Come on, Miles, one step, two step, uno, due, tre..." Led by Lettie, the debate

215

encompassed every possible interpretation of the words between mother and daughter from "parading the woman in public" to being "caught with her – you know."

What I do tell Leonard is that when we moved back into the kitchen and started making our cocoa and tomorrow's porridge, with half-milk, half-water to cater for any requirements Miles might have before the fresh milk arrived, Mrs. Fuller came down and told us that her daughter had had a distressing time and would not be returning to Italy but staying permanently at Apple Tree House. "I apologise for all the inconvenience this will cause." "Nonsense," we had assured her. It was where Beatrice and Miles should be, their home. At this point, I voiced what Lettie and I had already agreed. "Would they like our room? We could swap.""Certainly not. No one is to be compromised," Mrs. Fuller said.

"So, Beatrice has left her husband?" says Leonard.

"Not officially, though between them they have parted. If anyone asks, we're to say that she is here for her health and to put Miles's name down for her husband's old school."

"H'm, it sounds as if a number of compromises have been made already," says Leonard, "not least," he gives an almost roguish smile, "a breaching of the female stronghold."

"He's a little boy."

"So was I, once – and look what happened."

Our eyes meet, though we are laughing. It re-establishes a yearning thread between us as fierce as hunger which, in these days when we work flat-out side by side like two farmhands or factory workers, sometimes seems obscured.

I carry that moment with me through the rest of a day which for me, now, is always overshadowed. I am glad that the volume of customers and their demands prevents further thoughts in the direction of its source. It has become Mr. Cutler's habit to present himself, neatly brushed, with pen and notebook ready, about half an hour before closing on a Saturday, his only free afternoon when we are open, a time at which our business for the day is usually winding down. He puts his head in at the shop and collects Mrs. Kemble from the yard, as I go through to the sitting room to greet them both. He is a bright and capable student, keen to do well. Already his prose is less verbose, his use of language better. I am pleased for him, but my heart sinks at the prospect of his lesson. I can never quite forget his former manifestation, even though he clearly is reformed.

I feel the weight slip from me as he cheerily says good-bye for another week and Mrs. Kemble packs up her knitting and carries her sleeping baby back across the yard.

I have been aware, through the open door between us, that there has been at least one customer in the shop and, judging by the lightness of pitch, probably female, which is no surprise. As I walk towards the door, to say good-bye to Leonard, it also comes as no surprise to see that it is his star pupil of the trainee-teachers, Miss Haydon, who has glossy brown hair, blue eyes and a pretty, turned-up nose. She is both well-read and well-spoken and, to cap it all, writes her own poetry, and it is over this, I think, that their heads are bent at the moment.

"No, it doesn't create suspense, splitting the definite article from the noun to which it refers. It just makes a weak line, ending on 'the'," says Leonard.

217

"There! I knew it, but I needed you to tell me," says Miss Haydon, looking at him aslant from under her lids.

"Well, I just have!"

They both laugh and look up at my approach.

Something inside me turns to ice.

"How is your student?" asks Miss Haydon, with a smile.

"Able, progressing well, thank you." I don't know how I manage the words in a normal voice.

"Do feel free to go, Miss Alleyn," says Leonard. "I'll close up here."

"And I must fly, or I'll miss dinner," says Miss Haydon, absolving me of the need to respond to my employer.

I walk back into the sitting room, as I hear her saying how much she's looking forward to Leonard's lecture. He has been teaching German on Saturday evenings at the Training College since the beginning of term. Although the students are taught French as part of their curriculum, there is, apparently, no member of staff with the capacity to instruct in other languages.

I still feel icy and shaking, but with a cold anger. How could I have been so deluded? I stay exactly where I am, controlling my breathing, thinking what I am going to say. I hear Miss Haydon leave the shop and Leonard locking up.

I shall be late home, but it can't be helped. I'm beginning to feel almost noble and tragic. I must hold that strength of conviction. There will be time enough to let the tears flow when I reach the sanctuary of my room.

"Oh! Rose, I thought... Rose...? What on earth's the matter? You look white."

He hastens to me and grabs my cold hands. I pull them free.

"A lot has changed, Leonard, since you asked me That Question. If you've met someone else, I'm not going to beg you –"

"Met someone else?" He looks thunderstruck. "What are you talking about?"

"You know very well, Leonard."

"No, I don't, so stop playing games with me. A lot has not changed as regards my feelings for you. I should have thought that was obvious. I love you, Rose."

"And I love you, Leonard," I say, evenly, "but with all these young women –"

"Oh... You don't mean Miss Haydon?"

"Of course I do."

"Good Lord!" He looks genuinely bemused, running a hand through his hair. "I've never thought about her... in that light."

I have to believe him.

"She has an enquiring mind, I grant you, but when it comes to depth you leave her standing."

I must be bright red.

"Besides, she's a Byronist."

Oh well, that's that, then.

"If you recall, Rose, during our very first conversation, in the grounds of Sawdons, we shared our admiration for the poetry of Keats and Shelley. I think I must have known then, even if it hadn't come to my consciousness, that there could be no other girl for me." He picks up my hands again and I don't resist. "And I'm always thinking of you, my love, in that light." He places the back of one hand to his lips, then the other. "Does that convince you?"

219

I am melting. We stand, locked into each other's eyes until I have to look away, blushing, for fear of leaning towards those lips whose touch I can still feel upon my skin.

We pull apart and he says, "We've allowed your sister long enough for her scheming. I must see your father."

I resolve to write to Hilda.

As I walk home, I think about Leonard's letter, written weeks ago now, which although addressed to Father had to be read by Hilda on his behalf, since he can neither read nor write much more than his name. Her response, that "it will not be convenient for you to call in the near future" had brought forth the sardonic quip from Leonard, "I didn't realise your family led such a hectic social life." I knew, of course, that it was about her courtship with Mr. Armstrong. Father would need time to come to terms with the idea of a second daughter's marriage so soon after Dot's, let alone a third. If we were to jump in ahead of her suit he might, by Hilda's reckoning, refuse permission to that unlucky last person.

I had no need to recall Phyllis's dire warning in order still to be concerned about the implications of marriage. Although Leonard and I had yet to have our Serious Discussion on the subject, which I think we both had assumed would follow naturally from Father's consent, these reservations had all but vanished in the face of Hilda's blatant manipulation. I now had an almost perverse desire to embrace the married state wholeheartedly. I told Leonard I would write in tactful language to try to ascertain how things really stood. I got a barbed answer from my sister: "I know what you're hinting at, Rose. If it's any of your business, things have reached a very delicate stage and I don't want to rush them. Not wishing to be unkind, seeing as you are my sister, but it's high time you thought of someone else besides yourself. When Gerald finishes the Curacy here, he could be given a parish anywhere. If it pleases God that I should be his wife, you might care to reflect on the problem of who is going to look after Father."

That old chestnut again. On the very day of Mother's death, I had been due to start in service at Sawdons Hall, but Father said that when I went there, as the bearer of our dreadful news, I must tell whoever was in charge I would be needed now as his housekeeper. It was only Hilda's desperate plea to let her come home, after the funeral, in place of me that changed what would have been my role – both destinies vanquished by my meeting Leonard. I was so dismayed not only by the tone of Hilda's letter, but the reality of the prospect for me, I hadn't answered till I could keep a civil pen in my hand, which I did by speaking only in generalities. Hilda must have regretted her tone and picked up my emollient one because, after a longer interval than usual had elapsed, a similarly bland letter had arrived from her, which I have yet to answer.

Our initial correspondence took place... I pause at the gate... in the days after the opening of the Training College and viewing of Mrs. Fuller's mural. On Monday, it will be October. A month has passed and we have barely noticed.

I enter the kitchen and am plunged into another world. The sisters are poised with plates of bread and butter waiting for Beatrice who is in their way placing, with infinite precision, table napkins in silver rings and cutlery laid in a formal setting. Lettie follows her and, with a casual, unobtrusive gesture, manages to push each knife and fork further towards the centre of the table, so that little questing fingers should not

221

grasp one of these shiny objects. At the range stands Jenny, one eye on our sardines, one on the prowling cats, and a third, in the back of her head, on lightning, unpredictable little legs which might toddle too close to danger. Mrs. Fuller emerges from the scullery, holding a towel: "Come to Granny, Miles. Time to wash your hands."

Somehow, my letter to Hilda doesn't get written.

After Sunday luncheon, while Miles and his mother are resting, we quickly clear the table and then fetch from the shed the step-ladder, taking it round the side of the house to the apple tree. Leonard, of course, has no truck with any question about whether picking apples is a suitable activity for the Day of Rest. When I mentioned that we were having difficulty reaching all but the lowest boughs, laden with a bumper crop, he upbraided us for not asking sooner for his help.

Now, he appears in clothes I've never seen before consisting of an old pair of corduroy trousers, an open-necked shirt and neckerchief, a cloth cap and a worn jacket. He could pass for any working man at the brickfields, even more so when he discards cap and jacket and rolls up his sleeves. I know that he follows a routine of physical exercise every morning. It evidently pays off. I can hardly tear my eyes away from him to hold the ladder steady, feeling the weight of his footfalls as he ascends. I gaze up at him.

"Be careful!" I gasp, as he steps onto a branch and reaches to the extremity of another.

The apples yield to that little twist of the stem, falling into his cupped hand. He places them in his pockets and in the basket we pass up to him. Those branches he cannot reach he shakes, the elusive apples falling into the stretched sheet which we all stand holding underneath the tree. We are joined by Mrs. Fuller and Beatrice who, when Leonard descends, introduces herself and Miles. Then we all, Miles included, carry the apples down to the disused byre next to the studio and lay them out in the hayloft and on the ground floor. The room, when we have done, smells softly of its harvest.

Although the heart aches at the absence of those dipping, flitting arcs of darkest blue, which imprint themselves as much on the mind as on the azure summer sky, this last afternoon of September bestows a welcome calm in the stillness of the hollyhocks' graceful spires. The borders are awash with a mellow beauty in the jewel-like colours of the dahlias and chrysanthemums under trees still dressed in green.

We shake the sheet used to catch apples and place it on the grass, Leonard needing no second invitation to stay for tea.

"I must come and patronise your bookshop," says Beatrice, sitting on his other side from me. "It sounds as if you've made it a wonderful place – lucky Rose to work there."

"Its character is as much to do with Rose as me," says Leonard, turning away from Beatrice to gaze directly at me, "she's indispensable."

I blush but, until Lettie nudges me and I catch the others' indulgent smiles, I can't stop looking into his eyes, the blue of swallows' plumage.

By the time Leonard had sat Miles on his knee and gone through 'this is the way the farmers ride'–"Again", Miles knows that English word – and we'd both tested our repertoire of nursery rhymes while the others cleared up and before his mother came to fetch him for bed, there was once more no opportunity to write to Hilda, so I take her last letter with me to work and bring it out at lunch-time, noting its date. Is it really two weeks old? I scan its neutral contents for anything upon which to comment but decide instead, after enquiring about her health and that of Father, to tell her briefly of the new arrivals and then to ask: "Do tell me what's been happening to you. Any new developments?" She can answer this as she chooses.

When I get back to Apple Tree House, I find my letter has crossed with one from her. It is not until we retire to our room that I have a chance to read it.

"Goodness me!"

"Not bad news?" Lettie stops, hairbrush in hand.

"No – well, not really."

"What's that supposed to mean?"

I tell Leonard the following morning about the letter, omitting the opening, in which Hilda says she assumes I must be very busy as I haven't written. I do tell him what she goes on to say, that our two brothers, Rob and Ted, who live and work in New York, are coming home for Christmas. Three exclamation marks. With business on the continent afterwards and in London before, they will come and see us "for the entire twelve days!!! Father is in such a state about this that any plans you and I might have, Rose, must simply wait till he calms down or it'll be too much for him. Your loving sister, Hilda."

"I knew I should have gone and seen him last month, regardless," says Leonard. He takes his displeasure through into the shop, but is soon engrossed in daily routine, our future life together temporarily forgotten.

We don't look back in terms of business. This is, of course, reassuring. It crosses my mind that if we were married, time when we were not working in the shop would become available and precious. We might even re-discover the leisure to pursue our mutual interest in literature, the Arts in general and who knows what else?

At Apple Tree House, the Munns family fender-cum-fireguard is now installed round the range. We have to step over it to cook, but at least it keeps Miles from harm, for the time being. He can already reach the doorknobs. It won't be long before his fingers gain the strength and dexterity to turn them. Mrs. Munns keeps an eye on him for part of the day. "I know all about little boys," she says to him, and to his mother, "at least he's clean and dry." "I couldn't leave Italy till then," says Beatrice, "knowing I'd have to cope alone." We all have good reason to be relieved on this account.

Mrs. Fuller has given her daughter part of her studio, for Beatrice is a portrait painter. Needless to say, she has already sketched Lettie and is making a start on a painting but, with the evenings closing in and all of us at work, her ambitions are somewhat thwarted. She sketches the rest of us but, when it's my turn, I fall asleep. "That doesn't matter, Rose. It gives me the opportunity to try to capture your face. It's... interesting." I can hear Father's voice: "Well, that's a very nice compliment, Rose."

I have missed the last two Fabian Society meetings. I was too tired after work. Understandably, they have both been about the General Election, taking place over the period of a month this September and October. Since I am excluded from the vote, I feel I have lost nothing by my non-attendance except, perhaps a chance to inform myself in a debate where my views count for nought.

Leonard informs me that he decided, yesterday, to ride over on his bicycle and speak to Father.

"But your father wasn't there. Hilda says he's been going out on the horse these Sunday afternoons of late. She never knows what time he'll be back. Rose, I couldn't wait for him."

"No, of course not. You had to get back before nightfall."

"It wasn't just that. I couldn't bear the thought of having to make small-talk with your sister, possibly for hours."

If only Leonard had not acted with such impetuosity but had intimated his intention, I could have spared him a wasted journey. Hilda had written to me, worried about Father's absences. Although when questioned by her he is non-committal, she wonders whether, as the year turns towards darkness and the anniversary of Mother's death, his grief is re-awakened and he takes himself off alone to give vent to his sorrows. Hilda may well be right. It is a source of anxiety to us both.

"I think we should go ahead with our plans," says Leonard. "We need to have a talk."

As it happens, today, Tuesday, the trainee teachers and their tutors are going to South Kensington to visit the museums. Towards the end of the afternoon, one of damp and chill with, consequently, few customers, Leonard closes the shop and we go through to the sitting room where he makes us tea, which we take and sit in our respective chairs. I feel nervous.

"Rose, I want to allay your fears if I can – about the physical side of marriage."

I can feel a blush starting already.

"I just want to reiterate that I would never put you through –" he speaks gently, "what your mother went through."

"That's very kind of you to say so, Leonard, but..." With my free hand, I make a gesture suggestive of fate.

"Let me be clear. I'm not a man who must have a son – or a daughter for that matter. Indeed, we don't have to have any children at all."

I put my cup down, having spilt the contents in my consternation. "But... it's what happens, Leonard. You get married. You have children. As night follows day –"

"No, it doesn't have to be like that." Now Leonard puts his cup down, too. "I don't know exactly how sheltered – or incomplete – your education has been in these matters, but there are methods widely available to avoid unwanted consequences. I'll be direct, Rose. I am talking about ways of putting a barrier between the man's seed and the woman's egg. - I can, and I will, use what is called a sheath which can be applied to my penis."

I gasp, both hands to my mouth.

"Yes, I've got a penis, Rose. You must have thought about it, given your concerns."

"I have not thought about your..." I can't say it.

"I'm sorry, would you prefer it if I called it something else?"

"I'd rather you didn't call it anything," I blurt, for now – oh, no! – nerves and embarrassment have come together in a giggle. "I understand what you're saying," I gulp, trying not to think of what I've just heard, but I'm helpless.

"I was hoping," says Leonard, "that we could have had the kind of practical, down-to-earth discussion of sexual matters which would take place on the Continent rather than the British way, as if it's a dirty joke."

When we've calmed down, we apologise and agree to postpone the meeting. It turns out that we both feel we could have conducted ourselves better, Leonard with more tact and kindness, he says. As for me, I know I could have behaved with more maturity and decorum.

We seem to have got over yesterday's regrettable situation, thank goodness, aided by the shop's return to full custom. I realise I am tired, my shopping bag heavy on my arm, but I manage to quicken my pace up New Road, anxious to get home. The sun is setting and suddenly, a shock I had forgotten since earlier this year, the street lamps spring on. Their pools of light have the effect of intensifying the surrounding darkness, as if they wish to add their contribution to tonight's revels.

I enter by the back door and unpack my goods onto the pantry shelves with the speed of habit. In the kitchen, I am confronted by Beatrice, on a chair, attaching apples by their stalks to strings suspended from the lowered pulley. She adjusts them, with the aid of her mother, so that they are within reach of our teeth. Winnie and Meg are trying to serve jacket potatoes and check my apple crumble, while Miles is running up and down the hall with Jenny at this end, pretending to catch him and Lettie keeping him from the stairs.

"Good, you can have a turn," she says, as I walk through, "I'm busting to go."

She disappears upstairs, leaving me to grab at Miles who reminds me, yet again, just how strong and flexible a toddler can be. I feel myself break out in a sweat. I haven't even got my hat and coat off.

After the meal, we bob for apples in a bowl, to Miles's delight, and then we all try for his mother's ingenious pendants, holding the boy up to have a go, with much laughter from all concerned. The room feels hot and crowded. Beatrice has lit candles in two ornate candelabras. "Suitably grotesque, if I may say so, Mother," she comments, to which Mrs. Fuller replies, "You can say what you like, they were a present from your father's side. Ghastly." I can smell hot, fatty wax.

When Miles has gone to bed, Lettie suggests that we should perform the ritual of swinging a length of apple peel round our heads to find out, when it falls to ground, the shape of the letter which will foretell the initial of a truelove's name.

The others enter into the spirit of the thing with predictable results: "Well, it could be a 'C'......a definite 'S'."

"Come on, Rose, you are slow."

I take the peel and twirl it, feeling dizzy.

Lettie shrieks. "You see, an 'L'."

"With a short, curly base," someone says. Her voice clangs in my head.

"What about that bit?" someone else's voice resounds.

"If it's broken off, it doesn't..."

And now I'm going. I grab at the table. I know nothing.

Sweating... I kick the sheets off... now, I'm freezing, but I'm too tired to... too tired... ...eyes, all looking... coming closer... can't scream, no sound... I sink back... ...dry... dry... ...my mouth is... ah... water... ...so tired... so tired... ...dry clashed the dint of... ...ifs and ands – what...? Nonsense... ...sleep... must sleep...

Beautiful feeling... serene... I feel well... ...sunlight... on my lids... I'm bathed in sunlight... sit up... open my eyes... Ah... Mother... how lovely to see you!

Chapter Twelve

...Cool skin... ...the back of a hand...

"You don't feel quite as hot, thank goodness."

...brushing my forehead, cheeks...

"This moistened flannel should help, too."

...Whose voice?...

"And a sip of water – that's right."

...Mother?...I must be home...

...My head... ...block of stone... ...chest... ...raw...

"Try to sit up, Rose, lean against me. Now see if you can swallow this. Well done."

...Phyllis... ...Phyllis?!

"Let's put these pillows behind you. Now, can you lean forward over this bowl?"

...It can't be Phyllis!

"That's right – and I'll put the towel over your head."

...Aaaah... ...menthol vapour... ...bliss... ...I can breathe...

"I've got you, Rose. I won't let you go."

It is Phyllis! – Isn't it?...

...Net curtain fluttering... ...smell on the breeze... ...roasting barley... ...Lettie's bed stripped. Of course, I've been infectious... ...Footsteps...

"Oh, you're awake, that's good. Yes, it's me behind this surgical mask. Meg and Winnie insisted."

"What are you doing here, Phyllis?"

"I'll tell you all about it when you're a bit better."

"Are you staying?"

"No more questions. Time for your invalid food. That's it. Good girl."

...Phyllis...? Lettie...? Where's everyone sleeping...?
"Now, you must rest."
...Yes... ...rest...

It is the second of December. I have lost a month to illness. Lettie's birthday and Guy Fawkes's Day both passed while I was in the oblivion of fever and its aftermath. The circus came and went. "You should have seen the elephants, Rose, walking down the High Street." Life went on, but I was at one remove from it. Halfway through November, when I was beginning to struggle out of darkness, a letter came:

Dearest, darling Rose,

You cannot imagine with what relief and joy I greet the news that you are getting better. In this knowledge, I dare to write, but beg you do not tire yourself by trying to reply.

Knowing you as I do, I expect you have been worrying about how I have been coping in the shop. (I had been, once back from the Lethe of sickness.) You will, perhaps, be pleased to hear that November seems to be a quieter month, most students having purchased the books needed for this term and customers yet to bend their minds towards Christmas. You will also know that Phyllis has been standing in for you whenever she can spare the time. (She told me, as soon as I was able to take it in.) She is a great help, not least in her immediate kind offer to deliver this.

Much as I long to see you, therefore, I beg you not to return to work until you are completely well.

All my love,

Leonard

I could not have held a pen, let alone focussed my sensibilities. I had no choice but to accede.

My recovery, though, has been steady, helped no doubt by the cod liver oil and malt extract for invalids brought from Hallambury's by Meg and Winnie. Just as sustaining has been Phyllis's beef tea and calf's foot jelly, the balm of her loving care, and the constancy of Leonard's love.

Today, the first Sunday in Advent, I am feeling better. I intend to stay dressed and only take a rest in the afternoon rather than going back to bed. I have coped with the crowd of us at table, animated voices all around me and Miles, until shushed, repeatedly banging his spoon on the tray of his high chair, another loan from the extensive Munns family. Now I am enjoying the sudden quiet. Meg and Winnie have gone to First Day School. Beatrice and Miles are already resting. Lettie is also upstairs making her bed, once more, in our shared room. "I shall be glad to get off that ottoman." Jenny and Phyllis are in the scullery. Their amiable tones soften the clatter of crockery and cutlery.

Having seated me in the armchair by the range, Mrs. Fuller stands, waiting for her tea to draw. "How would we have coped without your sister?" she says. "You do know she appeared on All Saints' Day?"

This much I have learnt from Phyllis. She arrived on the first of November when I was delirious, thrashing in burning heat or shaking in icy cold, and Mrs. Fuller was on the point of fetching the doctor. Phyllis stepped in from the start, looking after me and taking on the cooking. Each night, at Jenny's invitation, she would roll her mattress out next to Jenny's bed in the cramped space of her little room, which once would

233

have been a servant's. They would leave the door as wide as it would go, the better for Phyllis to hear any sounds of distress coming from my room, past the bathroom and lavatory, a few steps along the corridor in the well of the house.

"I was standing here, as I am now, making tea," says Mrs. Fuller, "and I heard the sound of a bicycle. I looked up and saw – the light was fading – what I took to be a young man dismounting."

Lettie has slipped back into the room and sits down quietly at the table. Phyllis and Jenny do the same.

"I was wearing my working clothes. I mean the ones I wear when I'm working for myself, Ralph's cast-offs," says Phyllis.

"I have never been more pleased to be mistaken, when the lad turned out to be your sister," says Mrs. Fuller, picking up her tea.

"Wait till you hear what happened, Rose," says Lettie. "You will tell her now, won't you, Phyllis?"

Phyllis makes a small dismissive movement, almost as if bored.

"May I be excused?" asks Mrs. Fuller. "I'd gladly hear your account again, but I must have a nap before Miles wakes up from his."

When the door has closed behind her, Phyllis says, in a matter-of-fact voice, "I had to fight Greville off. I lost my job for it."

I gasp.

"At least it was only your job," says Lettie. "Go on."

Phyllis sighs. She gestures towards her striking features – pale blue eyes, fair springy hair and strong-boned face – whose handsomeness she has always underestimated. "For

234

obvious reasons, I'd always thought I was safe from his attentions, but I think I became a challenge. I'd managed to avoid him for weeks on end but that morning, he found me alone. We were in the drawing room with the grand piano. The misses had both been ticked off by the maestro for not practising enough. Miss Caroline threw her scores on the floor and, of course, her sister followed. The maestro walked out and the misses stalked off in the other direction, telling me to clear up the mess, which is why I couldn't move quickly enough, although I tried, when Greville came in and made straight for me. He seized my hand and forced me back against the desk they use to show off their framed photographs."

I am feeling faint.

"I love this bit," says Lettie.

Phyllis gives a bleak smile. "Fortunately, he'd never bothered to notice that I'm left-handed. I grabbed one of the photos by its stand and slammed it into his face. He gave a great bellow, letting go of me. There was blood everywhere – his nose – and then his mother, who was supposed to be out at some event, came sweeping in and understood the situation at a glance though, of course, she would never have admitted it. 'Instant dismissal and no references,' she said to me. It turned out I'd whacked him with the Royal Photograph."

"Oh!" I clap my hand to my mouth. We all start tittering in a rather unpatriotic way. "I didn't know they were on terms with Royalty."

"They're not. It was in the time of the previous squire. The Queen felt poorly once when they were travelling somewhere and an equerry was sent ahead to have a room prepared for her. She and Prince Albert left a signed photograph, which has been on display ever since. I think Madam was more concerned about damage to that than to her son. I didn't stay to hear what she said to him. My heart was pounding, not only from having escaped unscathed but, in a strange way, with relief it was all over at that place, even though I didn't know what I was going to do next. I went and told them downstairs. A mixture of predictable reactions, mostly shock. Dot sympathetic but guarded in her response. Mrs. Gilliatt, poker-faced, gave me the wages I was owed. Then I went upstairs to pack. I knew I couldn't go back home with Father and Hilda. Unthinkable. We'd be rowing in no time. That was when I decided to come here. It was seeing my shirt, trousers and cap I wear when I'm woodworking. I realised I could pass unnoticed in them. I just thought, Well, I'll walk to Widdock and hope they can squeeze me in at Apple Tree House while I look for work. So I got dressed and went to say good-bye to Jack and Ralph."

"I bet they were upset," I say.

"Angry on my behalf, but they both agreed with my plan to come here. Jack tried to press money on me and Ralph gave me his bicycle. It's the one that came from home. He doesn't need it. He's going to a big house in Sussex in the New Year – a step up."

"I loaded the front and back baskets with my valise, tool-bag and some things I'd made. I was about to leave the courtyard when the Squire appeared. I could see him sizing up my outfit, but he made no comment about it. 'I'm sorry it had to end like this,' he said. 'If you write to me for my personal attention, I will give you a reference, Phyllis.' I was surprised he knew my name – his wife calls me Joan, as she does to summon any of the maids. I just nodded. It was all the thanks I could find. Then, I pushed off. I didn't hear his

236

footsteps on the cobbles, so he must have stood there under the arch watching me till I was out of sight."

Dearest Rose,

I should have liked to send you love letters every day, but didn't want to wear you out. (I wouldn't have minded.) I'm delighted to hear that you are doing so well. I cannot wait to see you for a short spell of light duties at the shop, starting on Wednesday, if you are restored to full enough health.

As ever, all my love,

Leonard

I pass Phyllis my reply to be delivered when she goes to the shop tomorrow:

Dearest Leonard,

I have been walking up and down the hall for exercise, just like an Elizabethan lady in her long gallery! I will see you on Wednesday, (I change God willing to) all things being equal.

All my love to you,

Rose

Here I come, arm in arm with Phyllis, hoping to surprise Leonard by being back at my usual time and there he is – and my heart leaps at the sight of him – standing at the counter, looking at a ledger. There is something stiff yet resigned about his stance. My eyes prick.

He looks up. It is as if a weight has fallen away from him. He looks again and holds out both arms. Now, he's rushing to unlock the door and let us in the shop. My eyes are misting, his face is working and – heavens – he's trying not to cry. He dashes an arm across his cheeks while the tears stand on mine and we walk forward and, just for one moment, we take each other's hands regardless of anyone outside.

"You're a good man, Leonard Pritchard, letting me read your newspapers," Phyllis says, as she joins the two of us in the shop after her break. They have clearly developed an easy working relationship. "Never having time or opportunity to inform myself – it's what I've been missing since you left Sawdons." I gather that Leonard has been buying both The Manchester Guardian, his daily newspaper, and The Times, his occasional one. I, too, like to read them but, in my weakened state, the thought of lifting those great pages daunts me, and I would not presume to fold them.

"That was one of the things I disliked most about that place," says Leonard, "living in a vacuum. You'll recall how I used to have to sneak out to buy my newspaper. It felt like an act of political defiance."

"Like that time when Madam came in and heard you telling me about the Dreyfus rally in Hyde Park. Do you remember?"

It comes to me that, of course, these two were firm friends long before I met Leonard.

Being in Leonard's company once more, after a month without seeing him, has brought back to me that feeling of unaccustomed masculine proximity, which I experienced when I first worked with him. If this weren't unsettling enough, there is now the re-awakening of romantic feelings. I blush to think of how, in a dream last night, I kissed him.

It is strange how the mind orders itself. All the time that I have lived in Widdock, nearly a year now and, indeed, the foregoing years when Phyllis and I have not lived as sisters in our parental home, I have carried an image of her in my mind's eye. It is something from which I have drawn comfort. Having her before me in the flesh is heart-warming. She is in every way her old self, but she is dazzling, too, in her physicality. And now, here she is opening the door and coming through from the sitting room.

I suggest to the two of them that I am well enough to work all day tomorrow.

"Would you agree, Nurse?" asks Leonard.

"It's a question of what's worse, the usual Saturday crowd ignoring us because they're so pleased to see her or having to answer all those endless enquiries about when we think she might be back," says Phyllis.

"See how you get on, Rose," Leonard says. "You can always go home if it's too much," he adds, misinterpreting my dismay as I recall – how could I forget? – the shadow that falls across the last day of the working week.

"Oh! I thought I told you," Phyllis says, when I explain myself, "he's gone."

I am speechless.

"Yes, he came in when you were first ill," says Leonard. "Bledington's opening a malting north of here on the River Tib. Access to Cambridge one way, a different part of London the other via the new railway line. That's his thinking. Cutler's been put in charge. He was very sorry to have missed you to say good-bye. There's a thank-you letter somewhere here." He starts rummaging in the counter drawer.

I feel as if I have been given an elixir of joy.

Now that the factory workers are back to their winter hours, Lettie, Phyllis and I are the first to arrive home. We encounter each other in the hall and walk into the kitchen together.

"You see, Ruskin and Morris weren't here when Mummy was your age and sat in that little armchair. They think it's theirs." Mrs. Fuller is crouched at her tearful grandson's height, stroking his hand. "They don't mind sharing it, but you must be careful. You see, they can't say Ouch! You're sitting on me, Miles!" This is spoken in a cat-like voice and evinces a grudging smile. "A little scratch is the only way Ruskin could show that you were hurting him, and you wouldn't want to do that, would you?" Miles shakes his head.

Beatrice turns from the dresser holding a dampened handkerchief. The cooking sherry is open. She dabs her son's roughened skin.

"Is that necessary, do you think?" asks her mother. "He hasn't drawn blood."

"None of this would be necessary if Miles had a nursery."

The three of us exchange covert, awkward looks.

"I'm not sure I follow your logic, dearest," says Mrs. Fuller.

"I'm sorry Mother, you're quite right." Beatrice draws a hand across her forehead. "I think I must be over-tired."

We know that they have been up to London to see Mrs. Fuller's gallery owner. Perhaps things didn't go as well as they had hoped.

The Fabian Society Party heralds the Festive Season. They are celebrating the election of Keir Hardie and Richard Bell, the first Members of Parliament from the Labour Representation Committee. Mrs. Cooper and Mrs. Fuller have formed a sub-committee to promote women's suffrage. At the shop, Leonard says, "We'd be fools not to display A Christmas Carol. The same goes for The Night Before Christmas. I'll just have to grit my teeth."

Phyllis and I dress the larger window with these and a selection of children's books. We rather enjoy ourselves. Phyllis also has Leonard's permission to make a feature of half a dozen or so books held between two, beautifully-turned bookends in polished oak. "I had the idea as soon as you started working at the bookshop, Rose. It gave me something to look forward to for a couple of hours on Sunday afternoons, if I was lucky." She has five more pairs at home. Next to these is her discreet card bearing the price, and the fact that orders can be taken.

"What are you going to do if there's a rush?" asks Leonard.

"Panic. I wish I had a workshop."

As an antidote to Christmas, Leonard has placed three poetry books in the smaller window: The Oxford Book of English Verse 1250 -1900, edited by Arthur Quiller-Couch and two by G.K. Chesterton, his recently-published The Wild Knight and, in answer to the child-centred theme of the main

241

window display, but on a more light-hearted note in keeping with the season, his Greybeards at Play: Literature and Art for Old Gentlemen, delightfully illustrated by the author with, on the cover, a drawing of one such old gentleman riding his hobby-horse.

Second post brings a shout of "Hooray!" from Leonard. He reads out a letter, from the editor of a magazine called The Monthly Review, accepting the three poems he sent them, the one about skating, the one about gathering flowers in the mist for his mother, and the other one which he had not shared with me.

It is quiet in the shop after three o'clock. Phyllis and I sit on the counter stools and Leonard reads:

"Taking A Step

'It's cool in our cellar,' she said, and I knew it to be an invitation.

Then I sensed it was more than that, it was a reckoning.

So I didn't tell her how this heat, which sapped a hard-won vigour

Regained after winter's harsh punishment of their malnourished bodies –

How this heat, which left them limp as the rags they wore,

Was no worse than mild discomfort to someone who has known

The streets of Buenos Aires, smouldering in blazing sun.

I followed her down, smelling root vegetables, coal and mould.

I saw, when my eyes could fathom the darkness, the shapes of the other women,

Children dozing on sacks spread out on the uneven floor.

Propped against sagging pillows, an old couple lolled, heads nodding together.

I felt honoured to be there, dignified by my neighbours' kindness.

The earlier thought, that the offer might be a kind of test

To see if I'd show a class fastidiousness, dissolved in shame.

The reckoning, I admitted to my conscience, had been mine with myself."

We both applaud. I'm taken back to the enervating heat of the summer, yet a window in my mind opens onto another world: Leonard's life in South America, a subject of which I'd like to hear more, one day, when we are at leisure. "That's an evocative piece of writing," I say.

"I admire the honesty," says Phyllis, "but is it a poem?"

Leonard laughs. "That's the question the editors have asked of my work, but they recognised that I'd been reading an American poet, Walt Whitman and, as they like to think they're in the vanguard of literary and artistic developments, they were prepared to give me a chance."

"You ask me what I'm going to do if I get a lot of orders. What are you going to do if they want more of your poems?" Phyllis asks, not altogether joking. "You run a bookshop, you lecture and you're learning Dutch."

"Yes..." says Leonard, momentarily disconcerted, "I'll have to relinquish something."

Rather than being intimidated by Leonard's literary success, I am impatient to take up my pen again. The Christmas holiday may be my first chance. I resolve to pack my writing book, which has lain untouched throughout my illness. If I can simply write a line or two a day, I shall be satisfied.

The Misses De Vries are the first to give us a card, saying, vrolijk kerstfeest. They leave for Holland, and Leonard gives his final lecture before term ends. The shop fills again with our old customers, the more thoughtful wishing to find the right book to give a loved one pleasure, others just trying to buy something which will satisfy expectations without costing too much. We are asked to give advice on numerous occasions. It is an activity we all enjoy and not like work at all, which is just as well because we have never been so busy. Lettie, too, is engaged all day in helping ladies with their seasonal requirements in the garment and haberdashery line. The three of us fall into bed and even she is too tired to chat before being overcome by sleep.

A Norway spruce, carried in by Mr. Munns, appears in the bay window of our parlour. It is a formidable but benign presence, its piquant scent supplanting that of coal-dust and stirring in the mind's eye dark northern forests, branches heavy with snow and, between straight black boles, the glint of frozen fjords. We housemates attach candles and festoon the branches with strings of beads, but the three generations will finish dressing the tree on Christmas Eve, when Miles will be lifted up to crown it with a golden star, a tableau to be imagined by us all with pleasure.

It is our final evening all together. As Christmas Eve falls on a Monday, the factories will not trouble to open for that one day only. Instead, the men will work a full day tomorrow, Saturday, but the women will have fulfilled their statutory hours by one o'clock, so Jenny, Meg and Win will be free to leave for home.

Phyllis has been teaching Beatrice how to cook, in preparation for the Christmas turkey. "Really, it's just like roasting a big chicken."

"How do you roast a big chicken?"

She is a quick learner. We had roast pork last Sunday. Tonight, we have a piece of topside, beautifully tender, roast potatoes and gravy. She has even baked apples, stuffed with dried fruit and dark brown sugar, to be served with cream. The port bottle has been uncorked for anyone who likes it (Mrs. Fuller and Beatrice) to have as an accompaniment to cheese. We raise our glasses of pop and they follow, firstly to Meg and Winnie, whose birthdays, respectively, are in two and seven days' time. Then, we wish each other a Merry Christmas.

"What a year we all have had," says Mrs. Fuller, cuddling a sleepy Miles in her lap. "But we've gone from strength to strength," she says to cries of "hear, hear".

"Thanks to you," I say, raising my glass with heartfelt sincerity, the others following suit, much to our landlady's embarrassment.

"Well, I like to think this is a happy home, even if it is bursting at the seams," she says.

Phyllis and Jenny exchange a look.

Beatrice says, "Don't wait till the New Year, tell Mother now."

Jenny swallows. "We were wondering, Phyllis and I, whether we might renovate the cowshed. We could make the hayloft into our bedroom. There'd still be plenty of room for the apples."

"And then, on the ground floor, I could use the milking parlour end as my workshop," Phyllis says.

"They've said I can use the rest of the ground floor as a studio," says Beatrice. "Then, I won't need to share your studio, Mother."

"Well, what can I say? Go ahead."

It feels slightly strange not being Phyllis's primary confidante, though why should I be, now that we are no longer children? I'm glad that she and Jenny are such good friends.

"It would release a bedroom," says Jenny, after thanks have been expressed.

"Perhaps, we should mention..." says Meg, eyeing her sister.

"Yes," says Winnie, "we've put our names down for one of Mr. Hallambury's workers' dwellings near the factory. It's his next project."

"It would give you a room large enough to be a nursery," says Meg.

"Or a dining room again," says Mrs. Fuller, before Beatrice can speak. "Now that we shall be entertaining guests from London."

She has received a substantial cheque from the picture gallery. The owner and one of his colleagues, who specialises in portrait artists, are coming to Apple Tree House in the New Year when Beatrice has sufficient canvases to show them.

"Well..." says Mrs. Fuller. "Lettie? Rose? Any surprises up your sleeves?"

"No, we haven't," says Lettie in an emphatic tone, "have we, Rose?"

"No," I say, rather lamely, aware of Phyllis's raised eyebrow, "well not personally," after which, of course, I have to tell them about Mr. Hallambury's visit to the shop, just before closing, to ask Leonard if he would be interested in a cottage to rent. Leonard has asked us to go with him, before work on Monday morning, to view it. I'm flattered that he values our opinion but, really, it's his business not ours. Not ours at all.

We turn into East Street, one of Mr. Buttleigh-Truscott's mediaeval alleyways running parallel with the High Street, as does its counterpart, West Street. We come to an archway. I glimpse a terrace of cottages, old but not rundown, in a tidy yard.

"I didn't know this was here," I say, as we walk under the arch. "How could I have missed it?"

"You weren't looking for it," says Leonard, handsome in his navy overcoat and new hat.

"It seems private, doesn't it?" says Phyllis.

"Only because it's so quiet," Leonard says.

The cottages are three stories high, white-washed wattle-and-daub, with a dormer window in the attic. A bench to catch the morning sun in a less hostile season is a feature of several. We stop outside one. Leonard produces an ancient key and turns it in the lock.

Phyllis and I exchange a smile of recognition. It is like our old home, that sense of confinement, which can be both constricting and comforting. The light, slanting through a generous casement window, falls on a pleasant living room with an open hearth, a comfortable elegant chair on either side. In the space under the stairs, where our bunk bed would be if this really were the house where we grew up, there is a round table with four upright chairs. I walk over and touch its polished surface, feeling a sense of warmth.

"This is beautiful."

"Walnut," says Phyllis. "A lovely pattern in the grain."

A door leads to the good-sized kitchen. It will benefit from the afternoon sun and, in that respect, is again like the back of our old home. Phyllis and I nod to each other in approval. While we inspect the range and larder and turn on the tap at the sink to see the water flow clear, we hear Leonard moving around upstairs.

He comes down and, at his invitation, we go up the narrow stairs. Although we only peep into the two bedrooms, I cannot help the thought flashing through my mind, of lying beside Leonard in that comfortable double bed with its white crocheted counterpane. Phyllis looks as if she has read my mind, but just says, "You can look at the attic," and returns downstairs.

I take the next, even narrower flight, careful not to stumble on my skirt. The room stretches the length of the house and has a dormer window at either end. I lift the catch of the one onto the yard and open it. To my right are the backs of the shops in East Street. Ahead are the gardens and terraced houses of New Road, with a malting beyond and, further off still, a glimpse of fields. To my left New Road stretches up its incline and – yes – I can make out Apple Tree House.

I come downstairs to find the stable door open and the other two outside in a slim rectangle of garden, inspecting the outbuildings which comprise, as Leonard tells me over his shoulder: "wash-house…lavatory… coal-shed…" They go back indoors, but I venture a little way down the path which runs beside the outbuildings. In the borders I can see, in their winter dormancy, the gnarled shapes of interesting perennials. Presiding over a small lawn, branches triumphant against the winter sky, stands an ancient apple tree.

Back in the living room, whilst Leonard and Phyllis are agreeing that this cottage more than merits its fair rent, I find myself drawn again to the table. I pull out one of the chairs under the stair well and slide myself onto it. I am feeling…an energy surrounding me.

Attracted by the scrape of chair on polished floorboards, Leonard says, "That table's rather an awkward shape for the space."

…warmth …presences seated all around me…

"Good job it's gate-legged," he says. "It might be better moved, though."

"No, don't do that," I say, with some vehemence. "There's such a lovely view both ways, the yard and the garden."

"Rose…?" Leonard is giving me a puzzled look. "There's a solid wall between us and the garden." He taps it.

"Sorry," I say, shaking my head. "I don't know what happened. Anyway, it's up to you. It would be your cottage."

"It isn't just up to me," says Leonard.

"I think I'll go and sit on that bench," says Phyllis, leaving us and shutting the front door behind her.

Leonard takes the chair next to me on the curve of the table. He says, gently, "I know this has come rather soon after your illness. I'd hoped that, before we reached this stage, we'd have had our talk about aspects of physical love in

249

marriage, but it seemed too generous an offer not to consider. So, dearest Rose, what do you think?"

I'm actually thinking all sorts of things at once. Arising from 'aspects of physical love', that bed upstairs imprints itself on my mind at the same time as I'm imagining how I could stretch my hand out and run my fingers through his hair, kiss his lips and pull him to me as I did in my tumultuous dream last night. And yet I see, as if for the first time, Phyllis's horror-stricken expression at the news of Leonard's proposal. I see two tiny lifeless forms, the one who lived a week, the other who never drew breath in this world. I see my mother, exhausted from loss of blood...I hear my pounding footsteps on the frozen ground as I run in the dark to fetch Dr. Jepp, as dear Mother's face comes to me, serene in death. Over all, though, what I hear is Leonard's voice, gentle but clear, I would make sure nothing like that ever happened to you...

What I answer is, "I like the feeling of this cottage. I believe it could become Home." As soon as I've spoken the words, I know I mean them.

"Well, that's a relief," says Leonard, and I realize how he had been bracing himself for my response. "Where do we stand on Hilda's embargo regarding your father's state of mind?"

"I haven't heard from her recently," I tell him. "I expect she's run off her feet preparing for us all."

"Well, frankly, I think it's ridiculous that I can't speak to him. When he comes to pick you up tomorrow, I could try to make an appointment with him, at the very least – Twelfth Night, perhaps, on my way back from Stortree. That's the return date for the Christmas coach. I'd simply get off as it goes through Markly."

We hear the Town Hall clock striking, and know we must go.

"Let's just see how Father seems to be tomorrow," I say, as we re-join Phyllis.

As we're walking to the shop, Phyllis says, casually, "The only drawback about that cottage is that it would be quite a place to keep clean, for anyone who wasn't there all the time. Those beams and nooks and crannies."

"Oh, that's all right," says Leonard. "Mrs. Munns mentioned weeks ago that her daughter-in-law's looking for extra cleaning work. I can afford her now."

It's different for Leonard, of course, being a man, but I'm not sure how I'd feel about expecting another to do work I'd normally do myself. Not that I want to.

The day is busy from start to finish, the shop full of our favourite Saturday customers and more. Messrs. Davidson, Nash and Vance arrive, ostensibly for gifts, although Mr. Vance says that he agrees with Scrooge about Christmas. Mr. Davidson seizes The Oxford Book of English Verse and Mr. Nash is "only looking for something for the wife to give her father. Ah! That'll do admirably", as he pounces on Greybeards at Play. Really, they have come in for their verbal constitutional with Leonard — Mr. Pritchard, as I must remember to call him. Phyllis sells all her book ends.

We get back to a comparatively quiet Apple Tree House. Lettie is still here and Miles, of course. Propped on the hallstand is a letter addressed to me in Hilda's firm hand. I start to read it. I re-read a sentence, scarcely able to believe it. Once I've recovered from the shock, I do as Hilda asks and share it with Phyllis. Over the whole weekend, we find ourselves returning to the subject. It's hard to come to terms with it. In another sense, it simplifies everything. There is only one thing left for me to do.

Now that Miles is resident at Apple Tree House, no one has the luxury of a lie-in, so the six of us and the two cats breakfast together. It is Christmas Eve. For a moment, after breakfast, Mrs. Fuller and I find ourselves alone in the kitchen. All our mutual thanks and love are expressed in a hug.

"Have a very good Christmas, Rose."

"And you, too, M – Mrs. Fuller." I almost called her Mother.

We leave with Lettie, all three of us carrying our valises. Lettie's brother will collect her when she finishes at Gifford's. Father will come to the bookshop for Phyllis and me and our two brothers from America, whose train arrives mid-morning.

Mrs. Fuller, Beatrice and Miles stand at the front door, waving.

"Merry Christmas..."

"Merry Christmas..."

"Happy New Year..."

Then they are out of sight.

I feel tight-chested and my stomach clenches. It is a fine morning, sunny, with a little easterly breeze bringing a vestige of roasted malt. I savour it so that I will be able to remember it, and all it means to me, once I am back at my old home.

On the corner of New Road and the High Street, regardless of early shoppers, Lettie and I clasp each other for a moment. We exchange those seasonal valedictions again and then she's off to her job.

Phyllis and I pass the men on the bridge and the baker's with its aroma of fresh bread. We wave to greengrocer Kate, who is hanging a bunch of mistletoe on a hook. "Merry Christmas," the three of us cry. Now, I'm hurrying across the road to the bookshop, Phyllis behind me. There is Leonard. He looks up, as I clatter under the arch almost running now, and he's already through to the sitting room as I come pounding in, chest heaving.

"Rose, Phyllis, you're early – whatever's happened?"

I can't get my breath.

"I'll go through and start tidying," Phyllis says, and does so closing the connecting door behind her.

I hand Leonard Hilda's letter:

Dear Rose,

In haste. I had it out with Father today about his disappearances, as I was so worried. It turns out he has been courting!!! He met Cousin Grace in town, shortly before her husband died. They were in a tied cottage at Steadling. She had come in to see if Aunt Mary would have her afterwards at the mill. Father visited them both until the end, and he has helped her with her move. This means that you won't have to come home to look after him when Gerald and I are married, to which he has given his consent. So Leonard could speak to Father, if you are both still of a mind to wed. Father knows I'm writing to you. Please tell Phyllis. It takes some getting used to and no mistake, doesn't it?

Your loving sister,

Hilda x

Leonard hands the letter back to me, with a wry smile. "I'd already made up my mind I was going to approach your father, but this should mean he's amenable, I hope."

There's a knock on the door into the sitting room and Phyllis says, "Just to let you know, I've seen Father go past. I should think he's taking the horse to the trough."

"He is early," says Leonard, as we go through.

"That's Father," I say.

Leonard unlocks the door, but doesn't alter the sign. Phyllis and I step outside and wave when we see Father returning. He gives Iolo his nosebag and enters the shop.

"Phyllis... Rose..." He nods, turning his hat in his hands. Our own moment of awkwardness, wondering how we would feel, passes. Here is a man who has suffered and needs our compassion. As one, Phyllis and I step forward and each squeeze a hand, then let go as we see him blinking and pulling himself together. He shakes hands with Leonard who, for once, seems lost for the appropriate word.

"I believe you'd like to speak to me," Father says to him in a kindly voice.

"Yes, Sir, may I make an appointment?" My love recovers himself to ask.

"Their train's not due till eleven o'clock. We can talk now, if you like. Shall we take a turn round the block?"

My stomach lurches. This is it.

The two dear men leave the shop and walk in the direction of Bridgefoot.

Phyllis and I stand there, looking after them. "It'll be all right," my sister says, with a thoughtful smile, "you marrying him. But even if you didn't, you know, it would still be all right."

We both laugh and grasp each other in a swift hug.

254

"Thank goodness we're both here in Widdock," I say.

Phyllis agrees. Then, we start tidying the books. A short time later, the men walk into the shop with a genial air, though Leonard still looks nervous.

"I've always liked this young man," says Father and, turning to him, "You've made a success of this place. I'm very happy to see you marry my lovely girl, Rose." I'm astonished to hear the description. Father turns to me. "And since I've found some solace when I thought I'd spend the rest of my life in pain, I can only wish you happiness." He grasps at all our hands, clumsily. "And Phyllis, if ever…"

"Father, I think we should go and buy some mince pies for the journey."

"Oh… I see, yes…"

They leave the shop and Leonard locks up. "Just for a moment. Come through to the back so I can ask you formally in private."

"You don't have to go down on one knee."

"Thank goodness for that."

I follow him into our dear sitting room. We stand looking at each other, suddenly shy. He offers his hands and I take them. I feel slightly light-headed as he speaks.

"Will you marry me, Rose?" His lovely eyes search mine.

"Yes, I will. Yes."

"Would you mind if I kissed you?"

For answer, I take a step forward as he opens his arms.

I close my eyes as our lips touch.

I dissolve.

And now I know, I think I know.

Epilogue

All the Days

A soft summer downpour is all the permission I need to sit here musing,

Instead of slipping out to the garden before work, to pull and snip at the ivy,

That stealthy invader, masquerading as ground cover, linked in the mind

With its seasonal partner. I see Phyllis, Hilda and me cutting holly,

The white of our pinafores heightened by twilight.

I cut juniper, as I did on the morning of Mother's passing.

We decorate mantelpiece, dresser. The room is alive with fragrance. Midnight,

The old carols. Greenery mingles its scents with the wax of church candles.

These are no brighter than Hilda's smile lighting her face, reflecting her love's.

The pungent odour of coffee, 'cawfee', as my brothers from New York pronounce it.

They drink it black. I remember the flavour, which reminds me of malt, but more bitter.

It is tasty, but cloying and not at all soothing. They have brought us an angular pot,

Solid silver. 'Good Lord!' says Father. A hamper from Fortnum's ('Good Lord!' again)

With ham, glacé fruit, Stilton, champagne. And an American children's book, a bestseller,

'The Wonderful Wizard of Oz', with sumptuous illustrations. No, my brothers never read

Poetry, have not heard of Whitman. Our gifts are modest but thoughtful: knitted gloves;

Shoehorns crafted by Father. Throughout the exchange, the scent of the turkey,

Gently roasting, tantalises the taste buds and lifts the spirit like a well-loved refrain.

Three pairs of eyes. One seeing parkland and borders in a new place, bulbs, spring buds.

In thought, Ralph's already there, planning a garden. Another pair, tender with love, is full

Of joy for my future as much as his own bright one, dear Jack. The last pair pleads, tries

To coerce. Mine must look shocked. Inside, I'm reeling at what's being asked of me.

My heart breaks for Dot, who is showing now, for George mourning his sister. I search

For a way to say 'No' with kindness. Cousin Grace gives Father a questioning look.

Slowly, he nods, breaks into a smile, encouraging her to make a great-hearted offer.

Transformed, Dot tells us to open the boxes from Sawdons yielding flans and curd tarts,

Her light touch rivalled only by Hilda's mince pies. All, we agree, equal to Fortnum's.

A postcard: City Hall and Newspaper Row, like Italian palaces stretched to the sky.

On New Year's Eve, there are always bands and fireworks, electric illuminations.

"To tell you the truth, I'm getting a bit fed up with N'Yawk," mutters Father.

Twelfth Night. The Wassail Cup and the blessing of fruit trees. For me, three apple trees,

Three homes. In the newest, night cloaks the garden bringing the scent of imminent snow.

A winter kiss. Chill lips spark fire, a promise of heat to come.

Now I look up, reflections pleasantly ended. As I catch the perfume of our climbing rose

And notice raindrops which gleam on its petals, a thought comes to me,

A curious blessing: this meditation will take all the days of my life.

Acknowledgements

I should like to thank my husband, John Freeman, who was my first reader, and my daughter, Nell Dawson, who was my second, for their detailed feedback and unfailing encouragement. Thanks, also to my son, Trevor Dawson, and to all my extended family and my friends, and to 186 Publishing for their ever-sustaining support and belief. I am grateful for useful conversations and correspondence with Valerie Don, Dr. Gavin Goodwin, Marc Harshman, Rev. Rhiannon Jones, Anne Maskell, Cheryl Ryan, Louise Thayer, Dr. Reina van der Wiel and Valerie Warren. Finally, a big thank you to Gill Stoker and colleagues at The Mary Evans Picture Library, and to the kind and helpful staff of Hertford Museum.